JUST HIS BOSS

A SWEET ROMANTIC COMEDY

SOUTHERN ROOTS SWEET ROMCOM
BOOK 2

DONNA JEFFRIES

ISBN-13: 978-1638762065

CHAPTER ONE

TARA

I GLANCE UP AT THE TELEVISION PLAYING IN MY kitchen, hearing the words "Fowler International" and then "Dawson Houser."

My knife doesn't slow as I move it through the onions I'm chopping, though my gaze is now trained on the screen showing my best friend's fiancé. I expect to see Callie appear on-screen too, but the media doesn't seem as enamored with her as they do Dawson.

Of course, Dawson's the one with all the power and prestige. The one with the huge bank account. The one with the handsome face, the straight-teeth smile, and the Carolina charm.

I scoff and scoop up the onions with the blade of my knife. They go in the pan behind me, where half a cube of butter has been melting gently.

I know the truth behind Dawson Houser, and that's

that Callie's his backbone. Callie puts together his speeches and his outfits, and Callie's the one who reminds him to smile, coaches him on what to say, and cares for him before and after all of the publicity surrounding their upcoming wedding.

They should be here in about an hour, and I'll get to see the real Dawson Houser. I've met the man loads of times, and I can admit that he's changed a ton since he and Callie started dating.

I season the onions with salt and pepper, something I've done so often I don't have to think about it. That allows my mind to wander down a semi-dangerous path toward dating.

I haven't been out with anyone in a while, because when a chef has a business, that's the intimate relationship in their life. At least for me, I've had a hard time devoting myself to anything but Saucebilities.

Since I catered the Fowler Founder's Gala a couple of months ago, my business has exploded. I can't keep up with the requests coming in through my online form, and I've hired someone part-time to tackle that job for me.

Callie keeps telling me to hire new chefs, because then I'd be able to keep up. But I'm not sure I want to. A new chef eats into my profits, so while I might be able to do more events, I'd have to pay those chefs.

Most of them think restaurant work is more prestigious than catering, and I'll train them up, give them great experience, and then they leave to go do "bigger and better" things. I've actually had a few of them say those exact words to my face.

Familiar bitterness creeps through me as I add several cloves of chopped garlic to the pan. Celery and carrots go in next, and the mirepoix really starts to scent my house.

I shouldn't even be cooking today. One of my goals this summer was to only work six days a week. No one can go, go, go all the time, though I've been tempted. Plus, I hate cooking at home. Sure, everyone sees those celebrity chefs on TV, talking about all these dishes they make at home for their loved ones.

I think they're all liars. I work so much in the kitchen at Saucebilities, there's no way I'm slaving over the stove when I get home too. Nope. I call for take-out almost every day, and the food from someone else's restaurant is a treat for me.

Not only that, but I've been really trying to cut down on how much I work. Six days a week, twelve hours a day, should be enough.

"This isn't work, Tara," I tell myself. I'm making soup for Callie and Dawson. They've hired me to cater their wedding, which will be a small, private affair at an undisclosed location. Dawson's had some nuptial issues in the past, and he doesn't want a traditional wedding.

That's why he and Callie are performing for the press so often these days. They've made it very clear everything surrounding their forthcoming I-do is off-limits.

Even I don't know where the wedding will be yet, and

it's in only another month. They've had a short engagement—one of the shortest I've ever heard of—and I need to
ask Callie about the kitchen at this place again.

She's assured me it'll be fine, but my nerves seethe
at me.

Maybe that's because I lost another chef a few days
ago. I've told myself I'm not going to hire another one. I've
got four working with me now, and the four of us will have
to handle whatever we've got.

I push all thoughts of work from my mind. I'm not
working today—I'm making lunch for my friends. This
could be the soup they choose for their wedding dinner.
That's it.

I've just added tomato paste and a dash of oregano to
the pan to start to draw out the deep, rich flavors of it
when my chef-cell rings. It's a low-pitched tune that
steadily moves up an octave, and I know to ignore that call.

"Someone from work," I say. "And I'm *not* working
today."

Anxiety eats at me, because I am the boss, and it's my
catering company. I assign all my employees the same ringtone on the chef-cell, so it could've been any of them.

My mind moves through who's working today—Jared,
Barley, and Alec.

Oh, Alec. My thoughts freeze on him, and it's a good
thing I know how to put together a sausage and orzo stew
without thinking too hard.

Alec Ward is like six chefs in the kitchen. He works

faster than anyone I've watched cook before, and his palette is incredible. We went to the Food and Wine Festival in Florida a couple of weeks ago, and he could identify the minute spices and tangs in the dishes we sampled even when I couldn't.

He's been a real Grumpy Cat to have in my kitchen, but I'm terrible at firing people, and he's really the best chef in the South. I'm lucky to have him.

You just want to get lucky with him, I think, shocked the moment the thought fills my mind. Once it's there, I can't get it to leave, and I actually start to fantasize that he was the one to call me, but only to ask me to dinner.

A private dinner he'll have cooked himself, with all of my favorite things. Eggplant parmesan, with homemade spaghetti noodles, and a deep, rich meaty sauce he's labored over for hours. Food really is the way to my heart, though I'm not male, and the extra weight I carry on my tall frame testifies of that.

"No one trusts a skinny chef," I tell myself as I lift a spoon to my lips to taste the broth I've put together. It's rich, hearty, salty, and perfect. I'll add the orzo, and that'll take some of the salt out of it, giving me a final product that will leave bellies full and mouths happy.

With the small, oblong pasta boiling away in the soup broth, I brown up the sausage and get out my fancy, only-for-important-company bowls. I hardly ever use my nice dishes, though I own a ton of them.

When it's just me eating, I don't need a gold-rimmed

plate to put my chicken Caprese sandwich on, even if it is a fancier sandwich than most people would eat for dinner.

I finish the soup and flip off the TV. Outside, it's time to let out the chickens. I breathe in the hot air that covers Carolina in the summer as I go down the steps to the yard. The coop sits right up against the corner of my house, and I worked hard to put up the fence between the chicken run and my yard.

Most people would've used that space for their dogs, but canines require too much human interaction. Chickens don't care if I work all day and all night.

"Cluckles," I say as I open the coop door. "Time to get some fresh air. Come on, guys." Cluckles comes bopping out, her head thrusting forward and pulling back. Just the way chickens walk makes me smile. "Go on, now. Get some good exercise in the yard."

I'm like a chicken warden, letting the bird inmates out for their one hour of exercise. I smile at myself and watch as Nog, Nuggets, and Fluffers follow Cluckles. All of my chickens have names, as they're good friends.

They know all about Alec and his attitude, all about how Gene quit last week to go work at a premier steak-house in the city, and all about my pathetic, non-existent love life. Only Hennifer has ever given me any judgment at all, and my smile straightens as the black and white hen bobs on past me.

"You stay in the strip this time," I tell them as they continue to come out of the coop. I own thirteen chickens

—a baker's dozen—and their eggs go with me to my catering kitchen every day.

Between my house and my neighbor's, there's a strip of pasture. The Reynolds used to put a calf on it every year, but Mr. Reynolds didn't do that this spring. I look across the wild strip of grasses and weeds to his house. His wife died last year, and I try to take over all of my new recipes for him to taste. It gives us both someone to talk to—for me, someone who I don't employ, and for him, just someone.

"Getting Puffles out?" Callie's voice sounds above me and to my left, and I look up to the deck.

"Puffles?" I ask in a disgusted voice. "Don't be ridiculous. Who would name their chicken Puffles?"

She grins at me and leans against the railing. She always looks like a million bucks, and today is no different. She's wearing a pair of shorts that do amazing things for her legs, a silk, peach-colored blouse, and her hair all wavy as it cascades over her shoulders. She's stunningly beautiful, and I smile at her. I wish I wasn't quite so tall, because I feel like I loom over people, especially some men, and it's awkward.

"Who—besides you—names their chickens at all?"

"A lot of people," I shoot back at her.

"Yeah, people who are ten years old," she says with a grin.

While she's been heckling me, Alfredo and Omeletto have exited the coop. Of course, there's still one stubborn chicken inside. "Come on, Benedict," I say to her. "Get out of there." I bend to pull the farm animal out, and she warbles at me.

"You need some fresh air," I tell her. Plus, I need to gather the eggs. "Grab that basket," I tell Callie. "And come help me with the eggs."

Callie joins me, and she holds the basket while I fill it with eggs. "You're all fancy," I say, putting the last egg on top of the others. "I love this blouse." I grin at her and give her a hug, the basket off to the side of us.

"Thanks." She sighs and laughs lightly. "It's nice to be here," she says. She's always liked my house; she says she feels safe here. We've known each other for over ten years, and she's my safe place too. She's been there through another near-engagement, through the opening of Saucebilities, through everything. She was the one who picked me up and dusted me off after my husband, Otis, left.

I swallow against those still-raw feelings, wondering how much time has to pass before they'll go away. A decade seems like long enough, but perhaps not. The Good Lord doesn't think so, at least, because my heart still quivers a bit in my chest.

That might be from the disastrous relationships I've tried since my marriage ended. Or the way I eat butter pecan ice cream for breakfast each morning. I've heard all that sugar and cream isn't great for hearts, but I can't stop myself.

"There you are," Dawson says, coming outside. "It smells great in there, Tara."

"Thanks." I put a grin on my face for him too. "Howdy, Dawson." I start for the deck, Callie in tow. "You guys must've had a press event. I saw you on TV this morning."

He looks down at the blue blazer-white polo-with jeans combination he's wearing. "Yeah, we had breakfast at the country club."

My heart taps out an extra beat. "You're surely not hungry for lunch then." I glance at Callie as she reaches the top of the steps.

"Sure we are," Callie says with a smile. "When have I ever not wanted to eat your food?" She hands me the basket of eggs, her blue eyes dazzling at me. "Plus, I know you ate breakfast. I saw that empty ice cream container in the trashcan."

"You're rifling through my trash again?" I tease as I follow her and Dawson into the house. "After that doughnut incident, I thought you were going to stop doing that."

Callie bursts out laughing, and I join her. We'd literally seen someone fish a doughnut out of the trashcan at the coffee shop last week. It really was too bad it had turned out to be the guy Callie was trying to set me up with. She'd had to think fast on her feet then, and I'd ducked into the bathroom to save us both some humiliation.

Inside, I set the eggs on the kitchen table and step over to Dawson to give him a light hug. He squeezes me back, but his expression is more nervous than I've seen him in a while.

"What's going on?" I look between him and Callie, as I'm now standing in the middle of them.

"Nothing," Callie says, her voice as false as my granddaddy's teeth.

"Nothing," Dawson mimics in the same, fake tone, and every hair on my arms stands up.

"Someone better tell me," I say. "Or I'm not serving the soup." I fold my arms and glare from one of them to the other.

"Tara," Callie says in a soothing voice. She links her arm through mine and starts to tug me further into the kitchen. I don't want to go with her, but my feet move anyway. My chef-cell sings out another chefy ringtone, and I have most of a mind to answer it. I have a feeling I'm not going to like what Callie says next.

"What's going on?" I whisper as I reach for the bowls I've gotten out. I hand them to her, and we go into the dining room. I hardly ever use it, because I can eat my midnight sandwiches at the regular kitchen table. Or my bed. "You two are still getting married, right?"

"Yes," she says in a voice only a few decibels louder than mine. "Here's the thing."

"Oh, boy," I say, sliding my arm out of hers. My mind fires through things, as if I've forgotten something. The soup is ready to eat, sitting benignly on the stove, the lid keeping everything hot. The chickens... "I left the coop

door open. Come with me, because I have a feeling I'm
going to need the wide Carolina sky to help me compre-
hend what you're about to say."

Dawson's at the kitchen table, his attention on his
phone as I step out my back door and walk across the small
deck, Callie right on my heels. She's wearing some immaculate ankle boot things, because she's a petite, beautiful
woman who works in an office. I'm the lumbering, tall oaf
wearing orthopedics because I stand all day long.

We go down the steps and back to the coop, where
sure enough, I've left it open. The birds could've come
into the yard, and I wouldn't have been happy about that.

"Your back yard is so wonderful," Callie says, and I
turn to find her with her face turned into the sun, the
slight breeze kissing her cheeks as it flows by.

I close the door to the yard, trapping the chickens in
their prison pasture strip, watch Callie. "Yes, Morris has
done a great job this summer."

Callie faces me as I settle my weight on my right foot.
"Dawson and I want to get married here."

I blink at her, taking in the nerves in her eyes and the
way her hands rotate around each other. "What? Why
here?" I look past her to my yard, which is nice. I pay for it
to be lush, green, and landscaped, so it should be beautiful.
I never let Chick Fillet and her buddies back here. For all
accounts, there should be coils of razor wire between the
chicken pasture and my emerald green grass.

I have a lot of trees along the east-side fence that I

suppose act like the razor wire in a neighborhood-friendly way, and no neighbor on the west. It faces south, so I get a lot of great sun in the winter months, and not so much in the summer ones. Since we're moving into autumn in a couple of months, the sun is nearly overhead about now.

Roses bloom along the other side of the deck, and I have raised flowerbeds with dwarf trees, more bushes, and big, flowering plants around the side. As I look at the yard, I can see precisely where an arch would go to make a beautiful wedding scene. I can see trellises and tea lights, jarred fireflies and small tables and chairs for the few guests the wedding will bring.

"We don't want somewhere commercial," Callie says, bringing my attention back to her. "We can't do it in one of our yards, because the press will expect that."

"What about the beach?" I ask. "You'd like that."

"It's public," Callie says. "Your place is perfect, and there's not going to be more than thirty people here. Maybe only twenty. You can cook right in your own kitchen, and serve from the deck, and you won't even have to move your chickens."

I glance at them, their little heads bobbing as they peck at the ground in their prison-pen. I have no reason to say no, so I say, "Okay, sure."

"Tara?" Dawson asks from up on the deck, and I turn toward him. "Uh, there's someone here to see you, and he doesn't look too happy."

"Who?" I ask, already going around the corner of the deck to get back to the stairs.

Alec muscles his way out onto the deck, nearly shoving Dawson out of the way. "Isn't it your job to answer your phone when one of your chefs call?" he growls at me. "Boss?"

CHAPTER TWO

ALEC

THERE'S NOTHING THAT ANNOYS ME MORE THAN someone who won't answer their phone. Just because Tara Finch is my boss doesn't mean I have to put up with that. Saucebilities is her company; doesn't she care?

Calm down, I tell myself as the gorgeous brunette reaches the top of the stairs. She glares at me with the heat of the sun, and dang if that look doesn't get my blood moving a little faster.

Something switched for me on our trip to Florida, but I can't quite identify what it is. I also can't tell her, and I've resorted to being surlier than ever just to keep the walls up around myself.

She certainly doesn't make things any easier on me by wearing such delicious jeans and a tank top that shows off the muscles in her arms and the curves of her female body.

"What are you doing here?" she demands, striding across the small space toward me. "How do you even know where I live?"

"He didn't know where you lived?" the woman she was with down on the grass asks. Her name is Callie Michaels, and I've met her plenty of times. She actually makes me smile, and I can see why she and Tara are friends. "How did he figure that out?"

Tara ignores her, so I do too. "I called you," I growl out. "Twice." I gesture toward her house as if it's the commercial kitchen in the retail space she rents. "I can't work with Barley. The man barely has any personal hygiene, and he shouldn't be allowed in a kitchen. He's going to get us in trouble with the Health Department."

I expect Tara's eyes to widen, and then she'll rush over to Saucebilities with me. Maybe we can go to dinner after we finish feeding the mayor and his office staff at their quarterly meetings.

Instead, she starts to laugh. "Us, Alec?" She tips her head back and laughs. The sound infuses me with a sense of joy I haven't felt in a while—and plenty of annoyance that I have. "Barley's fine. Besides, he's the very best at the grilled oysters Mayor Fielding likes."

"That is so not true," I say. "I can grill *lines* around that guy." Double lines. The kind that create perfect diamonds on perfectly cooked meat—which Tara knows.

She *knows*.

I've seen the way she looks at me, and she's not light on the praise either. I'll give her credit for that. Tara Finch compliments her cooks when they deserve it.

"Maybe you can," she says, taking an extra step toward me, as if she's really going to go chest-to-chest with me. She's tall, but not as tall as me.

She's scrumptious, and as I get a whiff of the scent of her skin, I get fresh air, something fowly, fully of sausage, and the deep, rich smell of that stew I saw on her stovetop.

She's got pretty-boy Dawson Houser here, along with his fiancée, both of whom have been dominating the social headlines in Carolina for a couple of months now.

I knew she was friends with them, and I'm not surprised to see them here on her day off. I am a bit surprised I left my post in the kitchen and drove over here to confront her. Barley just makes me see red.

Crimson red.

"But he does have a way he seasons and grills them that the mayor likes," Tara says, bringing me back to the argument at hand. "It's not always about being the best, Alec."

"Don't patronize me," I say.

"I'm not." She sighs. "Listen, you're a great chef. The best I've had, and you know it."

"That's the problem," Callie says, and Tara shoots her a glare. She blinks and says, "Sorry, Tara. Come on, Dawson. Let's go inhale that soup Tara made and let her handle this." She takes her fiancé inside, leaving me and Tara alone on the deck.

"I'm sorry," I say, the words thick in my mouth. I don't say them often, but with Tara, I find it easier than with anyone else. Especially my dad or my brother, and a sting of regret starts low in my gut.

"You are an amazing chef," she says again, falling back that extra step she took. "You need to figure out how to get along with Barley, number one. And number two, you need to understand that in catering, it's not about being the best. It's about—"

"Delivering what the client wants," we say together. This isn't the first time she's given me this lecture.

I sigh and run my hand through my hair. "Okay, Boss."

"What did Barley do?" she asks, cocking one hip and folding her arms.

She is downright lethal to a man's defenses, that's for sure. I force myself to keep my eyes on hers, so she won't discover these soft feelings I've been developing for her. It simply won't do, as she's my boss.

My *boss*.

I've gotten involved romantically with a boss before, and let me just say, that had ended badly. I see smoke and fire, and not just because we broke up. But actual smoke and fire from an accident in the kitchen that had left me humiliated and her in trouble with her financier daddy...and her *other* boyfriend.

I smile at Tara, because she runs Saucebilities herself.

No rich daddy in sight. "He answers his personal cell while he's cooking, Boss. It's gross. That thing could've been anywhere, and I just..." I shiver.

"Maybe you're a germophobe," she says, grinning at me.

"That's not a maybe, sweetheart," I drawl, pulling on my strong Southern roots.

Tara rolls her eyes, but I think her face turns a bit pinker. A man can hope, at least. I can't believe I let the hope in, actually. I know what a relationship with my boss looks like, and I know how it ends.

I actually like this job, because Tara is a professional. She plays by the book, has all the right permits, and puts out delicious food.

My eyes drop to her lips, and I wonder how delectable they'd taste. I yank my thoughts back to something more appropriate and move my gaze back to hers. "You better get back to the kitchen," she says. "Or..." Her eyes flicker over my shoulder. "Maybe you have time to stay for lunch? I tried a new spin on my sausage stew recipe, and I'd love your opinion on it."

My eyebrows shoot up. "Really?"

She shrugs as if she doesn't really care, but I suspect she does. She changed while we wandered the Food and Wine Festival a few weeks ago. Things are different between us now, and as a flush creeps up her neck and into her face, I see a more vulnerable version of her. It makes me wonder if I can be more laid-back, more open, and more...myself with her too.

Maybe I don't have to be the tough-as-nails chef with fifteen knives flying every which way. Not with her.

"Really," she says. "I put you on the mayoral dinner for a reason."

"I thought it was because of my knife jokes," I say.

Tara rolls her eyes, and even that accelerates my pulse. "The one about them being *cutting-edge* technology?" She scoffs. "You're no stand-up comedian."

No, but there's a great comedy club on the waterfront, and I wonder if she'd go with me. Instead of asking, I say, "I can call Jared right now. The cakes just have to come out and cool. Then I'll head back and decorate them."

"If you have time."

"I have time," I say, liking how she keeps up with the conversation as it moves from knife jokes to me staying for lunch. "You're a great chef too, Tara." My voice grinds through my throat, and I drop my chin toward my chest. I'm not great at giving praise, and that's only one reason I'm not the boss of my own kitchen anymore.

"Thank you," she says diplomatically. She steps past me and opens the door to re-enter her house. "I think that's the first time you've called me Tara and not 'Boss.'" She gives me a smile and another whiff of her scent before stepping inside. "Guys," she says. "I just need two more minutes, and then we'll taste what could very well be the soup course for your wedding."

I take a moment and take a deep breath. Tara has a beautiful back yard, and it seems to match everything else in her life. The cleanliness of her kitchen, the stark white chef jackets she wears, and the way nothing on her face, body, or head is ever a hair out of place.

I wonder what it will take to stir her up a bit. Make her stumble. Really light her fire, though I've seen her mad plenty of times. She has a shorter fuse in the kitchen than she does here at home, and I think about asking her to come sample some of my cooking, in my apartment.

Then I think of the giant bird cage in the living room. Yeah, having Tara over—or any woman—for anything other than a quick pit stop isn't the best idea I've had.

Not only that, but I have to go back quite a few years to recall the last woman I cooked for, and the memories are...nice. The relationship had turned sour, as most of mine do, but for some reason, I think maybe Tara and I could figure out how to get along.

She hasn't fired you yet, I think, and I also find it kind of pathetic that that's what I'm using as a measuring stick for my relationships now.

I sigh and turn back to the house, catching a glimpse of Tara's skin along the waistband of her jeans as she stretches to reach into a high cabinet. She pulls down a bowl and says, "C'mon in, Alec. We're not providing air conditioning for the chickens."

I smile and close the door behind me, then follow her into the dining room. "Can I help?"

"Nope. Sit." She sets the bowl in the newly made fourth place setting and brushes by me again.

I look at Callie, who's wearing a daggered look on her face, and Dawson, who offers me a semi-smile. I've dined with worse, and I pull out the chair across from Dawson. "When's the big day for you two?" I ask.

I can be nice if required. Besides, I'm not in a competition with either of these two people.

"September fifth," Dawson says, glancing at Callie. There's something going on there, but I'm not sure what.

Of course there's something going on there, I think. *They're engaged, duh.* But I think there's something more. Something's not quite right. But what that might be, I have no idea. My momma tells me every chance she gets that I have no tact, but I bite my tongue. I'll be sure to tell her next time I go see her. She'll be so proud I haven't pressed these two people I barely know for more information.

"So, Alec," Callie says, leaning her elbows up onto the table. "How are things going for you at Saucebilities?"

"Great," I say truthfully. "I really like it there."

"Do you?" she challenges. "You might could stand to be a bit nicer to Tara then."

"Callie," Tara says behind me, entering with a gorgeous serving bowl of soup. "Alec's fine." She shoots me a glance that sends electricity through my blood, and I offer her a smile. I do remember how to make the gesture, and she sends it back to me.

"Okay," Tara says, wiping the back of her hand across

her forehead, dislodging some bangs I didn't even know she had. "Oh, wait. I forgot the parmesan."

She turns to leave the dining room again, but her foot catches on the leg of my chair. We grunt at the same time, and then my whole world gets upended.

Literally.

My legs bang against something hard, and a horrendously loud crash fills my ears. They ring, and I hear people clamoring about me. The delicious scent of sausage soup fills my nose, so it makes no sense that I'm in so much pain.

Dawson's face appears above mine. "Can you hear me?"

"Yes," I say, realizing I'm on my back. I roll to my right, only to find Tara there, Callie rushing around the other end of the table to get to her.

"Sorry," I say, steamrolling her and taking her into my arms as I do.

"I tripped," she says, her eyes meeting mine. Her arms come around me too, and the whole world freezes.

"I think I fell too," I say, still not sure now that happened. I'm not sure what I mean by that either. I'm not falling for my boss. I'm *not*.

"She tipped you right over, man," Dawson says, extending his hand toward me at the same time Callie asks, "Tara, honey, are you all right?" She shoots me a glare as if I'm the one who lunged at Tara and knocked her down.

I start to disentangle myself from her, and I finally get to my feet with Dawson's help, sweat beading along my brow. My stomach growls, and my chest feels like someone's wrapped me in a tight rubber band and is twisting, twisting, *twisting* it.

Tara makes it to her feet too, refuses to look at me, and mumbles something about getting the parmesan. Callie goes with her, her arm around Tara's shoulders like a mother hen protecting her chick.

"Well," Dawson says, clapping his hands today. "I'm glad I'm not the only one who's ended up on the floor with his girlfriend."

"She's just my boss," I say quickly. "We're not seeing each other."

"Mm hm." His grin is as wide as the Mississippi. He leans closer, his dark eyes sparkling like diamonds. "I've said something *very* similar to that before too." With that, he rights my chair and moves back to his spot.

I don't know if I should take the seat or pick up the chair and throw it through the window. A storm rages inside me, because if Dawson can see how I feel about my boss, surely Tara can too.

She's smart. She's observant. She'll *know*.

"Sit, sit," Tara says, coming up behind me. "I promise not to take you out again."

I reach for the chair and sit down, my movement heavy and the back of my head sending an ache through my body. I realize I probably hit it against

the floor when I fell backward. Or got dragged backward by the most beautiful woman in the world.
Whatever.

She puts a lovely dish of freshly curled parmesan
cheese on the table. "Okay." She draws a deep breath.
"This is a spin on my sausage gumbo, and I've made it
sausage orzo stew, since I know Callie doesn't particularly
like gumbo."

Callie grins at her best friend, and Tara smiles back.
They have a tight bond, and I know if I want to win over
Tara, I'm going to have to get Callie to like me first.

I can't even believe I'm thinking such things, as if Tara
and I are anything but boss-employee. Still, my mind
wanders along that forbidden path, and maybe the fall
addled my brain, because I can see myself with Tara.

Tara starts to serve the stew, and I've missed the last
bit of her presentation. It doesn't matter. A chef's food
should speak for itself.

She places a bowl in front of me and offers me the
parmesan curls. I take a few and let them float on the stew,
wilting from the heat. It smells great, and looks great, and
she's ticking every box so far.

The first bite makes my mouth rejoice, with spices,
salt, and something rich and nuanced. I try to hold back
the groan of pleasure from how delicious the stew is, but I
can't.

I even close my eyes, something I don't realize until I
open them and look straight into Tara's. "I'd marry you for

this," I say, which is literally the first thing that comes to my mind. Also the stupidest thing.

Her eyes widen then as I'd imagined they would earlier, and both she and Callie gasp. Dawson, the devil, just starts to laugh.

CHAPTER THREE

TARA

I HAVEN'T FROZEN THE WAY I AM NOW SINCE CALLIE caught me crying in my back yard, over ten years ago. Fine, *almost* ten years ago. No matter the date—though I know exactly when it was—she found me sobbing in my back yard, as hers butted up against it.

My husband had just left, and I'd fallen apart with the divorce papers in my hands. I'd tossed them somewhere and escaped the house that had been closing in on me.

Very much like this dining room. I stare at Alec. Dawson's laughter bounces around the room. Callie blinks, and if Callie can't say something, that's serious.

I finally get control of myself, and I spin and walk out of the dining room. The rug nearly takes me down again, but I avoid its traps and make it out of the near vicinity of Alec Ward.

What in the world is happening? I wonder. The

kitchen isn't safe, because I want to grab a spoon and taste my own soup.

I'd marry you for this.

He'd marry me for this soup?

It's *soup*, for crying out loud. People don't propose over soup.

Alec's love language is clearly food, and surprise, surprise, the extra thirty-five pounds I carry says mine is too.

I bypass the pot of soup on my stove as I hear Callie's voice say something. She's probably excusing herself to come find me, but right now, I just need a minute to breathe.

Since Callie wears some sort of heel everywhere she goes, and she's scared of spiders, bugs, and other things that go bump in the night, I open the door that leads to the basement and hurry down the rickety, wooden steps.

The cellar is not really a basement, and I only store extra potatoes and onions down here if I've ordered too many for Saucebilities.

Once, I'd ordered enough spuds to kill a small army with all the eyes staring at them, and I'd brought them home during the first week I'd lived in this house.

I'd forgotten about them, of course. If I don't set an alarm or have one of my phones ringing in my face about what I need to do, the task sort of flies out of my mind.

The next time I came down into the cellar, the pota-

JUST HIS BOSS   29

toes had burrowed themselves into the earth with all these spindly, long, white tendrils.

The smell can't be described, but let's just say that it took me a couple of weeks to clean it all out, dig it all up, and then convince Callie that I had not, indeed, buried a body in my cellar. That's certainly how it had smelled.

She definitely won't come down here.

She thinks there could be dead bodies everywhere, and her constant habit of locking doors and windows and setting traps for serial killers is my best friend right now.

I reach the bottom of the steps without tripping—another miracle—and pause, taking in a deep breath. I run my hands through my hair and brace my palms on my back.

"What just happened?"

People say stupid stuff all the time. Heck, I've probably said a dozen stupid things today. I talk to my chickens, whom I've named things like Cordon Bleu, Pot Pie, and Curry, for crying out loud. The truth is, Alec gave me the perfect reaction to my food.

He likes it, and he's the best chef I've come across in my career.

"Why are you standing down here?" I ask. "Get up there and thank him."

"Tara," Callie calls from the top of the steps. "You did *not* go down into that creepy cellar." She doesn't sound happy about it. To her eternal credit, and a testimony for how close we are, her ankle boot lands on the first step.

"I'm coming down, so get ready to have my death on your conscience."

I turn back to the steps and put my clogged foot on the bottom one. "Don't come down," I say. "I'm coming up."

She ignores me in usual Callie fashion, and we meet somewhere near the top of the steps.

"Dawson stopped laughing," she says.

"Miracle of miracles," I say dryly.

"Alec just likes the stew."

"I know that." I can't really look down at my hands, and there's not a lot of light here for examining nails anyway. "I just...who is so...elephantenous that they can trip over a chair and topple the man twice their size sitting in it?"

Callie puts her hands on my shoulder, and I'm usually taller than her by a head or two. But standing down a stair, we're eye to eye.

"First off, elephantenous is a great word. I'm stealing that. Second, you're *not* elephantenous. You're gorgeous and talented. Third, it's that disastrous rug. I've told you to throw that thing away no less than four times. Fourth, he is not twice as big as you."

I look into her eyes, trying to believe her. We're roughly the same size. I'm taller so I look thinner, but really, my weight is just distributed in a more feminine way. I have little chicken legs that seriously can't hold up my body—at least if my boyfriend two ago is to be believed.

The man ran marathons, for the love of all things buttery, and just because I don't have muscled legs doesn't mean they're not functional. That was what I'd told him, at least. They manage to keep me working all day long in the kitchen.

It had been my idiotic feet who'd betrayed me today. Or maybe the rug.

"Come on," Callie says. "Chin up. It's no big deal. Dawson says the soup is *fantastic*."

"Glad he stayed to eat it," I say. "I feel so stupid."

Callie takes my hand and teeters as she tries to turn in her ridiculous shoes. She manages it and goes back up the steps. After leading me all the way into the dining room, she clears her throat.

"Tara would like to apologize for rushing away. She had a major emergency down in the cellar. She thought there might be a serial killer waiting in there, so she shooed him away." She grins at me and then the men still seated at the table.

I just smile and shake my head, noting that Alec has not eaten a whole lot of soup while I've been gone.

"She knows how much I can't stand the thought of any doors or windows being unlocked, and she's always watching out for me. So." Callie releases my arm and goes around the table to her seat.

"This soup should be bottled and sold," Dawson says. "Callie and I could put together the perfect marketing program for it." He flashes me a smile, and I appreciate his effort.

The man has changed drastically in the past few months, and I attribute most of that to Callie.

"Thank you," I say, being careful to check the placement of my feet as I move to take my seat next to Alec. That rug is going in the trash as soon as I can heft it out of the house. "So I guess you like the soup?"

"It's amazing, Tara," he says, a smile I've literally never seen appearing on his face. "Really."

The use of my first name isn't lost on me. He said it a couple of times in Florida, but since we've been back, it's *Yes, Boss,* or *You got it, Boss.* Or like earlier, *Isn't it your job to answer your phone when one of your chefs call? Boss?*

Callie once said Dawson had a lot of facets, like a diamond. Some of them just hadn't been shined up yet. I wonder if Alec is the same, and the insane part of me really wants to find out.

"Okay, thanks." I pick up my spoon and dip it into the sausage orzo soup. My parmesan has wilted, but I don't care. "Now, tell me what you really think."

Alec looks nervously at Callie. "I did."

"Right." I roll my eyes. "You think I don't know when I'm being flattered? This is for their *wedding*. Tell me what you really think."

"It is a big wedding," Callie says, her eyes wide and oh-so-serious. "There will probably be a dozen articles just on my dress."

His gaze flitters back to mine. "It's seriously the best *winter* soup I've ever put in my mouth."

I catch the adjective and look down into my bowl. Even the color is wintery. Dark red, as it's tomato-based. It's a hearty soup, almost a meal by itself.

My mind starts to move through something lighter that would still be tasty and elegant. "Maybe we don't need a soup course," I say, looking at Callie.

She's dipping bread in her stew—buttered biscuits, I've prepared a *stew* for their *summer* wedding—and doesn't even seem to know I've spoken.

I meet Alec's eye again, and I know he's thinking the same thing I am. "Unless it's cold," I say, and he nods, his grin widening by the second.

"A cold soup?" Dawson asks, and Callie chimes in with, "Why would you serve this soup cold? It's *so* good as-is."

A FEW DAYS LATER, mid-morning finds me in the kitchen alone. It's Wednesday, and we don't book a lot of parties and events on Hump Day. I usually give all my chefs the midweek days off, though Thursday can be busy with prep for the weekends. But Monday, Tuesday, and Wednesday are usually quiet.

I finish grating the lemon peel for the chicken marinade I'm making and turn toward the stove when a timer goes off. Some chefs claim they don't use timers and anyone who does needs to go back to culinary school.

I say I need the reminder that I put something in the oven, thank you very much. My star ratings and comments will tell people what kind of chef I am, and what kind of food they'll get from Saucebilities.

Sometimes, I still find myself hung up on what some chef-slash-boyfriend said to me years ago, and I have to push against those negative messages.

The lava cakes look absolutely divine, and they jiggle just the right amount. There are some things I can do just by looking. Knowing when a fried egg is done, for example. But knowing when a soft-boiled egg is done requires a timer, no matter what anyone says. Maybe Superman can see through eggshells with his laser-vision, but normal people should use timers.

Since I haven't met any superhuman chefs yet, I put myself and other chefs in the "normal people" category.

I made my glaze for the cakes the moment I slid the cakes in the oven, and it's been waiting for me to pour it over the desserts for a while now. I whisk the thin chocolate ganache all back together, getting a whiff of the mint I've put in there, and set the pot on the stainless steel counter down a couple of feet from where I'm working.

One of the hardest things about lava cakes is getting them out of the mold. It has to be done while the cakes are hot, but not too hot. An extremely well-greased, preferably silicon, mold is essential. A wire rack is a must-have.

I reach for my rack and turn it upside down over my molds. With a hot pad to protect me from the just-from-the-oven sheet pan, I press one palm to the rack and the other on the bottom of the rack.

Then I flip.

The silicon slips, and I know I'm going to be tasting broken chocolate lava cakes even as I say, "Peanut butter bars," as a form of swearing.

The rack clatters onto the counter as I try to catch the cakes. I get three of the four, and the last one slips to the floor with a wet *glop!* and chocolate immediately oozes out.

At least it's rich and dark and delicious-looking. See? I can be positive too.

"Peanut butter bars?" someone repeats, followed by a hearty laugh in a voice that has followed me into my fantasies every night since Sunday.

I'd marry you for this soup.

I spin toward the door to find Alec standing there, his bag of knives and tools with him. "Something smells amazing," he says, coming closer and still using that sultry, sexy voice against me. How have I never noticed it before?

Maybe because listening to him gripe about his co-workers and call you "boss" is ultra-annoying.

"My momma is very averse to swearing," I say.

"Mm," he says, putting down his knives. "At least it's not a mid-*knife* crisis."

I blink and take in his glorious grin. I want to laugh, but I really can't encourage his jokes.

"Come on," he says. "That was a good one."

"It felt like you've been waiting to use it." I turn away before he can see my smile. "What are you doing here?" I look back at him, still teetering on the edge of laughing. And flirting. And about ten other inappropriate things— like thinking about what his lips would taste like right now.

"You said I could come work on the Cornish hens." He takes in the glaze and the cakes. "Working on the Southern Ball dessert?"

"Yes," I say, looking down at the mess. Chocolate spreads across the counter beneath the rack, as I'd missed getting it onto the second tray I'd set out.

I reach for the glaze and dump it over the sunken cakes. "Well, the look of these would make a preacher cuss on Sunday, but don't just stand there. Pick up a fork and help me taste them."

CHAPTER FOUR

ALEC

"Bacon bacon bacon bacon," chirps from the kitchen, and I grin as I ruffle my towel through my hair and go toward the sound.

"You want some bacon, Peaches?" I ask.

"Bacon Peaches," the bird says, and I laugh.

"They don't really go together, baby," I say to the bird. She's perched up high, as birds like to do, and I hold out my hand for her. She's just taken a shower with me, where she likes to sing and tell me all about a "red motor-bike, motor-motor-motor-bike" while she stands in the spray. She doesn't take any time to get dressed, and she always beats me back to the kitchen.

She flies over, and I give her a little peck on her face. "Tonight, I'm making bacon-wrapped chestnuts," I say. "See, there's this big lodge that's having a party, and it's

Christmas-themed though it's only August. Don't ask me why we have to celebrate the holidays already."

The idea of sitting down to a family meal makes my smile dry right up.

"Don't ask me why," Peaches repeats back to me. She takes flight, and I let her go. I reach for one of the T-shirts I've left on the back of the couch, having folded them a few hours ago and left them there.

Sometimes I can only get my household chores done halfway. It's not the end of the world, and since I wear a T-shirt under my chef's jacket every single day, I can drop it in the laundry room on the way by at night, and pick one up from the couch on the way out to work in the morning. I don't wear a shirt in between all of that anyway.

Thinking about laundry makes my mind travel back to the inn where I'd worked last year. They had an amazing guest laundry facility that would've surely rivaled the royal family's. The Blackbriar Inn had the best of everything. The best rooms. The best rates. The best decorations. The best grounds.

The best chef.

I know, because I'd opened and operated The Blackbriar all by myself. At least until my father and brother had gotten involved.

"It's just a shirt," I mutter, and Peaches says, "Don't ask me why," again.

I grin in her direction, tug the shirt over my head, and enter the kitchen. I selected this apartment solely for the kitchen. I can sleep on the couch for all I care, but the kitchen must be the best it can be.

This one has gray quartz countertops, with a double oven next to the refrigerator. The stovetop is in the island, leaving the back counter as a long, beautiful prep area. The sink sits in the corner, and it looks out over six stories of the peninsula of Charleston.

I can always see the ocean over the tops of the dogwoods and live oaks, and as I go to wash my hands— chefy rule number one—I take a long look out the window.

My thoughts roam, as they often do while I cook. I don't need all my mental energy to chop onions and mix eggs and flour.

I do need all my wits about me to keep the tall, curvy, sexy Tara Finch out of my mind. My tall, curvy, sexy *boss*.

Tara is no-nonsense in the kitchen, despite the fiasco with the lava cakes a couple of days ago. Watching her pour that glaze and then dig right in had seriously boiled my blood. In a good way. In the way that had me wondering how I could feed her the cake off my fork. Then maybe taste the slightly minty glaze in her mouth with mine.

Yeah, I'm in trouble with her already. I know it, and it's only a matter of time before she does. I glance at Peaches, wondering where we can run to next.

But, see, I'm tired of all the running. I just settled here, and I kinda want to stay. Tara definitely has something to do with that.

The worst part isn't that she's my boss, and I'm never going there again. It's that I don't even know *why* she affects me the way she does.

I'm usually more into blondes. I'm usually more into someone who likes what she sees on the outside and doesn't worry too much about the inside.

In fact, Tara Finch is dangerous to my health, because the woman will want details. She'll want to *know* me.

And I don't do details, and no one in Charleston knows me. That's just how I like it and just how it's going to stay.

I shut off the water, as if I can punctuate my thoughts the same way and get them to stop.

They don't, of course, and all I'm doing is slicing chestnuts in half length-wise and then toothpicking the bacon into place.

The best part of any dish is always the sauce, which was what drew me to Tara's job listing in the first place.

Saucebilities is such a great play on words, and I enjoy that wit in a name. "In a woman," I mutter, still stuck on Tara.

I get the chestnuts roasting and turn to make the sweet and sour glaze that goes on them. Anyone can pour barbecue sauce out of a bottle and then add some vinegar and mustard to make some sauce.

I don't take shortcuts like that. I chop onions and start to sweat them to start the base for the barbecue sauce. I can take the sauce anywhere from there, making it as sweet or as spicy or as sour as I want.

I don't need a recipe card, and I listen to Peaches babble on to herself about *bacon, bacon, bacon* in her cute birdie voice.

The chestnuts come out beautifully, and I coat them in the sauce from top to bottom, side to side, and in all of the cuts and crevices.

Something thunks against the door, and I look up from my tasting. "What in the world?"

"What in the world?" Peaches says. "World, world, world. Bacon, bacon, bacon, bacon-motor-bike!"

"Enough Peaches," I tell her as I pass. It sounds like someone chucked something at my door, and I swear, if those twins from down the hall are fighting again, I'm calling their momma at work. Then I'll make them come clean my kitchen until she gets home.

I open the door and expect to see those rascally ten-year-olds.

Instead, the hallway is empty. I look down at my feet and find the newspaper. "Oh, of course."

I bend to get the paper and head back inside. Call me antiquated or geriatric, but I like reading the newspaper. Southern Roots does regional and local stories about the art, culture, and restaurants in the city, and I love it.

I love going to the restaurants and clubs and checking out the vibe. I love a good sports bar, with wings and club soda and a game on in the background.

I like walking the unknown paths around the city, and I like checking out the bands that set up in the parks.

Since moving here, I don't like spending time at home all that much. I don't like spending time with myself without much to do.

The newspaper gives me something to focus on that's not Tara Finch or listening to my parrot prattle to herself about bacon and motorcycles. I do love Peaches, and she's honestly the reason I'm not still in the Rocky Mountains. I try not to dwell on the fact that the living thing I talk to the most weighs less than four ounces and only knows fifty English words.

I unfold the newspaper and flop it down on the counter. Peaches flies over, chirping for all she's worth.

"No," I say, letting her climb up on my hand so I can put her on my shoulder. "I'm reading this one. You'll have to wait your turn."

That's another reason I like the newspaper; I need it for Peaches. She's got a giant cage in the middle of the living room, and I spread newspaper out all over the carpet to protect it. If my landlord knew...well, I'd probably have to give up this gorgeous kitchen, that's for sure.

Birds are messy, to say the least. I can't give up Peaches, though, because she's the only thing in the world that hasn't abandoned me. Well, her and Turner, one of my only human friends and the veterinarian here in Charleston who kept Peaches for me while I did a little running without her.

I've just popped a water chestnut into my mouth when I see a headline that makes me spit it right back out.

No one trusts a skinny chef, but can the plump cooks in this town find love?

I can't read fast enough. I suck in a breath when I see Tara's name.

"No," I say. "No, no, no."

I read on, thinking the reporter—Brett Daniels—will focus on someone else. He doesn't.

He *never* does. The whole thing is about Tara, and wow, it's written in a cruel, spiteful, sarcastic tone that makes me wince.

I abandon the water chestnuts and reach for the phone. I call Tara, saying, "Pick up. Pick up, Tara."

I know she's got two phones, and she screens all of her chefs calls through the one device. I wish I had her personal cell, but my wishes rarely come true. I've actually given up on stars and eyelashes and dandelions and all of it.

Life and disappointment have a way of snuffing out things like wishes.

"Hey, Alec," Tara says, and just the sound of her voice sets my cells a'vibrating.

"Uh, I'm reading something about you."

She pauses for a moment. "You are?"

Suddenly, my mind takes a sharp turn, and I can't stop myself from saying, "Maybe you better get over here."

———

THE NEXT TIME there's a knock at the door, I jump from the couch and side-step Peaches' toy rope. She yelps like the doorbell, and I don't know how she learns the sounds so fast. Besides her bird-sitter, no one ever comes over, and we've only been here for four months.

I nearly yank the door off the hinges and stand there, staring at my boss.

She holds up her phone, a pure hurricane in her eyes. "I read it online at the stoplight."

"How long were you at the stoplight?" I ask. I'm glad she doesn't have anything but her device in her hand, or she probably would've thrown it at me.

She glares my face off as she pushes past me, old, familiar darkness emanating from her eyes. Oh, I know what that feels like. I've been there. I've been steeped in rage and hurt like that, and as I close the door behind me and follow her, I hope I'm strong enough to corral this wind.

The newspaper rustles, and I say, "If you've already read it, you didn't need to come over." Not that I want her to leave, especially now that she's here. Having another human being in my apartment lights up the whole place, and I tell myself that anyone would've done that. That Tara's not the reason everything in my life is suddenly better.

Heck, sometimes Jessie, my best human friend and

bird-sitter, is still in the apartment when I get back from Saucebilities, and it's nice to talk to her before she heads out.

"It's nothing," I say, though that article is something. "It's a *stabloid*. Get it?"

Tara spins back to me, clearly not amused if the fire shooting from her eyes is any indications. "Yes, so funny." She shakes the paper in her hand. "I just can't believe this."

"It's drivel," I say. I want to tell her that she's gorgeous as-is, *and* she's the best chef in the city. "Whoever that guy is, he's extremely jealous."

She looks at me with pure hope in her eyes. "Really?"

"Absolutely," I say with authority. "He's probably got a brother starting up a catering company, and he's trying to smear Saucebilities."

"He called me fat."

"This isn't about you being big," I tell her. "At all."

"Then why did he say that?"

"Because he's threatened by you," I say. "Because you're so amazing, and he had to pick something." I look at the paper in her hand and nod to it. "Do you know him?"

Before she can answer, Peaches launches from the top of her cage. I expect her to flap a couple of times, because my apartment's not that big, and land on my shoulder. Instead, Peaches flies in a straight line toward Tara.

"Watch out," I say, trying to step between Tara and the incoming parrot.

Tara flaps the rolled up newspaper, yelling, "This is *unbelievable*," and whacks me in the face with the hard tube.

This woman, I think right before my hands jerk up to cradle my now-bleeding nose. She already threw me to the floor a few days ago.

"Bacon, bacon, bacon," Peaches says, her feet out and aimed right at Tara's head.

Oh, this is gonna be bad.

Peaches lands, screeching, "What in the world?" and Tara screams as she tries to get the bird out of her hair.

Literally.

CHAPTER FIVE

TARA

I WAVE MY ARMS WILDLY, DANCING AWAY FROM whatever has just attacked me. "Get it off!" I screech before realizing it's gone. My chest heaves and I reach up to gingerly touch my head where the claws just were.

Claws...

I turn around and face Alec. He's holding a cloth to his nose, which is bleeding, and he's got a green and yellow bird sitting on his shoulder. The bird has black and white features, and those freaky, keen eyes all birds have.

A legit bird. On his shoulder. *Creepy.* "What is that?" I ask, as if I've never seen a bird before. I own thirteen chickens, for crying out loud.

"This is a Quaker parrot," he says, looking from me to the bird. "Tell her your name."

"Peaches," the bird says, her voice almost as human as

mine. Well, mine if I've been inhaling helium for eight straight hours.

"Wow," I say, not quite sure if I'm talking to the bird or Alec.

He grins, and that is so not fair. He's already wearing a T-shirt that's two sizes too small, if the bulging pecs are any indication. I get a woman trying to squeeze into a pair of skinny jeans, but does he seriously not know he needs a large and not a small?

I lick my lips and lower my hand, not finding any scratches or blood on my scalp. "Did I hit you?" I ask, sure I'm going to die of humiliation at any moment. I can't believe Brett has written this article. My whole body shakes, and I can't get it to stop.

"A little," Alec says. "I'm learning to stay ten feet from you at all times." He gives me a bloody grin and walks into the kitchen. I watch him, taking in the food on the counter now between us.

I start to calm at the sight of the bacon-wrapped chestnuts. That only makes my blood boil harder, because isn't that what Brett just said?

She soothes herself with food, and that's fine. Chefs need to taste what they're making, try new recipes, and impress their clients. I just wonder if it means chefs like Tara won't be able to find the true source of happiness... which doesn't come wrapped in bacon.

"How did these turn out?" I say, glancing at the knife still lying on the cutting board. The toothpicks splayed all over. The leftover cuts of bacon. At least he's just as messy at home as he is in my kitchen.

"Good," he says, his back still to me as he cleans up his face. "You can have one if you'd like." His voice is maybe a little nasally, but I can't have hit him that hard. I barely remember doing it.

"Bacon, bacon, bacon," the bird starts to sing, bopping her head along with the semi-music.

"Peaches," Alec says, and the bird goes quiet. He turns toward where she was bee-bopping on the counter and lowers the towel. "How do I look?"

"What in the world?" she chirps next.

I can't stifle the giggle that flies from my mouth, and when I look at Alec, I burst out laughing.

"What?" he asks, smiling at me. "I don't make the *cut?*"

"Bacon, bacon, bacon," the bird chirps.

I laugh until I cry, because it's literally that or start sobbing into my newest chef's now-bloodstained, two-sizes-too-small T-shirt.

Alec grins and finishes wiping his face. His dark hair stands at weird angles, and he wets his fingers and runs them through it, getting it to settle down again.

His movement is so graceful, just like when he's got a knife in his hand. I glance at the knife still on the cutting board, remnants of onion there too.

"Let's make something," I say, reaching for the knife.

"What do you want to make?"

"I don't know," I say. "I just need to cook. Cooking calms me down."

He eyes the knife. "I don't know if I trust you with that knife in your hand."

"Why?" I ask. "Because I'm *plump*?" Disgust fills me, though what Alec said about Brett being jealous is probably true. "Who even uses the word *plump* anymore? What gives him the right to body shame me?"

Alec's eyes fill with fire, but he wisely says nothing. He turns and opens the fridge. "I've got stuff for grilled apple and cheese sandwiches?"

"Hit me with the Granny Smith," I say, and he tosses me a green apple. Surprise pulls through me, because I wasn't expecting him to have one, though everyone knows the Granny Smith is the best kind of apple to put in your grilled apple and cheese sandwich, and he probably wouldn't have suggested it if he didn't have the right variety of apple.

I wash the cutting board, because I don't want raw onion flavor in my apples, and then I start slicing. "I just can't even process what he said."

"Do you know the guy who wrote the article?" Alec moves next to me and starts laying out slices of bread.

"Yes," I growl. "He's my ex-boyfriend." I wave the knife through the air, coming a bit close to his ear. Maybe. Probably not. It's fine. "Fiancé. You know, it's all just semantics?" I look at Alec for confirmation, but he just stares back at me.

I go back to the apple, imagining it to be Brett's head. *Slice, slice, slice.*

"He thought I was already *married to my job.*" I say the last four words in a mocking tone. "He just doesn't know what it takes to open a business." I look at him, desperate for someone to understand.

"I'm sorry," Alec says, his voice quiet in a way I've not heard from him. He keeps his head down as he layers cheese over the bread. Who is this guy? He reminds me so much of the man I wandered around the Food and Wine Festival with, but he looks like the guy who glares at my other chefs like he's imagining slicing off their fingers and feeding them to his bird—which I didn't even know he owned.

I shake my head. I have *got* to stop fantasizing about him. A relationship with him is never going to happen. *Even if it did,* I think. *It would end badly.*

My mind recalls all the more horrible parts of that maddening article.

"Can you believe he named me by name?" I bring the knife up and hold it in front of me like a shield. "Like, what a jerky thing to do. What editor on this planet would let that go through?"

"A pretty lame one. I'm telling you, this is about Saucebilities. They're just trying to discredit you."

"I mean, *plump?*" I rage, waving the knife a little. Maybe I start to spell the ridiculous word. "I'll show him plump."

P-L-U-M-P goes the knife tip.

"Okay, Boss," he says, and that only makes fury shoot to the top of my head. He takes the knife from my hand and backs up. "I'm just going to relieve you of this before you take off one of my limbs."

"Oh, you're fine," I snap at him. "And I'd really appreciate it if you'd stop calling me *boss*."

He faces me, and I face him, and I will not blink first. Part of me wants to punch him in that pretty-boy nose for a second time tonight. Another part wants to know what his mouth against mine will feel like. And the biggest part of me is about to break down into horrible sobs.

I turn away and walk around the island, stopping by the table to grab my purse. "I have to go."

"What about the sandwiches?" he asks.

"I have to go," I say again, my voice breaking on the last word.

"Beep, beep," Peaches says, and she sounds like a toy car. "Motor-motor-motor-bike."

"Tara," Alec says, and he hustles in front of me, blocking my escape.

I really don't want to cry in front of him. I can't believe I drove all the way over here. I could've read the article online—as I did in the car. I could be raging at home, with seven take-out meals on the table. Callie would've listened to me. I could've called Jason, my cousin, and he'd have come over. Even Macie, my friend down the street, would be rage-eating with me right now.

Why am I standing in Alec Ward's apartment?

No, I hadn't been able to read the whole article at one stoplight. Well, I'd tried, but I'd gotten honked at once the light turned green.

I'm his boss, and I will not break down in front of him. Not over some stupid article written by a jealous ex who's made it his life's mission to make sure I stay beneath him.

"Why don't you show him that women of all sizes can find love?" he asks, those dark eyes of his challenging me. I think it's in a good way, but I have so much racing through my mind right now. "Because you're amazing, Tara, just how you are. You're smart, and you're savvy, and he's stooped to the lowest level to get you to think you're not."

He sighs and waves the knife himself. "Leave a comment on that article or something. Tell him you have a boyfriend and he's dead wrong. Or not. You don't *need* a boyfriend for him to be dead wrong."

I blink, sure I haven't heard him right. He can't be this sensitive, even if his voice was a bit on the aggressive side. *You're amazing, Tara.*

Does he really think so?

"It's not like you walk down to the grocery store and pluck a boyfriend off the shelf anyway," I say.

"Just stay for sandwiches," he says.

"I can't," I say, the change in conversation whipping me around a little. I'm used to fast-moving parts in the kitchen. Sizzling meats and bubbling sauces. People yelling for this dish or that one.

But somehow I can't keep up with this conversation. Maybe his one-step-away-from-the-sun hotness has melted my brain. Callie will no doubt ask me all about it.

And when she sees this article...I actually want to call her right now and read it out loud to her. She'll have a few choice words for Brett Daniels, the loser I dated a couple of years ago.

"Why can't you stay?" he asks, putting one hand on my arm. I think he's asked more than once, and his skin against mine unfreezes my thoughts this time.

"Because, Alec, if I stay for sandwiches, then he's right. I *do* soothe myself and my loneliness and my anger and every other emotion with food." I wave toward the kitchen, and at least I don't have that knife in my hand anymore. "I'm not even hungry. I ate an hour ago."

"I'm not hungry either," he says. "But I'm going to have a sandwich."

"You're also not plump," I say, rolling my eyes. "You're not the one whose name was just dragged through barbecue sauce and skewed on a kabob."

Alec looks at me for a moment, a cough coming out of his mouth. "Kabob?" he repeated, his smile appearing.

For some reason, I can't look away from his mouth, and I loathe myself a little bit more.

"Bacon, bacon, bacon," Peaches chirps.

"Come on, baby," Alec says in that sexy, Southern voice that is seriously going to undo me, slipping his fingers away from my arm and lifting his hand for his bird.

Peaches flies over to him, settling easily on his shoulder. "Eating a sandwich is probably better than confessing your feelings to a Quaker parrot."

"Motor-bike," Peaches says. "Bacon, bacon, bacon."

"She likes bacon," I say, smiling at the bird. I think we'd be great friends, because there are few foods better than bacon for soothing one's ego after reading a hate-article about plump chefs named Tara.

"It's an easy word for her," he says, taking her over to the giant birdcage that literally fills the entire living room. He turns back to me, and I see a level of vulnerability in his eyes I haven't before.

"Just stay for a minute," he says. "You don't even have to eat the sandwich. I'm worried about you."

"Why?"

"I don't think you should drive when you're so upset."

Probably not. I once hit a stop sign I was backing up so fast. I keep that to myself for now and turn back to the kitchen. Alec steps to my side, and it takes everything I have not to lean into him and steal some of his strength.

I sigh and say, "Fine, I'll stay for a sandwich. But if I do, you have to tell me what you confess to Peaches."

He looks at me out of the corner of his eye, and it's not a flirtatious or teasing look. More like a death glare.

"Pass," he says.

"Fine," I say. "Tell me how you got Peaches. Tell me something about that blasted bird that attacked me. You owe me that much."

"So I have to cook for you *and* talk? Doesn't seem like a fair trade."

"Okay," I say in a sing-song. "My death will be on your hands." I pretend to turn toward the door.

His full hand comes down on my arm, and I expect his touch to be heavy-handed and demanding, just like he is in the kitchen.

Instead, the feather-light touch sends a ripple of fireworks through my whole body and causes me to freeze.

Again. What is it with this guy and his frostbite touch?

"Stay," he says. "I'll cook for you, and I'll talk."

No woman would walk away when Alec Ward says, "Stay," in that voice.

So I do what most women would: I stay.

CHAPTER SIX

ALEC

I've just finished Peaches' repertoire of words when Tara says, "I think there's something getting a little too crisp."

I smell the char the moment she says it, and I leap to my feet. "No," I say, pure embarrassment pulling through me. What kind of chef burns a blasted grilled cheese sandwich?

The kind flirting with his boss, I think, though there's hardly room inside my head for such a thought.

I yank the pan off the low burner where it had been hanging out. Burning. I flip the sandwich, and it's not salvageable.

"Maybe it's okay," Tara says from the tiny, two-person kitchen table on the other side of the island.

"It's nowhere near okay," I grumble, my face heating

past comfortable. I can't face her with this catastrophe on my record. Determined that she won't see how completely black these sandwiches are, I pick up the pan and open the trashcan with my foot. In the sandwiches go, and I exhale as I practically throw the pan back onto the stovetop.

The loud clatter makes Peaches start squawking, and while I love that stupid bird with the only heart cells I have that know how to do that, I just want her to be quiet.

"My word, Alec," Tara says, frowning those dark eyebrows at me. "It's fine. Remember how I'm not hungry?"

Yeah, but I want her to stay. If I don't have a reason she should, she'll leave. I try to think through what else would get her to stay. I brace my palms against the countertop and ask, "Coffee?"

Tara looks undecided, and I sense her moving away from me. I start to make coffee anyway, knowing what will get her to stay. Talking.

"I mostly tell Peaches about where I was and what I was doing while she stayed with a friend of mine here in the city." I open the freezer, another idea in mind. "Ice cream?"

"Oh, now you're talking my language," Tara says, the smile clear in her tone. "If you have butter pecan, I might marry you for it."

I jerk my head up and face her, more heat filling my neck and cheeks than is humanly healthy. "I didn't mean to say that, by the way."

She simply grins at me, and while I haven't dated in a while, I know what interest looks like on a woman's face. She's *flirting* with me.

Dear Lord in Heaven, help me not be a jerk to this woman.

My momma instilled praying in her sons, that's for sure. Most of the time, I think it's a waste of time, but right now, the few seconds are worth taking just to get God on my side.

"Do you have butter pecan?"

I turn back to the freezer. "No," I say, but I think I'll buy a couple gallons and keep it here from now on. "I've got blueberry cheesecake and mint chocolate chip."

"Blueberry," she says, and I get it out. "Peaches didn't go with you when you traveled?"

"No," I say, taking her a spoon and a bowl. She bypasses the bowl and goes straight into the container of ice cream with the spoon.

"You have friends?" Tara asks, her voice so full of surprise that annoyance sings through me.

I return to the kitchen and pour the water into the coffee maker and start measuring grounds. "Funny," I say, tossing her a glare.

"I mean, of course you have friends." She actually shakes her head as if trying to dislodge thoughts there. "I just...you seem like the solitary kind."

"I am the solitary kind," I say, and that helps me put

up a couple of bricks between us that she's knocked down. Somehow, and I don't even know how.

"What made you that way?" she asks.

"The Marines," I say.

"You served in the Marines?"

With nothing left to do with the coffee maker, I turn to get down mugs. I take one over to her, our eyes meeting. "For a few years," I say.

"Is that where you learned to cook?"

"No, ma'am," I say, wondering if she'll hate that as much as me calling her *boss*. I should probably apologize for that, especially since it's not her fault I'm salty toward head chefs. "I trained in the culinary institute in Paris. That was on my résumé." I cock my head, seeing instantly that she didn't even look at it.

I start to laugh and return to the island for spoons, milk, and sugar. "You didn't read my résumé? I'm shocked by that."

"Why?"

"Number one, you label everything. Literally everything. There's a spot on the shelves for persimmons, and you've used them one time." I look at her, daring her to contradict me.

"Labeling is not a crime," she says, sticking a bite of blueberry cheesecake ice cream into her mouth.

"I disagree," I tease as Peaches starts to imitate the doorbell again. "Come on, you." I scoop her off the counter and put her in her cage. I reach for the blanket I throw over her cage while she hops to the top perch.

"What in the world?" she asks as I toss the blanket over the cage. She falls silent, and I turn back to Tara, catching sight of my T-shirts laying over the back of the couch. Another wave of humiliation tugs through me, but I don't reach for the shirts. Maybe she won't notice them.

"She'll be quiet now," I say.

"Who was keeping her here?" Tara asks.

"My friend Turner," I say. "He's a vet."

Her eyebrows go up now, and I like how expressive she is with them. I wonder what will happen to those perfectly sculpted eyebrows if I kiss her.

"Turner Winn?" she asks, sending my heart plummeting to the floor

"Yes," I say. "You know him?"

"I have thirteen chickens." She smiles. "He's great, because he's one of the only vets in the city who'll see a chicken."

"He is great," I say. "He kept Peaches after I—while I was gone." I clear my throat and look away from Tara. She has a powerful gaze though, and wow, I feel it pulling me back to her.

"Where did you go?"

"Here and there," I say, and Tara sighs.

She reaches for her purse and stands. "Okay, I'm going to go."

"Why?"

"Because you're a big, fat liar, Mister Ward." She glares at me and strides toward the front door.

"I'm a liar?" I follow her, not pleased with how fast this conversation turned.

"Yes," she says over her shoulder. "You said you'd feed me and tell me what you confide in Peaches about, neither of which you have done." She opens the door and faces me, plenty of fire in those eyes. "I'll see you tomorrow at work. I would appreciate it if you'd keep the article to yourself."

I don't even know how to respond to that. Does she think I'm going to post it on my social media? Well, she'll be sorely disappointed, because after I lost The Blackbriar, I closed all my social media accounts.

She sighs again as if I'm the most insufferable man alive, turns, and leaves. The door drifts closed, and I get control of myself in enough time to get my foot between it and the jamb before it achieves the job.

Tara's walking away from my apartment, her hips swaying for all she's worth. A male growl starts in the back of my throat, because she really is a gorgeous woman. I have literally never thought the word *plump* when thinking of adjectives for her, and my chest tightens at the article her ex wrote.

I want that whole story, but I'm not going to get it today. She steps on the elevator without looking back to me, though I'm sure she can feel me watching her. My brother always says he can. Heck, Byron says he knows when I'm thinking about him, and he used to call me to find out what was on my mind.

Before.

I sigh as the naughty twins step off the elevator, both of them turning straight in my direction. "Oh, no," I say, realizing they've got their loud friend from downstairs with them.

"Alec," one of them calls. "Can we talk to Peaches?" They run toward me, and it's all I can do to get the door closed a little bit before they arrive.

"No," I say, trying to use my former military voice on them as the trio arrives at my door. "Peaches is tired."

She makes the sound of the doorbell, and my neck suddenly can't hold up my head. "Fine," I say to Frederick, Finn, and their friend, Johnny. "Ten minutes, boys. Then you have to go, or I'll tell your mothers you were out back with those snakes."

Their eyes all round, and Frederick glances at his twin. "How does he know?"

"Don't ask me why," Peaches chirps from behind me, and I step back to let the boys into my apartment.

———

I SWEAR TO YOU, I type, smiling at my phone. *I went all the way to the top of the Grand Tetons. It felt like the top of the world.*

I've been texting Tara for an hour, and it's so much

easier to talk to her via my device. I frown at that thought, wondering if it's easier for her too. She doesn't seem to have a problem talking to other people, and I'm sure it's my saltiness that's kept her at bay.

Something about her sweetens me up, and when she sends, *Sounds like a pick-up line, Alec. A bad one,* I grin.

Do you think that impresses me? she asks next.

"Yeah," I say to myself. I've left Peaches in her cage down the hall. I left the T-shirts too. After the boys left—their bellies full of grilled apple and cheese sandwiches that were not burnt, thank you so very much—I'd retreated to my bedroom to read more of the newspaper I'd gotten that afternoon.

It should, I send to her. *Hiking is hard. The air is all thin, and you can't breathe.*

I'll be sure to join the Marines and go through basic training before I take a walk.

I smile, wondering what makes her tick. *Why do you label things?* I ask, changing the topic. She's told me when and how she started Saucebilities. I've been telling her where I've been for the eight months before coming to Charleston to retake my role as Peaches's father.

I hadn't left the country, but there's so much to do and see in the US that it feels like I did.

I like things to be where they're supposed to be, she says. *Then I don't lose things.*

Is that a habit of yours? Losing things?

Yes, she says.

What's the worst thing you've lost?

My husband.

I suck in a breath, the conversation moving from light-hearted and fun to somber and serious with just two words.

I'm sorry, I tap out, and those two words are so easy to type and yet so hard to say out loud. *I once lost my business.*

I swallow and stare at the words. They're unsent, and I'm not sure I should send them. "It probably cost her something to send what she did to you," I tell myself.

I look up, the city beyond my window still lit up and thriving. I haven't left the apartment tonight the way I normally do. The scent of Tara is still here, and I want to hold onto it.

I tap to send the text, hoping I haven't made the biggest mistake of my life.

You did? she asks.

She doesn't ask more, but my fingers fly across the keyboard. *Yeah,* I type. *I conceptualized, built, and opened The Blackbriar Inn down in the Atlanta area.* I clear my throat, though we aren't talking face-to-face.

Maybe I shouldn't tell her the name of it. Then she'll look it up and see some Wards still own it. I'll have more to tell her then.

"You want to," I say. "Do it." I send the text, and the next thing I know, Tara's calling me. I stare at the incoming call, my heartbeat hammering in my chest.

I answer the call, and say, "Calm down," my mind still rotating through what I need to do to converse with this beautiful woman.

"Calm down?" Tara repeats. "Wow, Alec, what a way to answer the phone."

CHAPTER SEVEN

TARA

I GRIN TO MYSELF, REALIZING I'M FLIRTING WITH THE ex-Marine on the other end of the line.

"Sorry," Alec says. There's no chirping of his bird in the background, and I wonder if he covers her every night. Maybe he sleeps with her in the same bed as him.

I glance at Tommy and Goose, my two dogs who *do* sleep with me every night. There has to be another breathing body in the room with me, and I've had Tommy since the day my ex walked out.

Alec grinds his voice through his throat, and I glance at the TV flickering in the room. "So," he says. "You called me."

I flinch, realizing he's right. "Your text surprised me," I say.

"Which part?"

"You owning an inn," I say.

"Because I'm a man?" he asks, his voice turning hard. "Men can own inns too, you know."

I blink, because that's not what I was thinking. "Did you run all of it, or just the kitchen?"

"Primarily the kitchen," he says. "But I had my hand in all of it."

There are so many questions now. "And?" I prompt.

"And we were talking about losing things."

"I've lost so many things," I say. "I once had to go get a new social security card after I misplaced mine. I never did find it." I smile, because it's easy to talk about what a loser I am after the fact. "I don't even look for things anymore. If I can't find something, I just replace it."

Alec chuckles, and such a sound is so not fair. "Sounds like you have a system for it," he says. "But it's completely opposite of labeling everything so nothing gets lost."

"Well, I'm an enigma, Mister Ward." I reach for my laptop, which is like a third appendage when I don't have a knife in my hand. "The Blackbriar Inn?"

"You don't need to look it up," he says.

"Oh, I'm looking it up," I tease.

"My father and brother still own it," he says, and it sounds like he blurted it out.

I pause though I have opened the laptop. I knit together some of the things he's said that day.

He kept Peaches while I was gone.

I went all the way to the top of the Grand Tetons.

I used to own an inn.

JUST HIS BOSS 69

I swallow, the tension as thick as ever between us. "I'm sorry you lost it," I say. "Knowing you, I'm sure it was perfect."

"I worked hard on it at least."

"I won't look at it." I snap the laptop closed. "What made you want to open an inn?"

"I know what women want," he says.

I blink, sure we've changed topics rapidly, the way he did while we were texting. I start to giggle, and I can't stop.

"That's not what I meant," Alec says, clearly frustrated. That only makes me laugh harder. "I'm hanging up now."

He does, and I'm still giggling. I'm also seriously considering giving him my personal cell phone number so I don't have to flirt with him on the chef-cell. I have the two phones to keep the parts of my life separate that need to be that way.

Alec has blurred all those lines, especially with the way he said to show Brett that women of all sizes can find love, and that I'm amazing and smart, and that I should leave a comment on his biased, ridiculous article.

I open my laptop again, but this time, I go to the newspaper website and start typing.

———

THE NEXT MORNING, I leave my house with my purse slung over my shoulder, the same way I have loads of times. Across the street, I see a van I've never seen before.

It looks like a TV van, and when a sharply dressed woman emerges from the driver's seat, I nearly trip over my stupid feet. Again. Whoever makes orthopedics really needs to up their game in the steadiness department.

"Miss Finch," she calls, and I increase my pace to my own car.

A reporter. My worst nightmare.

If I don't say anything, she won't have anything to write. I still feel like I need a huge pair of sunglasses and a wide-brimmed hat to get out of this disaster.

"Why did you comment on Brett Daniels's article? Do you two have a history?"

Humiliation strikes me straight in the chest. Leaving that revenge comment was a bad idea, though it had seemed like a good one at midnight, with all those Thai noodles in my belly.

I hold my head high as I go around the front of my car. I duck my head as I reach to open the door. A man has gotten out of the van too, and he's recording me. Legit recording.

I get in the car, feeling a little safer, which makes no sense. It's not like the video camera can't see through glass.

I reach up and smooth my hair back, my heart pounding. The cameraman stands right behind my car and Miss Classy is at the passenger window.

I'll run this guy over if I have to. I'm not the one who wrote a 1500-word article on chefs in the city, but only named one of them. Focused on her love life—or lack thereof. Hypothesized that chefs are only in love with themselves and their food, and therefore have a hard time finding a human being to love.

My face burns, and I put the car in reverse and honk the horn. As I'm pulling out of my driveway, I see Mr. Reynolds coming down his sidewalk. He's waving his hand and yelling. Relief fills me at the older gentleman's help. He lives right next door to me, and I'll need to bring him some of the strawberry shortcake cupcakes tonight after all of our prep work for tomorrow's luncheon.

I make it to the stop sign at the end of the street and turn right. A car pulls out from the curb behind me. My heart races the whole way to work, and I see another TV van parked in front of my building as I go around to the back.

"What have you done?" I ask myself. I haven't hit any stoplights, and I couldn't delete the comment on the way over. In the back, a couple of cars and a truck sit there. Jared, Henry, and Alec are already here, though I'm not late.

Maybe I should call one of them to help me get inside. "Don't be stupid," I say to myself. I made it to my car just fine, and there are no camera crews back here. It's ten steps to the door, and my guys will have it unlocked.

I grab my purse and step from the car. I rush toward

the door and reach for the handle. It's one of those that lifts up to open, but my fingers miss it. The handle flaps and clangs as my fingers slide out from underneath it.

Frowning, I try again, this time getting the heavy metal door open. I step inside, my foot landing right in a puddle of water. It splashes up my leg, making me cringe and my mood to turn fouler.

"What's going on?" I ask, scenting something on the air that's not quite right either.

"The dishwasher is on the fritz," Jared says. "Alec's working on it." He reaches for my hand, and I take it. There's nothing between us at all but camaraderie and friendship. No sparks. No fireworks. No electricity the way there is with Alec.

I hate that as much as I like it.

I don't quite clear the pond still enlarging on the floor, because I really can't jump very far. More water flies up, splashing everyone within ten feet and making me feel like I just bellyflopped in the pool and lost the top of my bikini.

"Oh," I say. "I need to lock the door."

"Lock the door?" Jared asks. "Why?"

"Because this whole place is crawling with press," Alec says, appearing with a dishtowel in his hands. He glares at me like it's my fault the dishwasher malfunctioned. "They followed me to work too."

I stare at him. "Really?" Why would they follow him?

He steps past me and without even having to hop or jump at all and clears the puddle to the door in a single step. He twists the lock and turns back to meet my eye. "I think we need to have a staff meeting."

I hate his use of "we," though he's right. I turn away from him and head for my office. "Give me a minute."

"Tara," he says after me, but I don't turn back to him. I just need one freaking second to find a full breath, and I just know it's going to be in my office.

I step inside and dump my purse on my desk. I've sat here and typed out my recipes dozens and dozens of times. I've been writing a cookbook for over a year, and the only reason I haven't thrown it away is because Callie won't let me.

My pulse has started to settle when someone pounds on my door, and I jump out of my skin, sure it's one of my best friend's serial killers, come to make mincemeat out of me.

Then Alec opens the door and says, "They're coming in the building. We need you out here, Boss."

I brace myself against my desk and glare at him. "If you call me *boss* one more time..."

Alec gives me a sexy smile and ducks out of the office as Jared calls for him.

I've got to get myself and my kitchen together. But first, I need to delete my comment from Brett's article online and hope I can control the damage from there.

ALEC DOESN'T GET VERY FAR from me as we walk through the building and make sure all the doors are locked. I pull down every blind, though I'm one of those that likes the sunshine streaming through the glass the moment the day awakens.

I've had my meeting, explaining the article in as few words as possible to Alec, Jared, and Henry in person. Jared had put me on video for Barley, and now all the chefs at Saucebilities know about the article. I saw Henry shaking his head with a frown as he read something on his phone, and my face burns hot even now.

Alec is like a hulking shadow behind me, and I nearly run into him a time or two, my annoyance with him and the whole situation growing with every second. I finally turn toward him and say, "I don't need a bodyguard." I'm eternally grateful I didn't call him to come escort me the ten feet into the building. How embarrassing would that have been?

"Maybe I do," he says.

I'm not sure what to say to that, and the twinkle in Alec's eye says he knows as much. I need something to hold over his head, and I seize onto his inn. "You know what? I'm going to look up Blackbriar the moment I get home."

He rolls those beautiful eyes and says, "You do what you have to do." At least he doesn't tack a "boss" on the end of the sentence. If he had, I have no idea what I would've done. Claws would've come out, I'm fairly certain of that.

He cocks his head and folds his arms. "I saw your comment on the online version of the article."

I suck in a breath, my eyes going wide. "It was a moment of weakness."

"I found it articulate," he says. "Well-written."

I gesture toward the blinded windows. "And now the press is all over me. Us." I take a deep breath and sigh. "I'm not going to give them another comment, and I deleted the first one."

"Oh, they've all seen it already," he says. "I wouldn't be surprised if Brett whips out another inflammatory article in next week's edition."

My irritation grows at the same rate as my horror. "My word," I say. "I gave him fodder."

Alec smiles, a half-laugh coming out of his mouth, as if he hasn't done such a thing in so long. It almost sounded rusty. "Fodder. Good word. I'm surprised you didn't go into journalism yourself."

"Please," I say. "They're slime balls, parking outside of my house and yelling at me in my neighborhood."

His smile slips. "Did they come onto your property?"

"Yes," I say, and I wipe my hand through my hair. It's come out of its normally tight ponytail, which is so abnormal. Everything in my life is always so lined up. Buttoned close. Labeled.

Sure, I lose a few things, because there are so many

moving parts to keeping chickens, raising two dogs, and running a catering company. But I've never lost my sanity before. Standing in front of Alec, especially as his hand drifts toward my face and brushes that loose lock of hair back from my cheek, I feel completely crazy.

"I'll go home with you," he says.

A grin pops onto my face, cementing how completely loony this all is. "Is that a promise?" I ask, cocking my head. I scan him to his feet and back to those glittering eyes. Something flashes there, and I saw it in Florida too. I saw it in his apartment last night.

Oh, boy. I suck in a breath.

That's desire, I think, and I feel it coursing through my body at twice the speed it was a moment ago. I haven't had a man look at me like this in a long time.

Too long.

Doesn't mean I don't recognize it when I see it.

"Yes," Alec says, and then he turns and heads back down the hallway. "We better get this prep done if we want to get out of here before dark."

I don't tell him I wasn't planning on leaving once we get the prep done for tomorrow's banquet at one of Charleston's premier garden centers.

I have a strawberry shortcake cupcake recipe to perfect so it can go in my cookbook. "I also don't need him to make sure I get home safe," I mutter to myself. I can want something and not need it, something my momma instilled in me from a young age.

You need food and water, Tara. Not high heels. You just want those.

And now I want a dreamy ex-Marine who can cook circles around everyone else...but I don't *need* him, and I certainly can't have him.

Can I?

CHAPTER EIGHT

ALEC

I FINISH WIPING DOWN ALL THE COUNTERS, GLANCING over to where Tara is boxing up the last of the shelled edamame. We'll be back here in the morning to finish the dishes and get everything in the two vans she owns for transport to the garden center.

I don't mind working weekends, because I don't have anything better to do. My phone zings at me, and I pull it from my pocket now that I'm done cooking and cleaning. Jessie's texted that she has to go, and I quickly tap out a message that she can. Peaches will be fine for a while without anyone there.

Yes, I pay someone to come sit with my parrot and keep her company. Birds are really social, and I work a lot. I don't think Tara would be thrilled to have the bird here, and paying Jessie eases my conscious.

I look up as Tara sets the stand mixer on the newly-polished stainless steel countertop. "What are you making?" I ask.

"You don't need to stay," she says instead of answering. "I don't need help getting home." She glances at me, but she doesn't truly *look* at me. My heart pounds a little harder, as I was actually really looking forward to going home with her.

Not with her, I tell myself. I'd just drive behind her and make sure she got inside her house okay. That's it.

"I'm working on a new recipe," she says. "I'm not leaving for a while."

I look down at my phone as she goes into the pantry to get her ingredients. Jessie's leaving. She's been with Peaches all day. The bird will be fine alone for a couple of hours. Sometimes I leave the TV on for her, and she's learned how to say some words from it.

I almost always leave her after checking in to go sit in the hot tub in the clubhouse too. She'll be okay.

"Can I help?" I ask Tara as she returns with sugar, flour, baking soda, and freeze-dried strawberries. "Looks like you're baking."

She nearly drops the canisters, and they go clanging across the metal countertop. Honestly, the woman is somewhat of a klutz, but the moment she picks up a knife, she's like a ballerina. All grace and fine lines.

Her face shines a bit pinker as she says, "If you want. It's just cupcakes, but I want to take some to my neighbor. He tests all of my recipes."

Immediately, my shackles go up. *"He does?"*

"Yes," she says without looking at me as she rights the box of soda. "Luther Reynolds. He lost his wife a few years ago, and I'll show up with cupcakes and he'll make tea, and we'll have a little party." She smiles as she says it, and the softness of it makes me relax.

"So he's like your grandfather."

"Not quite that old," she says. "Maybe twenty or twenty-five years older than me."

"How old are you?" I ask, realizing a moment too late that I shouldn't have asked. "I mean—never mind."

"Thirty-three," she says easily. "You?"

"Thirty-five."

She does look at me then, and time suspends right then and there. She has to see how interested I am in her, because I can't hold it back. I can see something sparking in her eyes, but I fight against it.

She's my boss. I can't let my emotions get in the way again. "Tara," I say slowly, determined to tell her about Heidi. "Uh, the last time I got involved with my boss, I lost the inn."

"That makes no sense," she says. "You owned the inn."

I clear my throat. "Right, yeah, I know."

She starts measuring flour into a sieve. "So what do you mean? And who says we're going to get involved? We've worked together just fine for months." She focuses on her task, and I just want her to look at me. Be present for five minutes while we work through this.

Confusion riddles my mind, and I'm not sure which question to answer first. "I mean...I'm...not interested in losing this job."

"Great," she says. "Because you're the best chef I've had in a long time."

I sigh, this conversation not going the way I want it to at all. I don't even know what I want. "What kind of cupcakes are you making?"

"Nice try," she says, giving me a half smile as she sifts the flour, sugar, and soda together. "What do you mean about you losing the inn?"

"My brother stepped in to finance the inn," I say slowly, picturing Byron's face in my mind. He's even more stern than I am, but it doesn't matter, because he's married with a baby on the way. "Technically, he was my boss, though my name was on the ownership papers too."

"You had an affair with your brother?" she asks, finally stopping to look up at me. Those long eyelashes frame her eyes, which sparkle with a teasing glint.

"Funny," I say, rolling my eyes. "No, of course not."

"His girlfriend then," she teases, reaching for the clotted cream. I've never seen anyone make cupcakes with clotted cream instead of butter, and Tara fascinates me to the very core. Clotted cream isn't even something available in the United States, which means Tara's made it herself.

I fold my arms and say, "Well, she's his wife now."

Tara throws the clotted cream several inches, her

wide, shocked eyes coming up to meet mine. "Alec..." She lets her voice trail off. "That's why you lost the inn?"

"Well, I couldn't stay," I say. "Not when I found out she was kissing me in the refrigeration unit and him in the manager's office." I shake my head. "It doesn't matter. I made a decision to leave when I could've stayed. I signed everything over to them, and I...left."

I'm not even sure which order things went in after that. I remember calling Turner here in Charleston. I had to stop here and drop off Peaches. I've always loved South Carolina and the Lowcountry, as I grew up not far from here. This feels like a good place for me to be, but I don't say any of that.

Tara has walked toward me, and I didn't even know it. "I'm so sorry," she says softly, and then she takes me right into her arms. I can't remember the last time I've been hugged, and I'm fairly certain I melt right into her. Every defense against her that I've been building and then rebuilding when she knocks it down disappears.

She could order me to do a jig, and I'd do it.

I take a deep breath of her, getting sugar, sweat, and strawberries. I want to hold her for a lot longer, but I force myself to pull away. As I clear my throat, I take a step back.

"Okay," she says. "You can stay and help me with the cupcakes." She smiles, breaking all the tension between us. How she does that, I'll never know. "And if you're lucky, you can come eat one with me and Mister Reynolds tonight too."

"Oh, I can't," I say. "My bird-sitter has gone home, and I can't be out late. It sends Peaches into a frenzy."

Tara's eyes widen again. "A frenzy? Is that what happened last night when she attacked me?"

I laugh. "She did not attack you. Birds like to perch on the highest object, and that happened to be your head."

"My *giant* head," she says, moving back over to the mixer. "Great. I knew I was twice as big as you."

"Whoa, whoa," I say. "That's not what I said."

"It's fine, Alec." She doesn't look at me now though.

"Listen," I say. "I just wanted you to know that I like you. I like this job." I'm talking so fast, but I better get it out before she throws me out of the kitchen. "If I didn't work here, and you weren't the boss, I'd probably ask you out. There's this great place down on the water where they serve these tiny mousse cakes, and every Tuesday, they do all their flavors for a flat fee. So every fifteen minutes you can get another one. The lights shine on the water and—" I cut off, horrified at what I've said.

Tara's staring at me, an egg held in her hands that she's already cracked. The white leaks through the shell and onto the counter, but she doesn't seem to notice.

I barely notice, because when Tara's in the room, she lights me up. "I'm sorry," I blurt out again. "Forget everything I've said. I have to go. Peaches needs me." I practi-

JUST HIS BOSS   85

cally rip the apron off my waist and hang it on the wall near the front entrance to the kitchen.

Tara's gaze weighs a thousand pounds, and it sticks to me as I walk through the kitchen to the back door. It's locked, and I have to fight with it to get it open.

When I do, I simply walk out, telling myself I've said way too much as it is. It would've been nice had Tara said some*thing, but I don't wish for things. *Remember, Alec? Don't wish. Just work hard.*

"Alec," someone says the moment the door closes behind me. "Tara Finch was seen leaving your apartment last night. Did you talk to her about the article written by Brett Daniels? Can we get a comment?"

"No," I growl out, wishing Tara knew what waited for her out here. Perhaps I really shouldn't leave. I muscle past the man and his held-up cellphone and get in my SUV. I take a moment while the air conditioner gets nice and cold to send a text to Tara.

Reporters in the back alley. You sure you don't want me to stay?

I recognize the significance of what I've texted. Last night, I asked her to stay. She had. I've never really stuck it out and stayed anywhere, especially when things get hard.

The Marines wasn't hard for me. Culinary school wasn't either. Seeing Heidi with Byron...was. Astronomically hard. Letting go of The Blackbriar Inn had also nearly taken everything from me.

The only thing I had left was my ability to run away.

Maybe you better, she texts. *I promise these cupcakes are going to be worth it, and maybe we can call a Carry and sneak out the front.*

With Tara, there are an infinite amount of maybes, and I find myself wanting to explore them all. My heart wails at me as I kill the ignition and get out of my SUV. I can't promise it that Tara won't shred it up again, but at the same time, I want to find out if she'll handle it with care.

The reporter yells another question at me as I walk to the back door, and then Tara's there, opening it for me. I meet her eye, step past her, and do something completely reckless.

I slide my hand along her waist as I turn, whisper, "Smile," and give the reporter only a few feet in front of me my best grin.

CHAPTER NINE

TARA

I LAUGH LIKE I NEVER HAVE BEFORE. "YOU'RE LYING," I say through the giggles. Alec throws the empty container of strawberry ice cream in the trashcan, and he's laughing too.

"I swear, I'm not," he says. "I screamed like a little girl and reached for the nearest object. I had no idea it was Chef Florence's favorite ladle."

I pile the strawberry buttercream into the piping bag, still laughing.

"It wasn't a ladle when I finished slamming it on the countertops," he says, and he's a different person when he's not cooking for work. He'd layered all the cookies in the liners, as well as the topped the berries and put them in too. By then I'd had the batter put together, and I'd piped it around the fruit.

While the ice cream melted for this buttercream and

the cupcakes baked, I'd called Mr. Reynolds and told him I'd be by in a little bit with dessert. He'd told me there had been people by my house all day long, but he was keeping an eye on everything for me.

I squeeze down the frosting and twist the bag, gearing up to put a dollop on every cupcake. "You can dip these in those strawberries you chopped up." I start icing the cupcakes as Alec steps to my side.

"I've been talking for an hour," he says. "Are you going to tell me what this recipe is really for?"

I glance at him, my usually steady hand with a piping bag trembling a little bit. "I don't want you to laugh at me."

"Why would I laugh at you?"

"For starters, I tried to serve a winter soup at my best friend's summer wedding," I say. "I'm thirty pounds over-weight, without a boyfriend, and the entire city knows it. I threw you to the ground with my enormous feet, and I splashed water from here to the door when I got here today." I lift one of my orthopedic-clad shoes. "Oh, and your bird flew right at my head last night, causing me to pretty much freak out. Pick one."

"Peaches has a mind of her own," Alec says. "We don't get many visitors."

"Oh," I say, hurrying to finish the piping now. "My cousin is going to meet us at Mr. Reynolds's."

"She is?"

"He," I say. "I'm an only child, but I have four cousins

in the area. I'm closest to Jason, and he texted earlier today to make sure I was okay."

"Are you okay?" Alec asks, once again showing me his softer side.

"Yes," I say, not wanting to get into more detail than that. I'm still reeling a little bit from him admitting that he'd ask me out if I wasn't his boss. He obviously isn't going to act on that, and the familiar need vs. want debate runs through my mind.

"So who babysits your bird?" I ask.

Alec clears his throat, and that's his tell. He doesn't want me to know, but he doesn't want to lie either. "A friend of mine."

"Does this friend have a name?"

"Jessie," he says, and I force myself to finish piping before I look up at him. He picks up the last cupcake I've just iced, and he dunks it in the freeze-dried strawberries. "We grew up together. Neighbors."

They might as well have come straight out of a romance novel. Best friends. Grew up together. Lived next door to one another.

"Is Jessie a boy or a girl?" I ask.

"Girl."

I do my best not to wince, and I actually achieve it. Points for me. And I'll reward myself with three scoops of ice cream for breakfast tomorrow instead of two. Or maybe I'll order three number sevens from China Dream tonight.

Whatever. It's fine. His best friend is a female who clearly Peaches already adores. No problem.

"Where did you two grow up?" I ask, surprised at my level of professionalism. My voice didn't even sound sarcastic or hurt.

"Beaufort," he says. "Have you heard of it?"

"Everyone's heard of Beaufort," I say, impressed. "You must have old money."

"Not me specifically," he says, doing that throat clearing again.

"Does your family still live there?"

"Just my mama and my younger brother," he says. "Dad and Byron are down in Atlanta."

"Are your parents divorced?"

"Yes," he says. "Yours?"

"No," I say. "They moved to Miami after my dad retired." My voice gets quieter and quieter with each word. We've finished the cupcakes, but I don't want to leave quite yet. "I miss them."

"I'll bet," he says. "It's hard to be alone in the city."

"Jason is still here," I say. "We get along well, so that helps. And I have Callie—and now Dawson too." I have Mr. Reynolds next door, and Macie, my friend down the street who owns the coffee shop. I have the dogs and all the chickens. I'm not alone, even if it feels like it sometimes.

"Hm."

"Maybe we should go to Port Royal Island," I say. "See

the sights."

He glances at me, but we're done with the cupcakes. "It's the beach. You get the same view just down the street."

"Sure," I say, smiling at him. "Don't worry, Alec, I won't make you take me to the most beautiful town in the Lowcountry if you don't want to."

"Actually," he says, shaking his shoulders as if he's a dignitary. "It was named the best small Southern town, not the most beautiful town."

"Semantics," I say, remembering I'd said the same thing about Brett and him being my fiancé. He had technically asked me to marry him. I'd technically said yes. When he broke up with me, he said he wouldn't play second fiddle to a catering company, and that I was already married to Saucebilities.

"Words are powerful." Our eyes meet, and my pulse zaps through my body. He clears his throat again. "I really don't think you needed to take your comment down."

I straighten and start to put the cupcakes back into the cooled tin. It's really the best way to transport cupcakes, as they don't slide around. "You don't know Brett the way I do."

"Next time we bake," he says. "You'll have to talk for the whole hour, and then maybe I will." He gives me a smile, and I find myself wanting him to know.

"You know where I live?" I ask, raising my eyebrows.

"I remember," he says.

I pick up the cupcake tin and face him. "I've been working on a cookbook. This is the last recipe for the cupcake section."

He picks up the two empty wrappers from the treats he's consumed. He doesn't raise his eyebrows. His eyes don't get wider. He simply smiles at me as he puts the liners in the trashcan. "That's great, Tara," he says, and I sure do hear the absence of the word "boss" as my whole body heats from the Southern way he uses my proper name.

―――――

I CLOSE THE DOOR, aware I'm going to have to answer to Jason and Mr. Reynolds. I should've followed Alec out the door, but the tea hasn't even been served yet.

"He's handsome," Jason says, and I turn toward him.

"Don't make a big deal out of this," I say. "He just works for me, and we were bombarded at the kitchen with the press, and he wanted to make sure I got back home okay, especially after I told him there was a TV crew here this morning."

"Those people have no respect," Mr. Reynolds says, bringing a tray out into the living room. "I chased three of them off my property today." He smiles down at Goose as the little dog jumps up onto the couch as if eager for some of the herbal tea Mr. Reynolds is so good at making. "They rang your doorbell all day long."

"Not the sharpest tools in the shed," I say.

"I finally brought the boys over here," he says, sitting down and letting Goose sit on his lap. I once suggested he should get a dog of his own, but he says they're like grandchildren—he likes it when they're around, but then he gets to send them home for someone else to take care of permanently.

"Where's Tommy?" I ask.

As if on cue, the little black and white dog comes trotting into the living room. He's got a sock in his mouth, and I reach for it. "You devil," I say. "You stay out of Mr. Reynolds's room." I put the sock on the side table. "Sorry."

"It's fine." Mr. Reynolds leans forward, his longer hair flopping forward onto his forehead. He's completely silver now, though when I'd moved into this house after I'd sold the one Otis and I had shared, his hair had just started to turn gray. "Come sit down, Tara. I want to hear about this new chef."

"You've heard of him," I say. "He's Alec."

Mr. Reynolds hands me a cup of tea, and I wrap my fingers around the warming ceramic. "Alec? The rude one?"

"I don't think I ever said rude," I say. "Grouchy, yes. Grumpy, sure. Salty. I think I've used salty the most."

"She conveniently forgot to mention how good-looking he was," Jason says, and I throw him a death glare, hoping that will be enough for him to shut his mouth.

"Maybe his good looks have been overshadowed by his

forked tongue," I say.

"You two looked plenty cozy tonight," Jason says, accepting a cup of tea from Mr. Reynolds.

"He's...growing on me," I admit.

My cousin grins, and his mama would be so glad all the money she spent on braces has paid off. He's got straight, white teeth, and with his dark beard, hair, and eyes, I'm pretty surprised he hasn't been able to find someone to settle down with.

He's told me plenty of times that he doesn't want to settle down. If he did, he would've done it by now. I think it's just so convenient that he thinks he can do whatever he wants, when he wants to do it.

Jason has lived a somewhat charmed life, so he probably could get a woman and make her his wife if he wanted to. I wish I could do what I'd said to Alec before— go down to the grocery store and just pluck a boyfriend off the shelf.

It would be easier than trying to meet someone after working in the kitchen for twelve straight hours. A night at Mimi's, with all their mousse cakes coming every fifteen minutes sounds about perfect, and I sip my tea while my mind circles around Alec.

"Tara," Jason says, and I blink my way out of my thoughts. "There you are." He grins at me knowingly.

"What?" I ask.

"Tommy's licking your cupcake."

I glance at the coffee table and push the little dog back.

"Stop it." I pick up the cupcake and wipe my finger through the frosting where his tongue was. I put it in a paper towel and glare at my pup. "Naughty thing."

"I think you're the naughty thing," Jason says. "Bringing that muscley man here with those cupcakes."

"Muscley?" I laugh, though I have seen him in a two-sizes-too-small shirt. Still, his chef jacket is the right size, and he hadn't loosened it on the drive from Saucebilities to my neighborhood.

"Oh, come on," Jason says. "Give us something."

"There's nothing to give," I say. "He has a bird who attacked me. He fixed my dishwasher today. He's a fantastic chef." I shrug. "So he's a little grumpy sometimes, but you know...I think he has his reasons."

I think about what he told me about his brother and his ex-girlfriend. That can't have been easy, watching the two of them get married.

"We always do," Mr. Reynolds says. "Right after Karen died, I found myself yelling at a hostess in the restaurant where we used to celebrate our anniversary."

I put my cupcake on a small plate and look at Mr. Reynolds. "You never told me that."

"I try to keep the embarrassing things to myself."

"Hey," I say, smiling as I pick up my knife and fork. "You never let me do that."

"Yeah, like eating a cupcake with a steak knife," Jason quips as I cut into the dessert.

"I like seeing it," I say, nudging the two halves apart.

The strawberry is juicy and some of the redness has stained the vanilla cookie. It's perfectly baked, if I do say so myself, and I can't wait to taste that strawberry buttercream.

I take a bite of one half of the cupcake, and a party starts in my mouth. "I sent some home with Alec so he can tell me if they're good or not."

"Sure," Jason says. "You sent some home with Alec so you have an easy reason to call him."

"Your point?" I ask, grinning at my cousin.

"The point, Legs, is that if he's just some guy who works for you, why are you finding innocent-seeming reasons to call him?"

"Don't call me Legs," I say around all the delectable strawberry flavor. No one's called me that for years, and since it's not a nickname that comes because I have good legs, I hate it.

My chef-cell chimes, and I raise my chin and pretend not to hear it. My fingers itch to check it though, and Jason knows it.

He grins at me and grins at me, while a second chime and then a third joins the first.

"Oh, answer it already," he says. "I'm dying to know what handsome-hot-stuff has to say about the cupcakes you sent home with him."

I choke-scoff on "handsome-hot-stuff" and roll my eyes. My real phone rings, and I recognize the *boom-chicka-pop* of Callie's ringtone.

"Oh, there's your girlfriend," Jason says. "Who are you going to answer first?" He bites into his own cupcake, and his eyes roll back in his head. "Can I take a dozen of these home?"

"Forget it," I say, pulling out my friend-phone.

"I take back everything I said about Alec," Jason says. "Marry him for all I care. Just let me have one cupcake for breakfast tomorrow."

"Fine," I say as I swipe on Callie's call. "Hey, Cal. What's up?"

"I just turned to come down your street, and I saw Alec leaving. You tell me, and you tell me right now: What's going on with him?"

Jason starts to chuckle, his dark eyes dancing with delight. "Go on, Tara. Tell her what's going on with that really ugly man."

"I thought he was very symmetrical," Mr. Reynolds says. "I know how Tara likes that."

"You two are going to be the death of me," I say, getting up.

"I'm pulling into your driveway right now," Callie says. "You better have the door open for me, because there's a lot of sketchy vans and trucks parked here I've never seen before."

I go to Mr. Reynolds's front door and open it. "I'm not home. I'm next door having cupcakes and tea with Mr. Reynolds." I walk outside and down the front step. "I'm coming to get you."

Callie emerges from her car, and while it's not quite dark yet, she says twilight is a terrible time because one can't really see if someone's lurking in the shadows.

She marches toward me in a pair of platform sandals. "How are you after that awful article?" She takes me into a hug right there on the sidewalk, and I have to admit it's good to see her.

"I'm hanging in there," I say. "Come taste the cupcakes I want to serve at your wedding." I link my arm through hers and start back to Mr. Reynolds's. "Jason's over, and he will not let up about Alec."

"You better start talking fast then," she says as we turn to go down the sidewalk.

"Nothing to talk about," I say. "I'm just his boss; he's just my chef."

"Okay," Callie says, and even if she doesn't believe me, she doesn't press it.

"Where's Dawson tonight?" I ask.

"He and Lance are out getting a new doorknob for his back door. Finally."

I grin, because Callie has a thing for locks, and she's been badgering her boyfriend to get his fixed for months.

We reach the top of the steps, and Callie pauses. "Tell the truth. You and Alec?"

"Nothing," I confirm, deciding that if he can ignore the chemistry between us, so can I.

I can. I will. I absolutely can and will.

CHAPTER TEN

ALEC

I GROAN AS I LOOK AT THE SUNDAY NEWSPAPER. THE Local section has the picture of me and Tara, framed by the back door of the kitchen, grinning at the camera. It's grainy and not even all that focused, because that guy used his cellphone in bad lighting.

Definitely *stabloid* material.

"She's going to fire you," I mutter to myself.

In the living room, Peaches is chattering to herself, mixing her name in with motorbikes and bacon and now peekaboo. I have to leave for work in a few minutes, and I debate over calling Tara now or waiting to find out if she's seen the new article.

This one doesn't have a by-line with Brett's name on it, but Stephen Fyfe. I don't know him from Adam, and I wonder if Tara does. It's doubtful, but she has lived here for a while. Plus, if she did date Brett, maybe she knew other reporters too.

"What in the world?" Peaches asks, but I don't even look at her.

The article has us both listed by name, and I glare at it as if I can burn the letters right off the page with just my eyes.

Tara texted me a lot over the past week, mostly to get my opinion on the strawberry shortcake cupcakes, as well as whether or not she should hire another chef. I couldn't think of a single thing to tell her about the cupcakes, and we've been talking about our families a little bit more.

I know she's been asking Henry, Jared, and Barley about their schedules too, and yes, we all work a whole lot. If she's going to keep taking on events and parties the way she does, then she should hire someone else.

I'd thought about flirting with her every time my phone buzzed and her name came up, but in the end, I'd deleted all of those texts unsent. I can't stand in the kitchen and tell her I'd ask her out if she wasn't my boss and then flirt with her at night. How unfair is that?

"Peekaboo, boo," Peaches says, flying toward me. I brace myself for her birdie feet to grip my shoulder. She squawks and slips, because I'm not wearing a shirt yet. They're still on the back of the couch, as I can't seem to get them put away even when I think about it.

The past week has seen the reporters backing down quite a bit. They've stopped hanging out around my building at least, and Tara says she only had one at her house yesterday. With this new article, though, I'm sure the vultures will be out in force again soon enough.

She shouldn't have left her comment, and I feel like a schmuck for suggesting she should. I shouldn't have put my arm around her and smiled at that blasted camera. "Stupid," I mutter to myself even as I pull up my phone and navigate to the screenshot of her comment.

Peaches chirps and digs her claws into my skin. "Ouch," I say, and the bird repeats it back to me.

I find it disgusting that an editor and a supposed journalist would be so detailed as to name me and not use a single other example from the multiple restaurants and catering companies in Charleston.

Something wet lands on my chest at the same time someone rings my doorbell. Peaches mimics the sound, and I look down to see she's relieved herself on my chest.

"Come on," I say, already in a bad mood. "Really?"

"Alec," Tara calls from the hallway. "Open this door!"

"She's not happy," I say to Peaches. "Can you try not to poop on her?" I cross the room and open the door. Sure enough, an unhappy Tara stands there, a newspaper fisted in her hand.

"They printed that picture."

I lift my paper too. "I'm aware." I rip the picture out of the paper and fold it in half before using it to scrape Peaches's waste off my skin.

"This is a nightmare," Tara says. "Just when I thought

the press would move on to find someone else to harass." She slaps her paper against my abs, and I grunt out of reflex. "Why did you smile for that guy?" Her dark eyes flash with annoyance, and she stomps into my house.

I start to close the door when I hear, "Mister Ward, did Tara Finch just walk into your apartment? Are you two dating?"

"Dear Lord," I say, quickly closing the door. "What else are You going to send to us?"

Locusts? Drought? Rivers of blood?

I turn toward Tara. "You shouldn't have come here. They followed you, and now they think we're together."

"I don't care what they think."

"Yes, you do," I shoot back at her, giving her an identical glare. "If you didn't, you wouldn't be here chewing me out." Plus, she'd just called this situation a nightmare. If she didn't care what they thought—what the whole city thought—it wouldn't be a nightmare.

"I feel like a fool," she says.

"This isn't the end of the world," I say. "You haven't lost any clients, and—"

"Yet," she interrupts me. She pulls open my fridge and then slams it. "What am I doing here?"

"I have no idea what you're doing here. You weren't even going to be in the kitchen today."

"I should be feeding my chickens." She strides toward me, and I wisely get out of the way. She stumbles but manages to catch herself.

"Whoa," I say, reaching for her.

"That's what you say to a horse," she says. "I'm not a horse."

"I was just going to help."

"I don't need your help." She pauses in front of me.

"I'm not the one who dated Brett Daniels," I say. "Nor am I the one who left an inflammatory comment on a stabloid."

She ignores my pun, and while I've used it before, it's so stellar, I can't help myself.

"You said my comment was worthwhile."

"I said it was well-written." I'm not sure why I'm arguing with her, but wow, my blood feels like lava. She's wearing a pair of black shorts that hug her legs and a tank top with black stars on a pink background. I start to wish on every one.

I lick my lips, not sure why I haven't found a shirt and put it on yet. I clench my fingers, and every muscle in my body feels tight.

Peaches chirps along merrily, and Tara swats at her. "Peekaboo." Peaches bobs her head and whistles as if they're playing a fun game.

"She pooped on you," she says.

"Again, I'm aware." Humiliation fills me. I'm not sure how or why this woman makes me feel so small, but she does. "You should go." If she doesn't, I might grab onto her and kiss her. This past week since I admitted I'd ask her out if she wasn't my boss has driven me mad.

"You're standing in front of the door," she says.

I edge out of the way and she reaches for the door-knob. The moment she opens the door, a barrage of questions get yelled from more than one voice. She slams the door and takes a couple of steps back.

One more, and she'll hit Peaches's cage. "Tara—" I say, but I'm too late. She bumps into the cage and it starts to tip.

I can only watch in horror as she stumbles and tries to grab onto the cage to steady herself. But while it's big, it's already tipping, and it's not going to hold her up. Everything happens in slow-motion, and all I can think about is the huge mess I'm going to have on my hands once the birdseed settles.

She yelps, and I lunge forward to grab onto her hand. I grip her fingers, but I can't save her as she's already falling. "I got you," I say anyway as the cage clatters onto its side, the doors banging together.

Tara lands on the cage and rolls, dragging me with her. I manage to catch myself just before the bulk of my weight would've landed on her, and I grunt as I plant one hand next to her head while the other arm bends, and I balance on my elbow, my chest pressed into hers.

We're both breathing hard, and the metal cage settles as we look at one another. The power in the city has to have just gone out, because every bit of available electricity is now zapping between the two of us.

Tara starts to laugh, though she has tears in her eyes. I

do too, because it's better than the other thought in my head, which is to lean down and kiss her while she lays there on my living room floor, newspaper under her and a toppled birdcage beside her.

"Peekaboo, boo," Peaches chirps, and I realize something is dripping onto my floor. The bird's water. I refuse to think it might be anything but that.

"I'm sorry," Tara says, and together, we get to our feet, set up the cage, and start cleaning everything up. "I was so angry about the article, I didn't even get my butter pecan breakfast."

"I got you covered," I say, meeting her eyes again. That's it. Another power surge.

"Peekaboo, boo," Peaches chirps.

"There's butter pecan in the freezer, boo," I say, and Tara tips that gorgeous head of hers back and laughs again. Satisfaction fills my chest, but I know it's not going to be enough for long. I'm going to have to kiss this woman to be truly satisfied, and I distract myself from the thought by wadding up all the old and wet newspaper on the floor and laying out new sheets.

———

"NO COMMENT," I say an hour later as I press my way through the half-dozen or so reporters to the back entrance of Saucebilities. I keep one hand on Tara's lower back, having had to do the same thing at my apartment building.

We'd driven over together, the silence between us tense and thick after she'd eaten a bowl of butter pecan while I continued to clean up and re-feed and re-water Peaches.

I'd gotten all the feces off my chest before finding a shirt and pulling it over my head. We'd both said, "No comment," a bunch of times on the way to my SUV, but now Tara stays silent.

Since she's in front, she opens the door, and we escape into the kitchen. Someone tries to follow me, and I growl at him, "Not a chance," and make sure the door closes and latches before I lock it.

I breathe a sigh of relief, though I'm late and surely Jared is going to be up to his eyeballs in prep for that night's family party we're catering.

"I'll get the pasta going," she says, and she walks away from me. I'm not sure I can read this woman's signals, because I thought she liked me the way I like her, but she's been reserved and professional this past week too. Maybe she's been deleting flirty texts the way I have been.

I only have myself to blame for the relationship confusion, because I don't know how to relate to women. I don't know how to relate to other people at all. At least that's what Heidi told me.

I step over to the sink and wash my hands, then reach for a new apron.

"I could really use you out here," Jared says, bringing back a load of dishes. He gives me a dirty look, and I don't blame him for the blue fire in his eyes.

"Yep," I say. "Sorry. Where am I today?"

"You're on bread pudding," he says, and I go out into the kitchen. He's pulled a lot of the ingredients already, and Tara's standing next to Barley as he stirs something in a big pot.

I start cubing bread, determined to make up for the lost time, when the interior door opens. Tara's best friend, Callie, walks through it. "One week?" she screeches, holding up what looks like a printout. "He gives you one week?"

She strides toward Tara, slipping on the floor in her girly shoes. Callie grabs onto the counter to steady herself and keeps going.

"What are you doing here?" Tara asks, though she's brought this woman into her kitchen before.

"That monster says he gives you and Alec one week before you break up." Callie slaps the paper down on the table, and I exchange a glance with Jared.

"What a joke," Tara says as she bends over the paper with Callie. Her ponytail is slicked back as usual, not a hair out of place. I'd felt that hair last week as it had drifted near her cheek, and I haven't been able to stop thinking about it.

She doesn't wear much makeup, and now that she's buttoned herself into her chef's jacket, she looks like exactly the kind of woman I want to be with.

After scanning the paper, she says, "We're not even dating."

I pretend like her words don't knife me through the heart, though she's right. We're *not* dating.

The door opens again, and this time an unfamiliar man walks in. I turn to look at him too, as does everyone else.

Silence fills the kitchen, despite the few hissing pans and the bubbling of boiling water on a stove somewhere.

"Get out," Tara says, biting the words out through her teeth.

The man looks at her, and as he's frowning, I take in his features. He's got dark hair, like me. Dark eyes, like me. Broad shoulders, like me.

His gaze slides to mine, and I can tell he recognizes me. I think I know who he is.

"Brett, I mean it," Tara says, striding toward him. "If you don't leave right now, I'll call the police."

"I'm already dialing," Callie says, her fingers flying over her phone.

He looks from me to her, and I realize she's stopped right next to me. I've definitely lost my ever-loving mind, because I put my hand on her hip and tuck her into my side. "Is this the guy who wrote that article, baby?"

She looks at me, her eyes widening by the second.

I look back at Brett, my male protective streak rearing right up. How could a man like him—he's dressed well, with shiny shoes and pressed slacks—do something as despicable as he has?

"The lady asked you to leave."

JUST HIS BOSS 109

"So you two are dating, is that it?"

"Yes," I say, my voice strong. Beside me, Tara sucks in a breath, and I'm aware of all of the other chefs staring at us, not to mention Callie's gaping mouth. "And it's going to last longer than a week. You'll have to print a freaking correction." I take a step toward him, satisfied when he falls back, swallowing.

"In fact," I say. "I'll make sure you do."

"Alec," Tara says, and I return to her side. "It's okay."

"It's not okay, sugar," I say, drawing out the endearment in my Southern accent. "I have half a mind to file a slander lawsuit too. His completely-not-true article has cost you business."

Brett scoffs, but he doesn't fire anything at me. He's definitely the type to hide behind his pen and his computer.

"All right," Jared says, stepping between us. "Time to go, Brett. You got to say what you wanted, which was really untrue and completely cruel, by the way."

I wonder how long ago Tara dated him, and if Jared knew him. He has been working with her for a while.

"A week," Brett says. "That's all anyone ever gets with the mighty Tara Finch. Then her attention will be somewhere else."

"Get out," Barley says, moving next to Jared, making a protective wall between Tara and Brett. "Tara's an amazing chef, and you had no right to make it personal."

"You're a jerk for making this about her weight,"

Callie adds. "Is Lyon trying to get his Southern pizza oven off the ground again or something?" She cocks her hip and glares at him.

"Oh, he's worried about the competition," I say, putting a smile on my face. "Tara's pizza is the best in the city."

Brett waves his hand in dismissal, his eyes glaring holes in me, then turns on his heel and strides out.

I breathe a sigh of relief for the second time that morning and slide my hand away from Tara's waist. I let it linger along her lower back, because I like the way my blood fizzes as if someone's poured that popping candy in it when I'm touching her.

By the time I get my hand away from her body, everyone is facing us.

"Surprise," I say, and Callie latches onto Tara's arm and pulls her from my side.

"We need to talk," she says, and they head for Tara's office.

"Can someone find out how he got in, and lock us down?" Tara calls as she stumbles after her best friend.

With everyone still staring at me, I say, "I'll do it," and get the heck out of the kitchen. It's too dang hot in there anyway.

And only going to get hotter, I think as I start lowering blinds and checking doors.

CHAPTER ELEVEN

TARA

"I'M COMING WITH YOU," I SAY, TRYING TO SHAKE OFF Callie's vice grip. "Can you ease up?" My friend-phone rings, and it's the *sizzle-sizzle-plink* of dripping coffee for Macie. "That's Macie."

"Great," Callie says, finally letting go of me. "Put her on speaker so she can talk some sense into you too." She pushes open my office door and folds her arms as I pass. She steps into the office too and locks the door behind her.

I swipe on the call and say, "Hey, Mace. I'm going to put you on speaker, so I only have to explain this once."

"Oh, you're explaining," Macie says, her voice full of exuberance. She's probably drunk six cups of coffee by now. She runs a coffee shop as the morning manager at a shop on a very popular downtown corner. "You better start fast; my break is only ten minutes, and I've seen your smiling face a hundred times this morning already. Girl, who is that guy?"

"That guy," Callie says with plenty of bite. "Is her newest, saltiest chef."

"Hoo, boy," Macie says, and I can just see her fanning herself. "I better take up cooking to meet a man like him."

"You don't even know him," I say, flopping into my desk chair. I need a cold washcloth to press to my forehead. That's what my mama always did when I started getting upset about something. My back aches, and I'm fairly positive I bruised my tailbone when I fell backward onto a frigging bird cage.

I close my eyes while Macie says something else, imagining Alec hovering only a couple of inches above me. My skin crackles with energy now, the same way it had then. I wish I'd been brave enough to stretch up and kiss him. It's all I can think about, and it actually makes me frown.

"She's not dating him," Callie says, and I snap my eyes open.

"Hey," I say, sitting up and leaning forward. I've put my phone on the edge of my desk, and Callie's taken the seat in front of it. "This has to be a secret. We *are* dating."

"Fake dating," Macie says with a sigh. "That's almost as romantic as real dating."

Callie meets my eye, hers wide. "Is she kidding?"

I shake my head with a smile. Macie's had a worse time meeting someone than I have. I bend down and open the mini-fridge under my desk. I need ice cream for this conversation, despite the bowl I consumed at Alec's earlier.

"It is fake," I say. "He just sprung it on me, just now." I glance toward the door. "I need to talk to him." I open my desk drawer and pull out a spoon, offering it to Callie. She takes it, and I get one of my own. We only have a pint to share, but one cannot live on butter pecan alone, so it should be enough. "But Callie just whisked me away, as if that's the solution." I fix her with a cocked-eyebrow look.

"Her ex-fiancé showed up," Callie says, reaching for the pint I set on the desk between us. "He commented on Fisk's article that he only gives any relationship of hers a week." She scoffs and shakes her head, lifting the lid on the ice cream container. "He's just trying to paint her in a bad light so his stupid brother can launch his pizza oven."

"Well, I think his plan backfired," Macie says. "You should see the comments on both articles. The whole city is up in arms about his fat-phobia."

My heart warms. The whole city is behind me?

My phone chimes, and I glance at the notification that slips down from the top. Jason. He's seen the article too. The sense of being completely overwhelmed rams into my chest, and even the first spoonful of ice cream I put in my mouth can't quench that feeling.

"So what are you going to do?" Macie asks. "Prove him wrong? Not that you need to. You don't need a boyfriend to be a worthwhile woman or chef."

"I know," I say. "But yes." The idea starts to grow in

my mind. "Yes, I'm going to prove him wrong. Number one, Alec and I have been working together for months now." I knocked him to the ground two weeks ago, and that's when the fireworks between us really started. I'm already past the first week.

"Number two?" Callie prompts, and I focus on the conversation.

"Number two, I need a date to Callie's wedding, and that's still two weeks away."

"Oh, Lordy," Macie gushes. "Can you imagine that man in a tuxedo? I'm fanning myself."

Callie smiles, but I actually frown. I have imagined him in a tuxedo. And a suit. And a Marines uniform. If someone had been watching my Internet searches, they'd probably be concerned about me committing a crime and then trying to dress myself up to hide from the authorities.

"Number three, she likes this guy for real," Callie says, and I once again have to pull myself out of my fantasies.

"No," I say. "He works for me."

"She'll never fire him," Callie says, leaning closer to me. "So she might as well kiss him."

"No," I say again, my voice inching up in volume. I really hate the glinting light in Callie's eye. "It's just fake, Mace. I'll come by later today, okay?"

"Okay," Macie says. "I have that new blend you wanted to try. Bring something sweet with it, and we'll gossip some more."

"Sure." I hang up just as another text comes in, this one from Mr. Reynolds.

"Gossip some more?" Callie asks.

"Yeah, about me," I say with a bite to my tone. "She'll just want all the details."

"Well, honey," Callie drawls, and I look up from my neighbor's message. "I want that too."

"There are no details, Cal," I say. "Literally none. He stayed with me the other night to make the strawberry shortcake cupcakes. Remember, you came over? Anyway, he was going to leave, and he did leave, but there were reporters in the alley. So he came back in, and we just smiled at the camera for...funsies."

"Funsies," she repeats. "And now you're in a fake relationship with a man you *do* have a crush on, whether he's your chef or not."

"I'm just his boss," I say, though the words fall flat on their faces.

Callie giggles and says, "Honey, you've got to get up pretty early in the morning to fool me."

"And maybe not tell you everything," I grumble.

"That too," she says, shaking her hair over her shoulders. "Okay, so what are you going to do?" She scoops up another bite of butter pecan.

"Do?" I copy her and put my ice cream in my mouth.

"Yes, do," she says. "You need rules for a fake relationship. For example, Dawson and I agreed that holding hands was appropriate. Kissing was...not."

"But you obviously kissed him," I say. "You're marrying the man in two weeks."

"Yeah, we worked up to that," she says, looking away. "What is Mr. Reynolds saying?"

I know this tactic. Callie is very good at getting the spotlight off her, and I normally call her on that. Today, I don't. I don't have the energy. I still have a huge meal to cater for a family party tonight, and Jared was already upset Alec and I were so late.

I groan, thinking Jared probably thinks Alec and I were late because we had a late night. Or an early morning. Or were sneaking around, kissing.

"What?" Callie asks.

"Nothing." I blink and look at my texts. "Mr. Reynolds went to get the boys. He says the reporters are ringing the doorbell every other second, and the dogs keep barking. He's got them at his place."

"He's so thoughtful," Callie says. "I'll get him some Bryd's cookies. Dawson and I are going to get our order in there today."

"Oh, for the wedding?" I look up from thanking Mr. Reynolds.

"Yes," Callie says. "They'll be okay on the dessert bar, right? You're doing the cupcakes and a salted caramel ice cream still?"

"Yes," I say. "The cookies will be perfect for the dessert bar."

Callie smiles and gets to her feet. "Okay, you need to

talk to Alec."

"I need to get the asparagus roasting for tonight's party," I say. But I *want* to talk to Alec. *Needs and wants,* I think. I wish they lined up more often.

Callie waits for me to put the ice cream back in the tiny freezer, and she walks with me to the door. "You and Alec should come out with me and Dawson."

"Why?" I ask. "So we can have double the camera crews recording our every move?" I slide my eyes down to her feet. "You're always so cute and perfect. Can you imagine the headlines? Frumpy chef-girl out with Charleston's rich and famous." I shake my head. "No, thank you."

"You are not frumpy," Callie says firmly. "You're gorgeous." She eyes my shoes. "Maybe not in that exact pair of footwear, but they don't take pictures of your feet." She grins at me. "I'll let you borrow my little black dress."

I pull in a breath. "And the body shaper so I can be tall *and* curvy?"

"And the body shaper," Callie says with a grin. "You already have the perfect pair of heels for the dress. Those bright green ones you wore a couple of St. Patrick's Day's ago? Those."

"Okay, those have a pinpoint heel," I say.

"Just a reason for us to go shopping then." Callie opens the office door and turns back to hug me. "Rules, Tara. Just tell him the rules, and then don't be afraid to break them."

"I'm not breaking any rules."

"Oh, baby, that's just a shame." She pulls away and

grins at me. "It's breaking them that's so fun." She precedes me through the door, and I think about which rules I'd like to break with Alec.

All of them.

I'm in so much trouble.

Especially when he nearly collides with Callie as she leaves the kitchen and he tries to come in. He says something I can't catch from where I stand, and his eyes fly straight to mine after Callie gets by him.

He freezes, and my heart beats against the icy cage I've put it in. Luckily, ice breaks, because as he heaves a sigh that *can* be heard throughout the kitchen and comes my way, my heartbeat pulses heavily through my whole body.

"We should talk," he says, and I exit my office.

"Fine," I say, glancing at Jared, Barley, and Henry. They all shoot a look in my direction, and I honestly don't know what to tell them. I take a few steps toward the long, stainless steel counters that run down the center of the kitchen. "We'll be right back."

"Take your time," Jared says, his attention on the cabbage he's running over the mandolin. I'd be super focused on that too, because chefs lose fingers when working with the slicing tool. He's got the shredding blade on, because he's making cole slaw for tonight's party.

I turn back to Alec, meet his eye, and head for the same door Callie went through. He follows me, asking,

"Where are we going?" the moment we're free from the kitchen.

"I can't breathe back there," I say, my goal the conference room. I meet with clients and give presentations in here, and one entire wall is windows. Someone's closed the blinds, and I'm grateful for that as I step inside the dark room.

I take a breath, and it finally feels cool enough to hold in my lungs for longer than two seconds. I face him, my fingers automatically curling into fists. "Surprise?"

He frowns and folds his arms. "It *was* a surprise."

"Now everyone thinks we're dating."

"I'm sorry," he said, though he doesn't sound apologetic at all. "Did you *want* Brett to come into your kitchen, insult you, and then watch him walk away?"

"No," I bite out.

"I improvised. You praise me for it in a recipe."

"My life is not a recipe."

"Now this is my life too."

I take a step toward him, telling myself not to look at his mouth. "I didn't ask you to be my fake boyfriend."

"Yet here we are," he says, his eyes dropping to my lips. An insane amount of pleasure dives through me. When his gaze rebounds to mine, there's plenty of desire there. Plenty.

"I'm sorry," he says again, more gently this time. "Posing for the picture was reckless and hot-headed of me. But we're kind of in the bed now."

My eyebrows fly up. "We are?"

"You know what I mean."

"Do I?" I ask, grinning at him. He's so easy to tease with all the stuff he says.

"We just have to make the best of it. We made the bed, even if it was reckless, and now we have to lie in it."

All this talk about beds. My goodness. I can't breathe out here either. "I need some rules," I say, seizing onto what Callie said. "First, I'd love for this...thing—whatever it is—to last longer than a week."

"That's a given, Tara."

"I'd like a date to Callie's wedding. It's in sixteen days."

Alec's eyebrows go up for a moment and then right back down. "I suppose a boyfriend would go to your best friend's wedding with you."

"You're going to be there anyway," I say. "You said you'd help in the kitchen."

He nods, and I take another step toward him, this one much less menacing. He drops his hands to his sides, and I reach out and touch the collar of his chef's jacket. He sucks in a breath that makes me roll my eyes.

"I...think we should be able to touch each other without the gasp of the century being heard."

"The gasp of the century?"

"I'm surprised there's any air left in this room," I tease. "For how hard you just sucked it all in." I drop my hand and laugh. "Seriously, Alec. You acted like I'd just stabbed you with a knife and all I did was touch your collar." I hold up my hand. "Do *not* tell me a knife joke."

"Is that a rule?" he asks, reaching out to run his fingers down the side of my face.

I pull in a breath too, because his touch sends zings and zangs all through my body.

"I thought we weren't gasping," he murmurs, those dark, deep, delicious eyes locked on mine. Oh, this man knows how much I like him, and he's using it against me.

"No," I say, but my voice sounds like his parrot's.

"So I can hold your hand." He lets his fingers drip down my arm to mine.

I don't make a single noise. I also can't breathe, but it's fine. I can hold my breath for a really long time. My head only feels fuzzy because of the way he holds my hand, as if he really wants to make sure as much of his skin is touching mine as possible.

"Yes," I say.

"Put my arm around you," he says, doing just that.

"Yes."

He steps closer to me and tucks my hair behind my ear before letting his other arm envelop me in an embrace. "This is okay?"

"This is great," I say, giving away so much.

"Mm." He ducks his head and traces the tip of his nose down the side of my face. "Kissing?"

"I...don't see why we'd need to do that in public," I say.

"When are we going to go out?" he asks. "Have you

seen this week's schedule?"

"Yes," I say, because I make the schedule. "We don't have to go out. They already think we're together."

"So Tuesday night?" he asks, somehow getting his feet between mine as we sway right there in the conference room. "Mimi's? Mousse tasting?"

"All right," I say, my brain misfiring at me.

"Great." Alec steps back, half a smile sitting on that perfect symmetrical face. It would be easier to punch him if he wasn't so perfect already. "So no kissing in public. Holding hands and touching is okay. This has to last through the wedding, which we're attending together as a couple, and we're taking off on Tuesday night for a mousse tasting." His eyebrows go up. "Did I get it right?"

I frown, because he's not touching me anymore, and I can think more clearly. "Did I say yes to a date on Tuesday night?"

"Yep." Alec steps back and turns around. "I better get back to work. If you need a minute, feel free to take one." He leaves the conference room right about the time my brain catches up to what he's said.

"I don't need your permission to take a minute," I grumble to myself, sinking into the nearest chair. Every cell in my body feels cold, because he's not holding me anymore. I also realize that he didn't say no kissing ever, he said *no kissing in public.*

Dear Lord, I'm as bad at making rules with my fake boyfriend as I am at firing people.

CHAPTER TWELVE

ALEC

"HEY, ALEC," DAWSON SAYS AS I SLIDE INTO THE booth next to him. We tap knuckles and he indicates the blond man across the table from him. "This is Lance Byers, my best friend. Lance, this is Alec, Tara's new boyfriend."

I almost jump in to say I'm not her boyfriend. She's just my boss. I manage to clamp my mouth shut just in time.

"Good to meet you, man." Lance shakes my hand over the table, and I glance around The Ruby.

"This place is great," I say, noting all the red on the walls, the floors, even in the wood.

"Something to drink?" a waitress asks, pausing at our table.

"Just water," I say.

"More coffee for me," Dawson says.

"Another." Lance lifts his beer bottle, and the woman leaves. "You don't drink?" he asks me.

"Not anymore," I say with a smile. "I had, uh, a thing go bad in Colorado while I was there this past fall. Plus, I'm driving tonight." I've learned that drinking and Alec Ward don't really go together, and since that's something I can control, I do.

Lance nods and looks out toward the main area of the club. It's full of couches, chairs, and other plush things for people to sit on. Small tables linger nearby for people to put their drinks on, but since it's not very late, the club isn't very full.

I don't know Lance's whole story yet, but he's putting off a very distasteful vibe. No one will dare approach our table with such a sour look on his face. I try to copy it to really keep people away, which isn't hard this early on a Monday night.

"How long have you and Tara been dating?" Lance asks, and I stare at him.

Dawson clears his throat, and I look at him. "This shouldn't be a hard question," he says with a smile. "Haven't you answered it a ton of times?"

"No," I growl. "I just bark at everyone that I have no comment and keep walking."

"You gotta work out this part of your story," Dawson says. "It has to be rock solid, because you tell it so many times."

"She's my boss," I say.

"Right, uh huh," Dawson says, fluttering his eyelashes at me. "So when did you start having feelings for her?" He talks in this fake, female reporter voice, and it actually loosens me up.

"In Florida," I say, immediately wishing I could suck the words right back down my throat.

"Whoa, man," Dawson says, reaching for his coffee as the waitress puts it down. He whacks a packet of sugar against the table while we all get our beverages, and I reach for my water and gulp it.

"Florida, huh?" he asks. "When'd you guys go there? Over a month ago, right?"

I nod, because the cat's out of the bag now. At least between the three of us. "I, uh..." Need something a lot stronger than water.

"You didn't tell her," Dawson says, smiling in a way that makes me feel comforted in his presence.

"Of course not," I say under my breath. "She's my boss."

Lance pops the top on his bottle and watches us. "I feel like I've been inside this conversation before." He smiles at Dawson. "I told him the same thing I'm gonna tell you: It's not like you have to report to an HR rep. If you like her, go for it."

"Mm, no," I say, though I'm kind of already up to my neck into a relationship with Tara. "I just got out of a bad relationship with my last boss. I like this job. I *need* this job."

I like my apartment on the north side of the peninsula. I like the double-ovens, and all the space for Peaches's birdcage. I like the vibe in Charleston, and I really like that it's not Beaufort.

You really like Tara, I think, but thankfully, I know how to keep my mouth shut when sensitive things try to come spilling out. Usually. That Florida comment befuddles me a little.

"You can have the job and the girlfriend," Dawson says with a shrug. "Right?"

"I don't honestly know," I say. "Didn't work out that way last time." In my pocket, my phone dings, and I dig it out. Jessie's name sits on the screen. "This is my bird-sitter."

"You've got a bird?" Lance asks.

"Yes." I read Jessie's text real quick.

I have to go, Alec. And we need to talk.

"Uh oh," I say, showing Dawson the text. "I think she's going to quit."

"Sounds like it," he says.

"I'm going to go call her," I say, sliding to the end of the booth. "Excuse me a minute." I tap on Jessie's name as Dawson and Lance tell me to take my time, and she picks up at the end of the first ring.

"Alec," she says breathlessly. She's always had a cute little voice, and I'd once entertained a crush on her. I'd been ten, and she'd been nine, and I thought she was the coolest girl ever when she swung out on a rope swing over a pond and dropped right into it.

"Why do we need to talk?" I ask her, aiming for the exit and less smoky air.

"I can't keep bird-sitting for you," she says, her voice pitching up. "I'm sorry, but you don't pay enough, and I can't keep living with my uncle." She blows out her breath, and I realize she's not upset, she's furious.

"Why?" I ask. "What did he do?" I push past a couple of guys coming in so I can get out. Finally free, I keep walking down the sidewalk. I have so much nervous energy, and I can't wait to get out of here and go lift weights.

Dawson had invited me for drinks tonight to "get to know me." What he didn't—and doesn't—get is that I'm not going to open up to anyone. I can hold Tara's hand and laugh with her and nuzzle her neck for the next fifteen days. Heck, I could do it a lot longer than that. But I'm not going to let myself fall in love with her.

"He's just as bad as Mama and Daddy," Jessie says. "He tried to set me up with James Birmingham last night. James. *Birmingham*, Alec."

"Well," I say, trying to conceal my smile though Jessie's not here with me. "The Birminghams have a ton of money, Jess. All that land on that plantation. Why, I daresay you'll never have to leave for anything ever again."

"Sounds like pure bliss," she quips, and I hear her take in a breath.

I'm fast enough to pull the phone away from my ear as she screams, and I say, "Get it all out, girl."

"I hate this," she says, and there's the high-pitched voice filled with tears I expect. "I hate not being able to do anything but baby-sit my dumb friend's dumb bird. No offense."

"Peaches is not dumb," I tease, hoping Jess can hear it. "She knows almost fifty English words, and she never stops using them."

Jessie half-laughs and half-cries. "I need a job, Alec. A real job, that pays real money. One where I can afford my own house or apartment or whatever. I have to get away from everyone, or they're seriously going to marry me off to the youngest and wealthiest land-owner they can find."

"Oh, come on," I chide. "That's not true. The Collins boy is what? Four? Five?"

Jessie bursts out laughing, and I chuckle with her. "James is forty-seven, Alec." The moment sobers, and I stop at the corner.

"What are you thinking, Jess? You're not going to go back to Beaufort, are you?"

"No." She sighs. "I can't. I won't."

My mind races along all the things I know about Jess and her family. "Okay, so you want to move out of your uncle's house. That's easy. Move in with me."

"I need a real job, Alec."

"Okay, so move in with me, and then start looking for jobs."

Silence pours through the line, and I can tell she's thinking about it. "What will your new girlfriend say?" she asks, and I spin around as if Tara will be standing right there, accusing me of cheating on her.

"Uh..."

"You do have a new girlfriend, right?" Jessie asks, her voice lilting and teasing now. "I've seen your picture in the paper and online. I'm honestly surprised Nell hasn't called."

"I am too," I say, thinking of my mother. It's been her greatest desire the last ten years to get me married and settled. I keep telling her a person can be settled without a band on the left ring finger, but she doesn't believe me.

Running away for nine months hadn't helped my case. I start back toward the club, still trying to think of a solution for Jessie.

"Maybe I better talk to Tara first," I say, because if she really was my girlfriend, I'd definitely talk to her before I allowed a female friend—no matter how platonic our relationship is—to move into my apartment.

"Mm hm, yeah," Jessie teases. "When did you start dating anyway? And why am I finding out about it online?"

"It's new," I say, thinking about the Florida trip, over a month ago. "And you know I don't call you up and tell you everything." I scoff as The Ruby approaches. "I'm not a woman."

"Does she have any single friends? Family members?

Maybe we could double, and maybe I could get Uncle Jack and Mama and Daddy off my back if I had a boyfriend."

"She has a single cousin," I say, pieces falling neatly into place.

"Set up a double date," Jessie says. "I'll keep sitting with Peaches until I find a job, but I'm going to start looking, Alec. Just so you know."

"Okay," I tell her. "I understand. Sorry about Uncle Jack."

"Yeah, I thought he'd be different." She sighs, says good-bye, and I let her hang up as I return to the booth.

"Sorry," I say. "She watches my bird for me during the day." I throw back another swig of water as if it's whiskey. "I should get going."

"Wait," Dawson says. "I'm supposed to get to know you." He wears panic in his eyes. "I can't go back to Callie with, 'he owns a bird, and his bird-sitter is quitting.'"

"Who has a bird-sitter?" Lance asks, grinning.

"It's a unique situation," I say. "Birds are...particular."

"Yeah, we had one once that plucked out all of her feathers every time we left the house," Lance says. "My mom got rid of it, and she moved on to potted plants. Less maintenance."

I laugh with him, but I'm not going to give up Peaches. She didn't give up on me.

"So what did you do before you came to Charleston?" Dawson asks, and I guess he's really going to do this.

I sigh and decide to give them the Cliff Notes. "I joined the Marines when I was nineteen, after a year of... doing nothing, trying to figure out what to do with my life." Some people think having a ton of money is oh-so-much fun, but it's not. It's a lot of sitting around in stuffy clothes, holding drinks you can't actually swallow, and talking about how humid it is that day.

"Did that for five or six years, then went to Paris to the culinary institute there. Did that for a few years. Came back to Carolina and started a restaurant in an inn. That didn't work out, and I took a few months to travel before landing here."

Lance and Dawson nod. "Your family has money," Dawson says as if he knows.

"So does yours," I say coolly, lifting my almost-empty water glass to my mouth.

"So does mine," Lance says. "If anyone cares. I mean, I don't know if it matters, but I thought I'd throw that out there." He grins again, and I do like him. He seems down-to-earth and like a decent human being.

I grin back at him. "I do care, Lance. Thanks for chiming in."

"Just don't let your girlfriend become your wife if you're not sure she really likes you, and not your money." Lance throws back the last of his second bottle of beer while Dawson shakes his head.

I look at him, and our eyes meet. So much is explained

in that single moment of time, and my heart goes out to Lance.

"Well, she's not my real girlfriend." I clear my throat, because I wish what I've just said wasn't true. "So I think I'm in the clear there."

"Yeah, he's said that before." Lance throws a look at Dawson, who gazes steadily back at him. "I should go. I'm buzzed, and I have to do all those stupid interviews in the morning."

"Interviews?" I ask, seizing onto this vital piece of information. "For what?"

"Lance is the managing partner of Finley and Frank Realty," Dawson says. "He's been burning through assistants the way I used to go through secretaries."

"Callie won't come work for me," Lance says with a frown. "And it's really not that hard to answer phones and emails. I have no idea why Amber quit." He tosses some money on the table and slides out of the booth. "Give me a ride home?"

"Sure," Dawson says, and we both get to our feet. "And dude, Amber quit because you're Mister Growly Bear all the time. At least that's what Callie told me."

"Mister Growly Bear?" Lance repeats, and I manage to wait to burst out laughing until the two of them walk away.

Back at my apartment, I change and head toward the clubhouse. The gym closes at ten, as do all of the amenities. I get through my weight-lifting routine before the witching hour, but it's past ten by the time I strip down to only a tight pair of bicycle shorts and ease myself into the hot tub.

I can get fined for using the hot tub after hours, but I'm quiet as a mouse, and Miss Opal's given me permission. She runs the HOA board in my apartment complex with a semi-iron fist...which I know how to soften.

Oatmeal chocolate chip cookies, and I happen to be a pro at making those. Miss Opal said I could use the hot tub as long as I laundered my own towels, brought by a fresh dozen cookies every week, and never breathed a word about it to anyone.

Thankfully, even though I grew up in a rich neighborhood, in a house four times too large for my family, with maids, I know how to start a washing machine.

I let the water hold me up and cover my ears and start to lap at my forehead as I lay in it. I love how the world disappears when I close my eyes. It's dark in the pool area, despite the street lamps outside and the moon doing her best to throw silver everywhere.

With my eyes closed, I only see blackness, and with my head almost underwater, I only hear the rushing jets and bursting of bubbles. Everything else fades away, and I just exist in this hot water as it unknots the muscles I just worked.

Lifting the fifty-pound weights didn't drive Tara from my mind. I don't think anything will, and I should probably tell her I don't want this relationship to be fake. I don't want to ask permission to touch her, and I don't want to worry about breaking her rules.

When I finally feel relaxed enough that I can go home and go to bed, I pull myself from the hot water. I've just reached for a towel when someone whispers, "*Psst!* Alec, is that you?" in a voice that sounds very much like my fake girlfriend's.

I spin toward the noise, and sure enough, Tara's standing next to one of the floor-to-ceiling windows that's been left open. It's not bright like daytime, but definitely enough light shines in from outside to illuminate me in my very tight pair of shorts.

"Wow," she says, her eyes sliding down the length of my body. "I've never seen a man wear a swimming suit like that."

CHAPTER THIRTEEN

TARA

"What in the world are you doing here?" Alec asks, reaching for his towel again. But he's not looking at it, and his hand simply claws at empty air over and over. And over.

I can't look away from that body. Wowsers. I mean, I knew he was hiding some serious muscles under that chef's jacket, and I knew he didn't have an ounce of extra fat on him. But seeing it so plainly... I can't even breathe properly.

"Tara?" he asks, giving up on the towel. "Are you okay? Why are you here?" He comes toward me, but there's no door here. Just a window.

In that moment, I realize what a creeper I am. I've lost my ever-loving mind, because I say, "I looked up your pin on Maps, and saw you were here."

He actually takes a step back, horror crossing his face.

"I mean—"

"Ma'am," someone says through an intercom system. I spin around to find a cop car easing up to the curb, the reds and blues starting to flash. "Step away from the building, ma'am."

When I don't move instantly, the cop makes his car go *whoop-whoop!* and I see my freedom flash before my eyes. At least the last thing I'll see before I'm hauled off to jail is Alec in a near-Speedo, his torso and chest rippled with muscles.

When my eyes land on his face, I see that trademarked frown, and for some odd reason, it comforts me.

"I'll be right out," he says, turning and striding back toward the hot tub.

I do my citizenly duty and turn around, putting both hands high above my head. "I was just talking to my friend —boy—boyfriend." The words trip out of my mouth, and I pray that'll be all the tripping that happens tonight. With my luck, though, I'll fall flat on my face as Alec stands over me in those tight booty shorts.

"Do you live here?" the police officer asks. He stands as tall as me, and we probably wear the same size. If I could knock him out, I could switch clothes with him and go on a joyride.

His partner emerges from the car, and all thoughts of that fly out of my head. I don't like driving that much anyway. I bet I could get a lot of butter pecan ice cream for free though.

"No," I say. "My boyfriend lives here. Apartment 6D-39. He was in the hot tub. I was just talking to him."

The officer looks past me to the dark building. In that few seconds, I see every decision that brought me here, and I wonder what in the world I was thinking. Just because I can see Alec's pin on a map doesn't mean I should leave my house and follow him.

He'd told me about drinks with Dawson anyway, and he'd actually capped it in the text he'd sent me, as if it were an event.

Drinks With Dawson.

I hadn't heard from him since, but because we're not actually dating, that's not unusual. What is unusual is how I want to tell him that I'd like to be his real girlfriend. That maybe we could just try it for a couple of weeks. I'm not sure I can prove Brett wrong about a relationship lasting longer than a week, and I'd like to see if he's right or not.

"There's no one here, ma'am." The officer focuses on me again. "Have you been drinking tonight?"

"No," I say, turning back to the building. "He is here. I just talked to him."

"Do you take medication?"

I spin back to the police officers, both of them standing shoulder-to-shoulder now. "No," I say, frustrated.

"*Should* you be taking medicine?" the second one asks.

"This is ridiculous. He was right there." I can't believe Alec has abandoned me. Panic claws at my gut, because perhaps I've ruined everything already, and it's only been forty-eight hours.

But not for the reason Brett said I would, I think, and that gives me some vindication.

"Honestly," I say when they remain silent. "I have all these chickens, right? Well, one of them has been acting kind of sick lately. Won't come out of the coop and stuff, right? So my boyfriend—again, his name is Alec Ward, and he lives in apartment 6D-39—has this Quaker parrot, and he knows a lot about birds. So I thought I'd ask him if there's anything we can do for Pot Pie."

One of the officers turns back to the car, while the other one lifts his eyebrows. "You have a chicken named Pot Pie?"

"Yes, sir," I say, swallowing. "I have thirteen chickens." Why am I telling him this? I command myself to stop talking, and I press my lips together to achieve the feat.

"You do know that chickens and parrots aren't the same at all, right?"

Relief fills me at the sound of Alec's voice. He emerges from the shadows, fully clothed, unfortunately, and carrying a gym bag in his hand. "Sorry, beautiful." He slings one arm around my waist and presses a kiss to my temple. "I had to change." He glances at the cops, both facing us now. "What's goin' on?"

His drawl is slow and spectacular, and I bask in the honeyed quality of it. The man oozes Southern charm, and he's been hiding it behind crusty layers of salt for months. I almost want to stomp on his foot and ask him why.

Then I remember his ex-girlfriend, now sister-in-law, and I know why. Still, I don't see how she was his boss, and the two situations are totally different.

For one, I'm not kissing his brother.

You're not kissing him either, I tell myself.

"Do you know this woman?" the first officer asks.

"Are you Alec Ward?" the second one does.

"Yes," he says. "And yes."

"Apartment 6D-39?"

"Yes, sir," he drawls. "I was just relaxing in the hot tub after working out."

"You do know this hot tub closes at ten p.m.," the first officer says.

"Do you work for the HOA?" he asks. "This is private property, sir, and I happen to have permission from the HOA president to use the hot tub after hours."

I want to tack on a "So there," but I'm in my thirties and beyond such juvenile behavior. I'm still wearing my orthopedics, so the cops probably think I'm in my fifties, as my hair's a bit wild from my fray with thirteen chickens not long ago.

They look from me to him. "It's time to go home," the second officer says. "Let's go, Jer." They both nod, and I actually lift my hand and wiggle my fingers.

My word. I've gone insane. I drop my hand to my side

and step away from Alec at the same time he moves away from me. "Thanks," I say.

"I'm still not sure what you're doing here," he says.

"You heard the chicken ramble," I say. "I need help with Pot Pie." I gesture toward the parking lot down the way a little bit. "She's in the car."

"Wait, wait. You legit brought your chicken for me to examine?"

"You know birds," I say, enunciating each word. "What am I supposed to do? Turner costs an arm and a leg for an after-hours consult, and he'll probably just tell me to butcher her and enjoy a feast."

Alec looks like he's going to agree with the vet. I must put out some powerful don't-you-dare vibes, because he doesn't. "All right," he says with a sigh. "But I hope you realize I take Peaches to Turner when there's something wrong with her." He starts down the sidewalk toward his building.

I fall into step with him, his stride a little longer than mine but not much. "I only looked at the pin after I went to your apartment, knocked, and you didn't answer."

He gives me the side-eye. "Is that so?"

"Yes," I say. "There was a woman down the hall, and she said you sometimes work out late at night." My voice trails into a whisper by the end.

"Who did you talk to?" he asks.

"I don't know," I say. "I didn't ask her. She was

wrestling with one twin and yelling at the other to go back to bed."

"Hannah," he says.

"She didn't look happy to see me." I watch him for his reaction.

"She's never happy," he says nonchalantly. "Would you be if you were a single mom of twin ten-year-old terrors?" He gives me a small smile. "She does the best she can, I know that."

I nod. "I'm sure she does."

"I think that's all any of us are doing," he says. "The best we can."

I edge a little closer to him, my car only about a hundred yards away now. I want to hold his hand, and if I don't grab it soon, I'll lose my chance. On the next swing, I extend my arm a little, and our fingers brush.

It takes all of my concentration not to pull in a breath. I hear nothing from Alec either, and on the next step, he settles his fingers right between mine. "Okay?" he asks.

"Okay," I murmur, the soft quality of my voice in complete contrast to the loud rejoicing singing through my body.

At my car, I have to let go of his hand to open the back door and take out Pot Pie. She's warbling, and she never does that. My worry for her increases, and I should've just called Turner and paid the after-hours fee.

I say as much, but Alec says, "Let me see her. Was she out of the coop today?"

"Yes," I say. "I let them out once I got home tonight so I could get the eggs and feed them. She seemed okay; maybe a little slower than normal. She's not as stubborn as Benedict."

He quirks one eyebrow at me. "You have interesting names for your chickens."

I grin at him, and surprisingly, he returns the gesture. I see a completely different side of him standing in the orange lamplight, holding my wounded chicken and flirting with me.

For the love of all butter pecan ice creams around the world, he's *flirting* with me. I put my best smile on my face. "So, Doctor Ward. What do you think?" I nod to Pot Pie, who I swear has curled up in Alec's arms and gone to sleep.

"I think she needs to rest," he says. "She just seems tired."

"Maybe I could stay and watch an hour of TV with you?" I suggest.

He looks down at the chicken in his arms, to me, and then up to the sixth floor where his apartment is. "I'm not even supposed to have Peaches," he says.

"How in the world do your neighbors not hear her?" I ask. "They must be bacon crazy by breakfast."

Something dark crosses his face, and he slides Pot Pie into my arms. "I'm tired and hungry, and I don't even have cable."

Uh oh. I said something wrong. "Wait," I say. "I know

that's not true, because you told me once you leave the TV on for Peaches sometimes."

"Fine, then I'm tired and hungry, and I can't keep your chicken in my apartment." He turns away from me and opens the back passenger door. "You should take her home. Back to the brood. She probably just needs to rest. If she's not better soon, you should take her to a real vet."

"I can order Thai food," I say. "I have them on speed dial, and I know all the best meals."

His eyebrows go up. "You order take-out?"

"Every night," I say, putting Pot Pie back into the cardboard box I'd brought her over in. "I mean, almost every night." I straighten and look at him. "I don't like cooking at home."

"You don't like cooking at home." He says it like it's a foreign concept. The darkness hasn't left his face. "That's weird."

My irritation with him spikes. "You know what? You're right. I'm tired and hungry and worried about Pot Pie. I'll see you later." I round the car and open my door.

"Whoa," he says. "Wait a second."

"I told you once I'm not a horse," I growl at him.

"You're the one who showed up at my apartment in the middle of the night and insulted my bird," he says, plenty of fire in those eyes. "You have no right to be angry with me."

"You just told me to leave you alone," I say, glancing

around like reporters might be hiding in the bushes. For all I know, they are. "When we're supposed to be dating."

"I—You said Peaches was noisy."

"She *is* noisy!" I say, flapping my arm. "And I'm not weird because I don't want to cook a gourmet meal for myself after being on my feet, cooking for others, for twelve hours. But thanks for saying so." I get behind the wheel and reach to close my door. I slam it closed and jam the key in the ignition, but before I can pull out, Alec is sitting in the passenger seat.

"What are you doing?" I ask. I just want to get out of these shoes, shed this bra, and taste four or five—or eight— Thai combination meals. *Please, God*, I think. *Get this man out of my car.*

"I didn't let you leave when you were this angry before," he says. "I believe you said something about hitting a stop sign once?"

I blink at him, sure he's not bringing that up right now. "You know what?" I ask. "I did hit a stop sign once, but it was right after my husband asked me for a divorce, so I deserve some leeway."

My chest heaves. I'd mentioned Otis once before, and Alec hadn't brought him up again. "I also tripped into a couple of rose bushes right after he left, and I had to stay with Callie for a few weeks, because my life suddenly had no purpose." I can't believe what I'm saying. No one gets to know these things about me. No one.

Certainly not Mister Grumpy-Cat, take-your-chicken-and-leave, Alec Ward.

"Tara," he says softly, and that is so not fair. "I'm sorry." He sighs. "There's a reason why I said you should go, and it's only an excuse, really." He looks at me, and I have no idea which Alec Ward I'm dealing with. The one who lets a four-ounce bird dictate his life? The one who gives a job to a friend because she needs it? The alpha-male, in-charge chef in the kitchen? The ex-Marine? Or the one who burns grilled apple and cheese sandwiches at home?

"Come inside," he says. "I have a mantra specifically for you, and it's 'don't drive angry.'" He grins, and he's so handsome, and so symmetrical, and I don't really want to leave.

"Mister Reynolds has the dogs," I say quietly, as if that has anything to do with the situation at hand.

"If you can smuggle Pot Pie into the apartment, she can stay while you order Thai."

My eyes light up. "Really?"

"I generally hate the TV on at night," he says, yawning. "And it's already late. You might have to fill the time with...talking."

I swallow, though there's plenty to talk about. "Okay," I say.

"Okay." He gets out of the car, collects my chicken-in-a-box, and leads me upstairs to his apartment. As I close the door behind us, I think we survived our first fight as a couple, and the thought warms me from head to toe.

"Bacon motor-bike!" Peaches screeches the moment we enter the apartment, and I need to have a heart-to-heart with her about using an indoor voice.

CHAPTER FOURTEEN

ALEC

"This is amazing," I say, chopsticking up another bite of noodles. "Really takes the *edge* off."

"Okay, enough already." Tara smiles at me though. She called for Thai take-out, and twenty minutes later, no less than nine Styrofoam containers arrived at my apartment. I can admit that such delivery is faster than I could've done here, even in the gourmet kitchen.

I moved Peaches's cage all the way against the wall and covered her with a blanket, despite her squawking protests. Jessie's been gone for a few hours, but Peaches will be fine. I'll take her into the shower with me once Tara leaves, and she'll forgive me.

That gave us a bit more room in the living room, and we're sitting on the couch to eat our Thai food.

"What?" I ask. "It's really good. I've never eaten at Thai Jungle."

"You've been missing one of Charleston's best kept secrets then," she says, grinning at me. She checks on Pot Pie, but the chicken doesn't seem keen to leave the cardboard box. Thankfully.

"So after Otis left, you went on a male fast," I say, bringing her back to her original topic of conversation.

"Mm, yes," she says, twirling up some noodles with a piece of broccoli. "For a few years. I started dating again, but it hasn't gone well."

"Define that," I say.

"Uh, let's see." She blows out her breath. "The first guy I went out with we dubbed Wally the Walrus. He had these huge teeth, which is totally fine," she hastens to add. "But he had this weird obsession with sea creatures. He like, loved them." She starts to giggle, and I do like the sound of that.

I grin at her as she continues with, "Then I went out with this really tall guy. He played basketball in college. I obviously like a tall man." She sweeps her hand up and down her body, though she's sitting. I take it as an invitation to check her out, which I totally do.

If she notices, she doesn't act like it. "Callie called us the Twin Towers, and...let's just say there's an incident we've labeled The Envelope, and leave it at that."

"Oh-ho," I say, chortling. "No way. That could be anything."

She shakes her head, her dark eyes sparkling like stars in the sky. Land sakes, she's gorgeous, and it's all I can do not to lunge across the few feet between us and kiss her.

"Fine, he slid this envelope under my door one day. I was home and everything, but he didn't ring the doorbell or knock. I picked it up and opened, and let's just say—"

"No, just *say* it," I interrupt, grinning.

"It was full of nude pictures. Of him. He had this whole secret life as a male model, and he didn't want to tell me." She giggles and covers her mouth. "There are some things you can't unsee, Alec."

I blink at her. "So he wasn't coming on to you."

"No, he was," she says. "I broke up with him immediately." She shakes her head and sobers slightly. "I can't be with someone who won't talk to me. I mean, if you're going to be a nude male model, *be* the nude male model."

"Strut it," I say, smiling for all I'm worth.

"Exactly!" She punctuates the word with both of her chopsticks in the air.

I can't remember the last time I've had this much fun with a woman. Maybe I never have. "So where does Brett play into all of this?"

"Brett's next," she says, finally closing the lid on her container. She stabs the chopsticks through the top of it as if she's done so many times in the past. Which, of course, she has. "We dated for a long time. Two years before he asked me to marry him. I was just starting Saucebilities at the time."

I nod, deciding that a verbal utterance will slow her

down.

"We set a date for a year out, which is totally normal, by the way."

"Totally," I say, because my mother would be mortified by anything less than a year when it comes to an engagement. Byron really freaked her out by proposing to Heidi and then marrying her three months later. Of course, they have that baby coming already, and anyone who can do math knows she was pregnant before the I-do.

At least I'd stopped kissing her before then.

"So it's getting closer and closer, and he's acting weirder and weirder." Tara reaches up and removes the elastic band from her hair, letting her ponytail spill down over her shoulders. My mouth heats up, and not from the spicy peanut sauce on my noodles.

"He finally comes to the kitchen one day and tells me I'm already married. To Saucebilities, and he's not going to live his life while I 'cheat on him' for the next thirty years." She uses air quotes around "cheat on him."

She shakes her head. "I honestly wasn't even working that much."

I want to argue with her, but I keep my mouth shut. Chefs don't even know how much they work, and Tara's definitely a chef inside her own head.

"And no one since?" I ask.

She shrugs, though this is no shrugging matter. "It's been a few years, and...I don't know. It hurt, what he said to me."

"I'm sure it did." I close my Styrofoam container and cover her hand with mine. I like that the physical barrier between us is flimsy and paper-thin, easy to break.

"I am really busy at Saucebilities," she admits.

"You've *cut* to the chase there," I say, smiling. "Get it? *Cut* to the chase?"

"You're literally the worst with jokes," she says, but she's grinning at me. The moment stills again, and I have the urge to do that lunging thing again. My couch is big and soft, and I could easily see myself making out with her right then and there.

An alarm goes off on her phone, making us both jump. Peaches starts dinging and donging like the doorbell, and Tara fumbles to find her friend-phone. I get up, clearing my throat, and take our food containers into the kitchen.

The clock hands near midnight, and I still need to shower. I pause at the sink and look out toward the ocean. I can see where the lights stop and the darkness takes over, but that's it. It's almost like looking out into a black hole, and I feel the vastness of the universe overcome me.

"I should go," Tara says from behind me, and I turn away from my thoughts.

"Okay," I say, approaching her. "Thanks for the food and the stories." I push her hair back off her face, enjoying the soft, silky quality of it. "I'm off tomorrow, but I'll see you for Mimi's?"

She smiles up at me, and it sure looks like a real, genuine smile. "Okay."

"Good luck with Pot Pie." I fall back a step, suddenly realizing I'm not ready to kiss this woman. I've been thinking about it for a long time. It's a fantasy that plays on repeat in my head, but I've got some baggage to unpack first.

Tara's expression flashes with an emotion I can't name before it disappears. She bends to get her chicken-in-a-cardboard-box, and I open the door for her. There's no way we'll kiss over a chicken, and she ducks her head and practically runs out of the apartment. "Bye," she says.

"Good night," I say, and I bring the door closed. I press my back into it and sigh. Then I straighten, uncover Peaches, and say, "Who wants to shower?"

"Peekaboo," Peaches says.

"No." I shake my head at her and chuckle. "I said, who wants to shower? *Peaches?*"

"Peaches, peekaboo," she says, and I laugh. "Peaches, peaches, peaches."

I put her on the perch in the shower and turn it on, then go discard my clothes in the laundry room. I normally like my late-night showers, but tonight's is filled with thoughts of Atlanta, a five-hour drive inland, while Peaches chatters to herself, plays peekaboo with herself, and tells me she loves me.

If I got up early, I could be there before lunchtime. Get my reunion with my father and brother over with, and be home in time for my solitary ten p.m. weight-lifting and hot tubbing.

If I go, I'll miss the Tuesday night mousse tasting with Tara

I know I need to make things right with Byron and my father, and I know I won't truly move on until I do.

"If you want to kiss Tara, you better drive to Atlanta tomorrow," I mutter into the spray.

"What in the world?" Peaches asks.

I chuckle and stroke one finger down her head and back. "Exactly," I murmur. "What do you think? Will you be okay if I leave early and come home late?" Jessie hasn't quit yet, and Peaches should be okay if I leave the TV on when I go in the morning.

Her only answer is, "Bacon motorbike!" and I figure she'll be fine. It's me who needs to get his head on straight, and I know if I don't, I'll lose a lot more than an inn.

I'll run again, which means I'll lose my job...and Tara.

———

I TELL myself in every mile I drive away from Charleston that I'm going to return. I am. I have no desire to stay in Atlanta, that's for dang sure, and I didn't bring anything with me except my phone and my wallet.

I have forgotten how amazing it is to be behind the wheel, the open road in front of me, and nothing holding me back.

Nothing's holding me back in Charleston either, and by the time I roll into Atlanta, I'm already ready to return.

I've kept my phone on silent, because I find the constant notifications drive me batty. I feel all this pressure to check them instantly, whereas if I don't hear them, I don't know they're there.

Tara's texted me a couple of times about Pot Pie, that silly golden hen she'd brought over last night. I smile, because Tara and her chickens simply make me happy. *I'm glad she's doing better this morning,* I send back to her. *Listen, I went to Atlanta for the day. I'm going to have to cancel at Mimi's for tonight. Rain check?*

My phone rings, and Tara's name comes up with (*Boss*) behind it. I should probably change that, as I certainly don't need to be reminded of who she is. I can't stop thinking about her for longer than ten seconds as it is.

"Hey," I say.

"Atlanta?" she asks.

"Yeah." I exhale slowly, in a controlled manner. It helps me keep my thoughts centered. "I need to tie up the whole situation with my dad and brother."

"Oh, okay," she says, and I press my eyes closed, praying she won't ask why. "Why?"

Because I want to move on sounds lame inside my head.

Because I want to kiss you is worse.

"I just need to," I say out loud, my eyes coming open again. "It's time, and I feel like they're holding me back in...some way." I shake my head and open the door of my

SUV. "I'm here, and I'm sorry about tonight at Mimi's. We can go next week."

"Sure," she says.

"And so you don't stop by tonight with any chickens named Piccata or something." I grin as I face The Blackbriar Inn, something I thought would never happen again. The last time I was here, I'd told my father he'd always chosen Byron over me, and I shouldn't have expected anything different. The problem was, I *had* expected something different. I'd been disappointed.

But I'd also been disrespectful and childish.

"Piccata?" Tara giggles over the line, and I can just see those dark eyes sparkling at me. Flirting with me. I can't even imagine what they'll look like full of heat and desire after I kiss her. My cells sing with want, and I turn away from the inn as Tara says, "I don't have a chicken named Piccata, but I'm noting that. It's a great name."

"What are their names?"

"My favorite is Hennifer," she says, a happy little sigh coming out of her mouth and over the line. "But I like Nog and Alfredo too. Oh! Benedict is great. Chick Fillet. They're all good hens."

"Do they answer to their names?" I ask.

"Not really," she says. "But I like calling them by name. It's better than, 'hey you, get out of the coop for your one hour of pasturecize, you lazy hen!'"

I tip my head back and laugh, the wide-open sky above the inn taking it all and absorbing it. "Okay," I say, still chuckling. "Well, I'm here, and check-out has to almost be over. Check-in won't start for a while, so I just need to bite the bullet and go talk to them." I turn to look at the front entrance of the inn again. There are hardly any cars in the lot, which isn't all that surprising, since it's between departure and arrival times.

"Okay," Tara says. "Good luck, Alec."

"Hey, Tara?" I ask.

"Yeah?"

"What are the chances of me moving from your chef-cell to your friend-phone?"

She says nothing, and the silence doesn't comfort me. Shoot. Maybe I'm the only one who feels like he's walking through a lightning storm when Tara's nearby. I could've sworn I'd seen interest in her eyes. I could've sworn—

"I think the chances of that are high," she finally says.

I breathe a sigh of relief, mostly because that means my female radar isn't as broken as I'd started thinking. "Great," I say.

"I'll text you from my friend-phone right now."

"All right." I want to tell her I want to be more than friends. I want to ask if she has a lover-line, but by the stars in heaven, that sounds creeptastic and sort of gross, so I keep my mouth shut.

"'Bye, Alec," she says in that sultry voice, and I actually say, "Yep," before the call ends.

Yep?

"For the love," I mutter under my breath. This woman

has addled my brain.

I get a text from her from a new number, quickly label it, and tuck my phone into my back pocket.

I look up...and take the first step toward the inn. Everything seems just as I left it, and I'm not sure if that annoys me or makes me happy. Byron had begged me not to go, but then, he hadn't known about me and Heidi. I certainly hadn't told him, and I doubt she ever did.

He'd said the on-site restaurant would fail without me, and I'd tossed something rude over my shoulder about having his girlfriend run it. She was *so* smart, after all.

No, it was not my finest moment. In fact, it was a moment I don't want to live inside again.

I open the door and glance around. Light pours in from the front windows, and the check-in desk stands straight ahead. No one waits for me there, and I sweep the lobby to my right and then the restaurant to my left.

My feet have grown roots, and I can't move. The restaurant is closed.

"Closed until further notice," I read on the colorful sign hanging from a velvet rope that bars anyone from entering the restaurant. "Sorry for the inconvenience."

"Alec?"

I turn toward the sound of my older brother's voice, and our eyes meet. I can't get my voice to work, and I can't even raise my hand in a wave. Nothing.

"It is you," he says, coming toward me now. "I could just feel it. I knew you were thinking about me." He grins, runs the last few steps, and engulfs me in a hug. That thaws me completely, and I embrace him back. "I've wanted to call you so many times," he whispers, and while he's wearing a dark suit, white shirt, and tie, his voice is choked with emotion.

He steps back and grips my shoulders. "Look at you. You look so good." He grins at me, and it's like nothing bad has ever happened between us.

"Thanks," I say, clearing my throat. I'm not sure exactly how I wanted this to go, but it's not talking about how I look. "You look great too. The inn is still amazing."

Byron drops his hands, a cloud shuttering over his face for a moment. "She's still open," he says, and his voice is so much like mine. His drawl is the same, and his eyes are just as dark. His hair is a touch or two lighter than mine, but his teeth are just as straight and just as white. If I had to spend my days in a suit, though, I might go ballistic.

I can button myself up and wear a uniform. I can follow directions. But I prefer the freedom to spread my wings and fly. Maybe that's why the rules in my relationship with Tara are choking me.

I don't want rules. I want to hold her, talk to her about how I really feel, and kiss her.

That's why you're here, I tell myself. *It's time to move on.*

"What are you doing here?" he asks. "Come into my office. Let's talk."

"I just came to apologize," I say, going with him as he

turns and starts walking. "Where's Dad?" I clear my throat. "And Heidi?"

"Heidi had the baby last week," Byron says, throwing a grin over his shoulder. Nope, he doesn't know about me and his wife. I'm not going to tell him either. I'd ended things with her before their relationship was public, and before they got engaged, and before all of it. He doesn't need to know.

"Dad's around somewhere," he adds. "Probably the housekeeping department. He likes to hang out there and inventory things." He chuckles as he goes around his desk. He sits, a great sigh coming from him. "We miss you here. The restaurant closed. I couldn't keep it staffed with someone who knew how to make a medium-well steak. No one wants to drive out this far."

"Hm." I nod, but I'm not here to talk about cooking. "Listen," I say. "I want us to be okay." I shift as I sit down, taking an extra moment or two to align my thoughts. "I've sort of got this woman in Charleston, and I want to move forward with her. I feel...I don't know." I reach up and push my hand through my hair, trying to find the right words.

"You feel chained here," Byron says, because he's always known me so well.

I seize onto the words. "Yes," I say.

"Because of Heidi." He leans back in his chair, his fingers steepling.

"Heidi?"

"She told me about you guys." He puts a sympathetic smile on his face. "I didn't know, Alec. I honestly didn't. I wouldn't... If I'd known what she was doing, I would've broken up with her and let you have her."

My eyebrows go up. "Really? But you married her. She has your kid." I find a smile slipping across my face. "By the way, is it a boy or a girl?"

"Boy," Byron says, his smile coming at me with the wattage of the sun. "We named him Lars Winters Ward."

Everything dark in my life lifts. Rays of sunshine fill me, and I nod. "That's a great name, Byron."

"Yeah?" He chuckles softly. "I guess so. Heidi really wanted her maiden name in there."

"So you're happy with her."

"Yes," Byron says, his eyes casting down to his desk.

"I'm happy for you," I say. "I just want that happiness too."

"Who's this woman in Charleston?" Byron asks. "And what in the world are you *doing* in Charleston?"

"Tara," I say, her name and the image of her that flashes through my mind making me smile. "Her name is Tara, and she's my boss. I work for her catering company."

Byron's eyebrows go up, but I don't care. I don't really have to explain anything to him, and as Lance said a couple of days ago, it's not like I have to meet with an HR rep to go over anything and get my relationship approved.

I just need to make sure I'm good with my family, and then I need to get back to Charleston so I can kiss Tara.

CHAPTER FIFTEEN

TARA

MACIE SETS A STEAMING CUP IN FRONT OF ME AND takes the seat across from me. "One vanilla chai latte," she says.

I smile at the beverage, the scent of it wafting up and making my mouth water. "You're the only one I'd drink coffee for in the afternoon," I say, wrapping my fingers around the warm mug.

She grins at me, and I think about dying my hair red like hers. With my dark brunette locks already, it would come out a sexy, deep auburn. At least I think it would. Her light green eyes sparkle as she sips her own coffee.

"Oh, please," she says as she sets the cup down. "If your hot boyfriend asked you to have breakfast with him, are you telling me you wouldn't?"

"First off," I say. "He's not really my boyfriend." I

glance around, because we are in a public place—Legacy Brew, where Macie works—and while the reporters have backed off a little, I know they're not gone completely.

Macie trills out a laugh. "Oh, please," she says again. "You can't lie to me."

"I'm not lying."

"Honey," she drawls out. "I've known you since you moved in down the street from me. You bought me with those cinnamon rolls, remember?" Her personality sparkles like a disco ball, and it's no wonder she gets asked out almost every day by a customer. Too bad her rules of not dating anyone who drinks coffee are so firm.

"How can I forget?" I ask dryly. "You text me on the weekly to make them again for you."

"You never do," she says with a grin. "So stop acting like I put you out or somethin'." She glances over to the door as the little bell on it chimes. A couple of businessmen walk in, but Macie doesn't move. She's got two girls behind the counter, and they can handle two people.

The after-lunch rush will start soon, as Macie said, but we still have a few minutes. She claims people need a mid-afternoon pick-me-up, but I don't see how they can drink hot liquids when it's so fiery outside.

"You want him to be your real boyfriend," Macie says, that smile oh-so-knowing.

"So what if I do?" I ask, lifting my chin. "Would that be the worst crime on the planet?"

"No," Macie says. "Wearing those shoes is the worst crime on the planet."

I look down, but the table blocks my view of my shoes. I know what I'm wearing though, and I roll my eyes. "I work on my feet all day."

"So do I, honey," she says. "Trust me, you'd get more dates if you upgraded your footwear just a little."

"I'm not looking for a date to come out of my catering kitchen," I say. "Or from a client."

"And yet," she says, hitting the T hard on the last word. "You're dating your super-hot, super-skilled chef."

I can't argue with either adjective, so I just lift my latte to my lips. "I wish," I mutter, and Macie laughs. I can't help smiling too, but familiar frustration fills me. "How do I... I mean, we set rules."

The door chimes again, and no less than six men and women in confining skirts and suits walk in. None of them are wearing orthopedics.

"Honey," Macie drawls as she stands. "Rules are meant to be broken." She throws back the last of her coffee and heads for the counter. "Bring me some cinnamon rolls," she calls. "They're the only lovin' I need."

I grin at her back and startle as my phone rings. I dang near fall out of the teensy chair in the café when I see Lila Houser's name on the screen.

Dawson's mother.

I catered the Fowler Founder's Gala a few months ago, but I have no reason to chit-chat with the woman.

My brain screams at me to answer the call; maybe she has more business for me. "Hello?" I say, getting to my feet. "Lila?"

"Tara, dear," she says in an ultra-smooth, I'm-rich-so-everyone-does-what-I-want voice. "How are you?"

"Just fine, ma'am," I say. I pick up my napkin and my cup to take them to the disposal area. "How are you?"

"Good, great," she says, and I imagine her patting her hair as she does. I smile my way out of the coffee shop and onto the bustling downtown street. The afternoon air is heavy with humidity, and it's terribly hot so I turn east and start walking. I'll hit the rowhouses in a couple of blocks, and then the water. The breeze will cool me off, and I actually consider wasting a few hours on the beach that afternoon too.

"I understand you're catering the wedding," Lila says, and my feet trip over themselves.

I immediately throw my hand out to catch myself, grabbing onto the first thing I come in contact with. Unfortunately, that's another human being, and the man grunts as he braces himself and saves us both from falling flat on our faces.

"Sorry," I say. "So sorry." I remove my hand from him and brush down the collar of his suit coat. I offer him a smile, but he's all frowns. I get the heck away from him before he can take my personal information and send me a dry cleaning bill for touching him.

"Are you still there, dear?" Lila asks.

"Yes." I decide talking to this woman and walking is not a combination I can handle at the moment. I stop next to a parking meter and take a deep breath. "Yes, I'm here, and yes, I'm the caterer for Dawson and Callie's wedding."

"Oh, good," she says, as if she's really pleased by this. "I was thinking we should go over the menu..."

Disbelief runs through me. "Ma'am," I say as politely as I can. My momma would be so proud. Being a proper Southerner, she did teach me to mind my manners and respect my elders. "The menu is set."

"Anything can be changed," Lila says.

I scoff, though she's right. Not only is she right, she's used to getting her way. Used to changing things last-minute and having her wishes obeyed.

"Have you talked to Callie about this?" I ask.

Her silence says no for her.

"I'm sorry," I say, deciding to be firm. I'm really not great with contention though. I'd rather hole up in my office and let someone else deal with the unhappy customer or the chef who wants to quit to move on to "bigger and better things."

"The wedding is in less than two weeks, and the menu is set," I say. "I've already ordered from my suppliers, and we have the timing down to only seconds." It doesn't really matter if none of that is true—for example, I haven't timed out how long it will take to make and serve dinner at the wedding.

I *have* ordered all the groceries I need for it. The best

meat and produce suppliers in Charleston will take overnight orders, but they prefer a longer lead-time. Especially for things like premium cuts of beef—which Callie and Dawson are serving at their wedding—and seafood. Again, Callie and Dawson are going with an upscale, surf and turf buffet menu for the wedding.

"I just think—" she starts.

"Didn't you request the oysters?" I ask. "I'm almost sure that's what I saw your name next to. Dawson said you love them." I smile, hoping I can talk and talk and she'll grow weary of me. Lila usually doesn't tolerate conversations that last longer than she wants them to. "There's going to be so many amazing options on the buffet besides those too. One of my chefs came up with this divine recipe for a chicken and steak kabob, and it's unlike anything you've ever tasted. Then, we're going to have Brussels sprouts and asparagus in a creamy Dijon sauce, and I came up with that recipe. And the desserts. Do not even get me started on the strawberry lemonade cupcakes. That recipe is going in my cookbook even."

I talk right over her sighs and attempts to interrupt me. But even I have to breathe, and in that pause, she asks, "Cookbook?"

"Yes, ma'am," I say. "I've been working on a cookbook for over a year now. I'm getting very close to finished."

"What kind of cookbook?" she asks, more interest than exasperation in her voice now. "What are you going to do with it?"

"It's a Charleston-inspired cookbook," I say. "I don't know what I'll do with it. My cousin said he knew someone who publishes stuff like that, so I'll probably talk to him."

"You do know I live in Manhattan, right?" she asks.

"Yes."

"There is a plethora of publishers here."

I can practically hear her brain ticking, though it's hard above the sudden hammering of my heart. "Oh? Do you know any?"

"As a matter of fact..." Lila pauses for a moment, and I blink into the brightening day. This can't be happening. How would Lila know any publishers? I don't even know what I need to do to get the book published.

Panic suddenly rears, and I spin in a circle, forgetting about the parking meter. I hit it with my clumsy knee, which buckles. I start to fall and try to catch myself, but there's a curb, and my ankle folds when my foot doesn't reach the solid ground it thought it would.

I grunt as I end up on my knees, my shoulder pressed into the pole of the parking meter. My phone flies out of my hand and skids into the parking spot with Lila Houser still talking on the other end of the line.

Before I can move, a car pulls off the street and into the spot, the tires going *crunch, crackle, crispity-crinkle* over my device.

"No," I moan, because that was my chef-cell, and I

need that. I don't have all my business contacts in my other phone, and my thoughts fly to Alec.

Wait. I have his number in my friend-phone, and that thought relaxes me enough for me to get to my feet. I hurry around the now-parked car to where my device lays in pieces on the ground. I sigh and start to pick them up.

"What are you doing, honey?" someone asks, and I barely glance up at them.

"This car just drove over my phone," I say. "I'm picking up the pieces so I'm not a litterer." I get the last one and stand, using the car for support, wondering how Pot Pie walks around on her chicken legs all day. Mine seem to have betrayed me just now.

A woman stands there, and she looks from my broken phone in my hand to my face. "Did I run over that?"

"If you just parked this car, you did," I say. "It's fine. You couldn't have known."

She wears a pair of celebrity-style sunglasses, a ton of bright pink lipstick, and a flowery summer dress on her slim frame. The dress seems a little young for her, but I'm not going to tell her that. I'm certainly not one who should be offering fashion advice, what with my orthopedics and bland wardrobe.

She seems horrified at the cellucide she's just committed. "I'm so sorry," she drawls. "I'll pay for the phone."

"That's not necessary," I say. "Really. It's a business phone. My company will pay for it."

Her eyebrows go up, and she lifts her sunglasses to

show a pair of baby blue eyes that probably haven't seen a day of hardship in her life. They have seen plenty of collagen treatments, as she doesn't have a wrinkle anywhere but on her neck. They always forget about the neck. Her face doesn't move as she smiles. "If you're sure," she drawls.

"I'm sure," I say, starting to edge away from her. "Thanks, though." I start toward the beach, getting as far from the Southern socialite as quickly as possible, but I really can't stride that fast for very long. I slow down and decide my beach afternoon has just turned into a trip-to-the-cell-phone-store afternoon.

And anyone who's ever gone to get a new phone knows doing that is like consigning oneself to go to the DMV. We're talking seventh-rung stuff here.

I sigh, because I do like having my work life separate from my personal life. I like knowing who I'm going to get on the other end of the line just by which phone chimes.

My mind flows to Alec, as it often does, and I realize with a stumble-step that I've blended him into both halves of my life. Luckily, there's no parking meters and no man in front of me to manhandle this time.

I right myself, hold my head high, and continue toward my cell phone provider. It's fine if Alec is in both halves of my life. I want him in the one, and I need him in the other. Maybe my momma's been wrong all this time, and you can have what you want *and* what you need. Maybe they're the same thing. Maybe they come in a tall, broad-shouldered frame, with a neat beard and dark hair, with gorgeous eyes and the lamest knife jokes known to mankind.

Just maybe...

———

LATER THAT NIGHT, I've just finished setting up my phone when the doorbell rings. I look down at Tommy and Goose, both of whom are sitting so perfectly at my feet. They just want all the chicken from my chicken and green bean stir-fry, and I have to admit they've gotten quite a few pieces each.

"Who could that be?" I wonder, glancing at the clock. It's almost ten p.m. Normal dinner time for me, but certainly bedtime for most people. Callie's voice screams through my head about opening the door at night for strangers, and how I'm just waiting to get shanked if I do so.

I look at my two phones on the table in front of me. No one has texted.

I stay stubbornly in my seat. If it's not a serial killer, it's likely a reporter. I don't want to come face-to-face with either of those. The people who know me know what I'm dealing with right now, and they'd have texted or called or told me they were stopping by.

I pick up another green bean with my chopsticks and eat it.

The doorbell chimes again, and this time, so does my friend-phone. Alec's name flashes on the screen with *Are you home? I didn't think you were working tonight, but maybe you're doing a cookbook recipe.* I lunge for the phone, a little shocked by how much I've missed him today. He's been present in my mind since he can't be present physically, and I keep thinking about what Macie said at the coffee shop earlier today. I need to tell him how I really feel. Or ask him if he's pretending or not. Maybe if he doesn't want to pretend, and I don't want to pretend, we can make this relationship into something real.

Is that you at the door?

Yes.

Coming.

I jump to my feet and leave the kitchen, forgetting that both dogs can get on the table and eat my food. Somehow, Alec makes the important things fly from my brain.

I unlock the doorknob, unbolt the deadbolt, and unchain the door before opening it.

The sexiest man on the planet stands in front of me, wearing a pair of jeans and a two-sizes-too-small T-shirt with the outline of a taco on it. I pull in a breath, because somehow, going twenty-four hours without seeing him has made him more handsome.

"I missed you today," I blurt out, not quite sure why my brain has let my mouth take over. I rein it in and clear my throat. "I mean, how was Atlanta?"

"I don't want to talk about Atlanta," he says, advancing toward me. He's wearing a dark, almost dangerous look, laced with what I can only describe as desire. One hand slides along my hip while the other comes up and pushes through my hair.

"What do you want to talk about?" I whisper.

"Us," he says. "And I actually don't want to talk at all." He lowers his head toward mine, and my whole body lights up. My eyes drift closed, because I've kissed men before, and my body seems to remember how to do it.

He pauses, and his lips have to only be millimeters from mine. My heart booms through my chest and into my ears, making hearing impossible.

"I don't want this to be fake," he whispers, and I do hear him. "I want to kiss you now, unless you have some major objection to that."

No objection! my brain yells, but I don't think anything comes out of my mouth. This man makes me freeze in so many ways, and I hate that.

"No?" he asks, teasing me now. He's probably got his eyes open, watching me while I'm this frozen lump of a fish in his arms, her eyes closed.

I manage to shake my head slightly, and he growls as he touches his mouth to mine. Explosions go off, and while his touch started out as exactly that—a touch—within the blink of an eye, we're fighting each other for control of the kiss.

I give it to him after a couple of strokes, because holy whipped cream and strawberries, the man can kiss.

He kisses me and kisses me, and I'm no longer a frozen lump in his hands. I'm warm and melty and gooey, and he can shape me however he wants.

As long as he doesn't stop kissing me.

CHAPTER SIXTEEN

ALEC

THE COOL AIR RUSHING AROUND ME TELLS ME I'M still standing on Tara's porch. There are probably a hundred flashbulbs going off. Or maybe those popping lights in my brain are from the way Tara kisses me back.

No matter what, I don't want to stand out on her porch for the world to see. I break the kiss and whisper, "Can I come in?" before claiming her mouth again.

She grips my shirt collar at the throat and backs up, taking me with her. This woman... This woman makes me think and feel things I haven't thought or felt in a long time. Maybe ever.

I cross the threshold of her house and kick the door closed, then pull away again, breathing heavily. "What are you thinking? Fake or not fake?"

"Not fake," she says, her breath moving quickly out of her mouth too.

I turn her around and press her into the now-closed door. "Not fake for me either." I grin at her and push her hair back off her face again. "I think you're stunningly beautiful," I whisper as I bend my head toward her again, this time slower than before. I lean into my hand, which is against the door where she's pressed too and touch my lips to her neck. She shudders slightly, and that makes me smile.

"I think you broke all the rules," she says, her voice made mostly of air.

"I don't care." I take a breath of her creamy, powdery scent and pull back. "Unless you care."

She smiles up at me, those sparkling, dazzling eyes exactly what sustained me through a ten-hour round-trip today. "Rules are made to be broken," she says. She reaches up and cradles my face in her hands. "I think you're a great guy, Alec. You're smart, you're hard-working, and you're...nice."

I have no idea what to say to that. "I haven't been all that nice."

"But deep down, you're just the man who came to Charleston so his bird would have a dad."

I smile at her and try to get closer, though we're plenty close already. "So I'm a birdy daddy? Is that it?"

"Mm, yeah." She pulls me closer and kisses me again. She takes her time now, and I let her set the pace. I could kiss her for hours, but a loud, eardrum-splitting clatter comes from behind me, and I pull away, my heartbeat suddenly ricocheting through my whole body.

"What is that?" I ask, taking a step toward her kitchen.

"Could be a serial killer," she says. "That's what Callie would say." She comes to my side. "My guess? It's my two ravenous dogs, whom I haven't fed in weeks."

I glance at her, the level of sarcasm in her tone not hard to hear. "Pizza tonight?"

"Chinese," she says with a sigh. "Come on. Let's see if they've scarfed it all or if there's any left for us."

———

SOMEONE KNOCKS ON MY DOOR, and my pulse shoots to the top of my skull. Peaches ding-dongs in her parrot voice and adds, "Motorbike," which I hurry to finish wiping the counter. I turn toward the sink and toss in the washrag. The oven clicks as I go by, and the casserole is in there humming away.

Everything is set.

By some miracle of miracles, there's no event this Friday night, and I've invited Tara, her cousin, and Jessie for dinner. I figure it's time they met, and Tara's been asking me a *lot* about Jessie over the past few days since we kissed. Jessie wanted me to set up a double-date, and Tara said Jason was game.

I tried telling Tara there's nothing to worry about when it comes to me and Jess. I've kissed her in the refrigeration unit, her office, my hallway, and anywhere else I could so she'd know she didn't need to worry.

I still think she's worried.

I pull open the door to find my best friend standing there. "Jess."

"Howdy, stranger," she says, her face lighting up with a smile. She's Southern born-and-bred, with plenty of money, power, and prestige. She doesn't want any of it, though it took her a long time to realize that.

She only left Beaufort a year or so ago, and she's lived with her uncle since. Her parents have tried to marry her off to a half-dozen proper Southern gentlemen, who own stables, land, and vast fortunes. Some women would probably really like that.

Jess is not some woman.

"Did I get here first?" she asks, peering past me.

"Yep." I step back. "Come in. You look nice tonight."

"So do you." She scans me from head to toe, and I try not to squirm in my black polo and jeans. "You must like this woman."

"I do like this woman," I say with a smile.

Jess tips up onto her toes to kiss my cheek, and I kiss hers back. "How's the job hunt going?"

"Terrible," she sighs and wipes her hand through her blonde hair. It's wavy today, so she hasn't spent an hour with the flat iron to get it straight. Since I've known her for three decades, I know a lot about her. "Turns out no one really has a job for someone who can't do anything."

"You can take people's money for coffee," I say, closing the door behind her.

"Come on, Peachy," she says, and Peaches flies over to her.

She lands on Jess's arm, and says, "Peachy, peachy."

"So that's where she learned that." I shake my head at the pair of them. "I wish I could pay you more, but I can't." Not if I want to keep the apartment, which I do. Not if I want to eat, which I do.

"It's okay." Jess collapses onto the couch. "I've thought about getting a night job, so I can keep doing this. Even the supermarket won't hire me."

"It's been five days," I say. "How many places have you applied to?"

"Just three," she says. "They all say they'll call you back, but then they don't. I don't know how to get a job." She sinks onto the couch, as I've pushed Peaches's cage as far out of the way as I can.

"I talked to someone this week," I say. "He was looking for an assistant. He runs a real estate office."

Jess's bright blue eyes perk right up. "He does? What's his name?"

"Lance Byers," I say. "I have his number. You should text him."

"Yeah, I will," Jess says with a smile. "Thanks, Alec."

"We can ask Tara if she's hiring too," I say. "She was talking about getting another administrative assistant or even a prep cook."

"I can't cook," Jess says, frowning at me as I walk into the kitchen to check on the casserole. It's bubbling away in the oven, the rich cheese sauce over the chicken and ham making my mouth water. With the crispy, golden bread-crumbs, it'll be the perfect dinner.

"But it's a prep cook job," I say. "You don't cook. You cut up veggies and de-vein shrimp and stuff like that." I lean into the counter and look at Jess. She's wearing a cute red, yellow, and white sundress with a pair of Converse.

As part of her rebellion from the Dunaway family, Jessie stopped starving herself when she left Beaufort. Probably even before then. I'd been in Atlanta at the time, but I can remember the texts about how she'd finally eaten a piece of toast, and did I know how amazingly crispy and buttery bread could be?

I smile now, just thinking about it.

She cut her blonde hair into a bob when she came to Charleston, but it's grown out a little bit. She still has a lot of clothes and shoes she brought with her, but her actual cash flow is quite slow.

"I don't even know what it means to de-vein a shrimp," she says, a look of mild horror on her face. "Maybe I should take some cooking classes."

"Maybe you should go apply at every retail store you see. It really doesn't take a college degree to be a cashier," I say. "It'll give you some confidence and bring in a little money while you look for something else."

I turn to pull down some champagne flutes and open

the fridge to get out the salad I put together an hour ago. The clock on the stove tells me Tara should've been here by now, but she did say her cousin always runs a bit late.

"Plus, can you imagine what Cornelia Dunaway would say about her daughter being a cashier?" Jessie giggles, the sound increasing into full laughter after a few seconds.

"What in the world?" Peaches asks, and that only makes Jessie laugh harder.

I grin at the two of them, silently hoping she gets a night job. I don't know what I'd do without her to come stay with Peaches during the day.

Something thuds against my door, and I turn that way. "What in the world?" I say, and that only sets Peaches into a frenzy. She barely finishes the saying before starting it again.

Scraping noises come from the other side of the door, and I hear a man's voice. I'm not sure if I should open the door or not, but I do, only to find a man with dark hair on his knees, picking up what looks like little gems.

"I'm so clumsy," he says, grinning at me. "I dropped this stupid basket Tara gave me, because she had to run back downstairs for something." He gets to his feet, and while he's not Tara's brother, he shares enough of her features for them to look related.

"You must be Jason," I say, reaching for the basket of disheveled items. "What is this?"

"Your guess is as good as mine, bro."

I meet his eye, not sure if I should laugh or not. I smile as a compromise and shake his hand. "Come in. You're not bird-adverse, are you?"

"Tara told me about the killer parrot," Jason says, walking into the apartment completely at ease.

"This is my friend," I say, indicating Jessie. She stands and looks at Jason, her eyes really zeroing in on him. "Jessica Dunaway. Jessie. This is Jason Finch."

"So nice to meet you," he says, all smiles and manners. Jess should like that.

Instead, she folds her arms and glares at him. "You cut me in line yesterday."

Jason tosses me a worried look. "I'm sure I don't know what you're talking about," he says airily. "Where?"

"Double Dutch." Her eyebrows go up, clearly challenging him to argue with her. "I remember, because you had that scar by your eye, and I remember thinking, 'I bet he thinks he's so good looking with that. So rough. Like, I bet he flirts with women and gets them to guess where he got that ridiculous scar.'"

Jason blinks and starts to laugh. I'm going back and forth between them like they're a fascinating tennis match, and I don't want to miss a moment of play.

He's laughing, but I've seen Jess mad, and it's not pretty. I try to mime to him to cut it out, but he doesn't even look my way. "Well, now the whole date is thrown off," he says, still chuckling. "I was going to try to get you to guess where I got this scar. Shoot."

To my great surprise, Jessie smiles and unclenches her arms. "You're such a liar. Just like how you weren't in a rush to get that hot chocolate for your nana yesterday."

"Oh, now, that was true," Jason says, and wow, he is smooth. Tara said he was, that he knew how to talk to women and the double date wouldn't be awkward with him around. "Oh, yes. Nana. She was so cold yesterday." He shivers falsely, and I watch Jess to see if she's falling for this.

Mighty stars in heaven, she *is*. She melts in front of me. Positively melts, and I realize I've been flirting all wrong. Number one, I haven't been flirting at all. Number two, if I'd been accused of cutting a woman in line, I'd just apologize and hope she keeps talking to me for the rest of the night.

Not Jason. He moves over to Jess and takes Peaches from her. He sits down but doesn't leave any room on the couch for Jess that isn't immediately next to him. "Tell me who the hot chocolate was for," she says, leaning into the armrest on the couch and twisting to face him. She's wearing a flirtatious smile now, and Jason's got one too, to go with his dark hair, eyes, and pressed, clean blue button-up. He's wearing khaki shorts with that and hiking boots that make him look like he's just come out of the mountains. I wonder if those are a lie too.

Thankfully, Tara steps into the apartment with a, "Hey, sorry about that. I left my keys in the ignition." She shakes her head. "Do not recommend." She surveys the living room, and I simply watch her to get her reaction. "Dear Lord." She sighed. "He's already won her over."

"Seems so." I chuckle and slip my arm around her waist. "Mm, there's never a *dull* moment when you're around."

"You did not just make a knife joke," she says, turning to face me. Delight fills her eyes, and I get the impression she actually likes my jokes.

"I just heard a new one," I say. "Wanna hear it?"

"If I must."

She follows me into the kitchen as Jason says something that sounds so much like, "...the hot chocolate was for my nana, I swear," and I reach for plates.

"Doctors say it's important to cut carbs," I say, reaching for the oven mitts.

"Oh, I see where this is going," she says, peering into the oven. "What did you make?"

"A poultry-inspired dish," I say. "You can choose if you want a knife or a fork to cut your carbs with." I grin at her and pull out the bubbling casserole. Some of the bread-crumbs on top have started to burn, and I frown.

Embarrassment heats my face. "I'm still figuring out this oven," I say, glancing at Tara to see if she sees I've burnt yet another dish. I swear I don't do that in her kitchen.

"Smells like Swiss cheese," she says. "Chicken Cordon Bleu." She meets my eyes. "You know I have a hen named Cordon Bleu."

"I've heard," I say with a grin. I slide the casserole onto the counter and call into the living room, "Time to eat."

Jess gets to her feet instantly and turns toward me. I can read her expression, and she's ready to leave already. I shake my head and say, "Jess, come meet Tara."

She switches her gaze to my girlfriend—I love thinking those words—and gives her socialite smile to her. "Tara, of course. You know, I can't get Alec to talk about anything or anyone else."

"That's not true," I say quickly, but Tara smiles as if she likes it.

"Is that so?"

"This was a bad idea," I say, looking from Jess to Tara.

Jess takes her right into a hug, causing Tara to say, "Oh." She tries to look at me from over Jess's shoulder, but she can't quite manage it.

"So great to meet you," she says. "Alec's had a rough time with women lately."

"Stop talking," I tell her, but she just shoots me a smile. "It's time to eat."

"What are we having?" Jason asks, sidling up to Jess. She trains her smile on him, and she's slipped into hostess-mode, so I'm not sure how she's feeling. Something must've happened in the few seconds after Tara came in, because Jessie's not soft and melty now.

"He baked a dish in honor of Cordon Bleu," Tara says, grinning at her cousin. "Your favorite."

"Actually," Jason says without missing a beat. "Alfredo is my favorite. Or Nog."

"Wait, wait," Jess says. "Who are these people?"

"They're not people," I say in a dry tone. "They're chickens."

Jess looks like I've picked up a couple of roosters and bopped her on the head with them. "What?"

Tara starts to giggle, and Jason's smile could fill stadiums with light.

"Don't try to figure it out, Jess. Grab a plate and a utensil, and let's eat." I hand a plate to Tara, who takes it easily.

She starts to dish herself some casserole, saying, "So Jess, Alec says you live with your uncle."

"For now," Jess says. "I'm looking for a better paying job."

"She's wondering if you have anything," I say, meeting Tara's eye. "She's highly trainable."

"You're doing that thing where you make people sound like animals," Tara says with a grin. "She's not a dog, Alec."

"If you need a job," Jason says, picking up a plate and taking the serving spoon from Tara once she's finished. "I've got an opening in my office."

Tara's already shaking her head, her eyes wide. I look from her to Jess, who sees her. "Uh, what do you do?" she asks Jason.

"I'm a lawyer," he says with a grin, and the polite one on Jess's face drops.

"I've never worked in a law office," she says.

"I'm not sure if I'm hiring," Tara says. "Maybe some nightly janitorial help?" She looks at me as if I have any say what she does with Saucebilities.

"I can do that," Jess says hopefully.

"I thought Alec was going to tell you about Lance Byers," Tara says, and it's obvious—at least to me—she doesn't want Jess working in her kitchen. I'm not sure why, but something tells me it's because she's my best friend and not my cousin. Or my sister.

"I did," I say. "She's going to call him." I smile at Jess, who seems to get the message that there's not a job at Saucebilities. *Sorry*, I mouth at her, but she just nods. Jess is tough; she'll find the right spot for her, and she'll move out of her uncle's house.

I want to put my arm around her and comfort her the way I have lots of times in the past. The way she has for me. Instead, I serve up some casserole and hand it to her. "There you go," I say. "Salad down there." I nod needlessly toward it and start to spoon some chicken and ham in the delicious Swiss cheese sauce onto my own plate. I simply mix the burnt crumbs into the sauce, where they'll soften up.

"So, Tara," Jess says, following her to the dining table I've pushed against the wall in the kitchen. "Tell me about your nana."

Jason inhales, and he's obviously gotten a piece of poultry stuck in his throat, because he starts coughing and waving his arms like he's bringing in airplanes.

Tara stops and stares at him, his face turning red. In fact, we all just stand there and stare at him as he very nearly chokes to death. "What on earth is wrong with you?" she asks.

"You know how cold nana gets in the...when the seasons change," Jason says, and I can see him begging Tara with his eyes. I roll mine, because this guy is a total player.

My protective side rears its head, but Jess doesn't need me to come between her and Jason. She's already got him figured out, because she asks, "What's her name? Age? Does she have blue hair?"

Tara looks from Jason to Jess, clearly confused. "We don't have a nana," she says. "Well, we did, but she died five years ago."

"Is that right?" Jess sets her plate down on the table and cocks one hip. "No wonder she needed that hot chocolate. It must be *so cold* six feet under."

I try to stifle my laughter, but I've never been very good at hiding how I really feel. My ha-ha's come exploding out of my mouth, and both women join in with me while Jason's face turns an even deeper shade of red.

"Sorry, bro," I say through chuckles. "She's got your number."

"Seems that way," Jason says darkly as I take the seat

next to him. Tara sits beside me, with Jessie on the other end of the table. He clears his throat as the ladies stop laughing. "So, Tara, I'm sure Jess would agree with me in saying we'd love to know how you two crazy chefs got together."

CHAPTER SEVENTEEN

TARA

"No, the burner in the back," I snap, wishing I wasn't so stressed.

Jared simply flips off the front burner and turns on the back one, nothing said.

"Sorry," I say.

"It's fine," he says. "I wish I could be there tomorrow. Alicia says there's nothing she can do about the baby." He grins at me, and I relax a little.

"I can't wait to meet your baby," I say, thinking about children suddenly. I've never thought too much about becoming a mother, but I guess that comes with getting married. Otis hadn't wanted children right away, and we'd gotten married when I was twenty-two, so I was fine waiting.

Our marriage had only lasted fifteen months, so I

didn't have any kids. Now, when I think about it, my children are all boys who wear smaller T-shirts than their actual size. They have dark hair and eyes, because both me and Alec do, and they all can zip around the kitchen and put together gourmet meals.

The past couple of weeks with Alec have been divine, and we're not even pretending anymore. I've had a few reporters on my stoop, asking me about Alec and if I have any comment about Brett's prediction that any relationship I forge will only last a week.

I have not had any comments. I'm done giving him fodder to write about. I'm done thinking about him.

Now, I spend most of my time worrying that Alec's best friend could become his boo, and then I'll be left to cry into my strawberry shortcake cupcakes.

"That's boiling over," Alec says to my right, and I pull myself out of my horrible self-doubts.

"Then get it," I call to him. "Turn it down. Something."

"I'm up to my elbows in this steak sauce," he says, plenty of bite in his tone. I'm using the Saucebilities kitchen to prep all the food for the wedding, which is tomorrow, because while my back yard may be the site for the "wedding of all weddings," as one reporter called Callie and Dawson's nuptials, my kitchen is sorely lacking.

It's not the anything of anythings, and the only reason I said Callie could have her wedding at my house was because she'd bring the awesome with her. She'd set it all up, and she'd pay someone to take it all down. That, and she said my chickens wouldn't have to move.

"Chef," Jared says, and I turn toward him. He's wearing a bright expression that makes my heart sink to the soles of my feet. "She went into labor."

"Go," I say, though his departure makes me angrier and more frustrated than I already am. We've split our manpower today, because I stupidly booked a librarian luncheon for today, and that meant we couldn't start the wedding meal prep until afternoon.

Three-thirty to be exact. Jared and Alec have been here since seven, and I made Henry go with me to the library while they scrubbed dishes and got the physical facilities ready for the second round.

"Burnt," Alec says, drawing my attention from Jared's retreating form. He tosses the sheet pan of streusel topping on the stovetop, where it clatters with a terrible fright.

"Corn chowder," I say, my heartbeat jumping around as adrenaline streams through my body. "Will you calm down?"

"Will you?" Alec barks at me. He reminds me so much of the growly, grumpy bear who first came to Saucebilities a few months ago.

We glare at each other, and I'm thrown back in time. "Barley isn't even here," I say.

"You're yelling at everyone," he says as if I've not spoken.

"Yeah, well, your station is a mess, so it's no wonder. I

don't even have somewhere to put the dang streusel, even if I had gotten it out on time."

He takes a step closer to me, his dark eyes so, so dangerous. "You make my blood boil."

"Yeah, well, join the club." It's not like I'm happy with myself right now. A timer goes off somewhere, but I have no idea what it's for. "I'm not exactly having a vacation here."

"You shouldn't have scheduled two events in the same day."

I start hunting for the stupid timer that's going to put me in a nuthouse. "Tell me something I don't know." I find it, remember I set it for the cupcakes, and reach for the oven mitts. "Can you *please* clear me a spot for the cupcakes? There are thirty-six of them coming out."

Alec huffs and puffs like the Big Bad Wolf as he starts moving pans and pots and cutting boards off the stainless steel counter. "We need one of those cooling racks," he says.

There's a lot of things I need right now, and only one of them is a commercial cooling rack. I say nothing though, and turn with the huge, hot 18-well muffin pan in my hand. He's cleared me enough room for one of them, and he picks up the mixing bowl he used for the streusel and starts scooping things into it to make more space.

He's clearly upset, and so am I, and I swear, if I can get my hands on a knife after I get this pan of cupcakes out, something's going to get cut. I carefully slide the cupcakes onto the table though I want to slam everything.

But slamming baked goods is a no-no, and I have enough control over my temper to manage the slide.

"I need a minute," I say, tossing the oven mitts on the counter beside the trays of cupcakes.

"We don't have a minute," he yells after me. "Tara? Tara, come *on.*"

With that, I spin on my orthopedic heel and march back to him. "No, you come on." I grab onto his arm and muscle him away from the stove where he's literally set a bowl with a bag of oats, brown sugar, and vanilla. Right on top of the ruined streusel too. Has he no shame whatsoever?

I'm not as strong as him by any means, but I get him going for a few steps, and the rest is easy. "Everything is going to burn," he says.

"Let it." I pull him into the office and slam the door good and hard behind him. My chest heaves, and my fingers curl into fists. "We need a minute."

He faces me, and I'm not sure what he sees, but he softens. I suck at the air, trying to find a breath that isn't full of charred sugar or the horrible stench of starchy water searing into a burner. I pace past him to my mini-fridge and pull out my pint of butter pecan. "Sit."

To my surprise, he does, and in a much calmer way, I pull open my drawer and extract a spoon. "Want a bite?" I glance down, but there's no more utensils. "This is my last clean spoon, so we'll have to share."

He looks at me, and I can't read his mood. There's nothing in his expression, and I find that as unsettling as Mr. Grumpy-Cat.

"There's more out in the kitchen."

"We can't go out there." I raise my eyebrows. "We need a break."

Alec leans forward, his chef jacket straining across that impressive chest. "You're not talking about us, right? Just the kitchen?"

I blink, unsure of what he's saying. "Do you want to take a break?"

"Not from you," he says.

I open the ice cream and dig my spoon into the hard treat. "Great. I was talking about the kitchen."

"You should really let me go turn everything off," he says. "This is going to take longer than a minute."

I study him for a moment, consider what might happen if I leave all the burners flaming the way they are. All the ovens on with things inside them. He can either go turn it all off, or this has to take sixty seconds.

I see ashes and smoke and this building I rent burnt to the ground.

I want more than sixty seconds, so I say, "I'll give you sixty seconds to get it all turned off and be back in here. Or I'm not sharing." I lift my spoon, which still holds just a touch of cream.

JUST HIS BOSS 197

He jumps to his feet and dashes out of the office, practically pulling the door off the wall in his haste. I laugh,
but I still reach for my timer and set it for one minute.

The air in the office is cooler, more breathable. Sometimes I get so worked up, and I just need...a break. I take a
deep breath and then a big bite of ice cream, and the world
starts spinning at normal speed again.

"Ten seconds," I call, and Alec appears in my office
doorway. He's holding a fistful of spoons. I think I fall in
love with him right then and there, because he knows I
need more spoons for my drawer. He knows how much I
love butter pecan ice cream. He knows how dedicated I
am to Saucebilities—and Callie—and that I want everything to be perfect for her wedding.

He knows it was really hard for me to let Jared have
tomorrow off, even if his wife is having their first baby, and
he knows I can't handle the conflict that would come if I
told Henry he couldn't leave after the library luncheon to
go take his aging mother to the hairdresser.

All of those things have caused me a ton of stress, and
it just piles on, and piles on until I'm over-boiling water
and burning streusel—simple tasks I *never* mess up.

He closes the door behind him normally—no Mr.
Slammy in sight—and crosses back to my desk. "Did I
make it?"

The timer goes off, and I grin at him. "Just barely." I
push the ice cream pint closer to him, and he takes a big
dig at it with his spoon.

"Look," I say. "I'm sorry. I—I don't know what happened. The heat melted my brain."

"It happens to all of us," he says quietly before sticking his ice cream in his mouth. Watching him eat is almost as good as kissing him, and I quickly pull my gaze away from those lips. I know if I round the desk and sit in his lap, he'll kiss me. I'll get to taste my all-time favorite ice cream on his mouth, and dang, my body is already vibrating and heating up all over again.

"It's cooler in here," he says. "We might need to nudge up the AC out there."

"We need to just breathe out there," I say. "There's no race for this wedding. It's not until tomorrow. We don't need to have all six ovens on, with every burner at full flame."

He meets my eye and smiles. "You know what? You're right. Where's the fire?"

"It's going to be right here," I say, gesturing with my spoon between us. "If we don't freaking calm down." I take another spoonful of ice cream and eat it as I sink back into my chair.

"I'm mostly talking to myself, by the way," I say. "Not to you."

"You do want to get on home," he says. "Because it's Monday night, and you love those game show reruns." He grins at me, and for some reason, everything that was wrong out in the kitchen is suddenly fine.

"I'll have you know that I solved the prize puzzle on *Wheel of Fortune* last night."

"Mm," he says, digging into my pint of butter pecan again. "Was it from 1985?"

"No," I say, laughing. "It was a new one."

He chuckles too, his dark eyes now only dark in color.

He really has lit up my world, and I really do like him.

No, I think. *You're falling in love with him.*

I know, too, because I've been married once before, and engaged once before. I've never vowed not to fall in love again, and this time, it feels...different.

We finish the whole pint together, and when it's gone, I feel like I can get back to work.

"I just realized we can't go to Mimi's tomorrow either," he says. "It's Callie's wedding. Duh."

"There's always next week," I say, though I'm not entirely sure what next Tuesday's schedule looks like. I'm more of the type of person who likes to live day-by-day so I don't get overwhelmed.

"Better pencil it in," he says. "Or label it."

"I haven't used that label maker in a week, I'll have you know." I glance over to where it sits on top of my filing cabinet.

"You're joking, right?" He gets up and retrieves the label maker. "I think these things have a history on them..." The machine whirs and a label comes out. He rips it off as I stand up. "This one has your name written all over it."

I approach him, needing a kiss before I get back to work. He puts the label maker back in its rightful spot and faces me. He holds up the dark blue tape, and I read VERY REAL GIRLFRIEND.

I freeze, as per my usual when Alec does something to surprise me. He grins as he peels off the back of the label and sticks it to my chest, right above my heart, where a name tag would go.

He cradles my face in his hands, and they're so big, it's almost like he's holding my whole head. Looking up at him, I'm definitely falling for him. The best part is, he seems to be free-falling for me too.

"I'm sorry I said you make my blood boil," he whispers just before kissing me. This kiss is just as explosive as our first, but we've learned how to harness that heat and speed and power, only letting it come out in doses.

"It's true," he says against my ear. "My blood is like lava right now, but I'm sorry I said it."

I simply run my hands through his hair and guide his mouth back to mine.

"Guys," someone says, and I pull away from Alec to look toward the now-open office door. "What's goin' on out here? Everything's off, but Jared called and said I better get over here, stat." Barley looks utterly confused, which only makes me giggle into my boyfriend's chest.

"Yep, coming," Alec says, and he steps away from me so fast, I nearly fall down. I move a little slower, first peeling off his label for me and pressing it to the corner of my desk. That way, everyone will know it's mine, and that I belong there.

Then I follow him into the kitchen, because we have a wedding to prepare for.

CHAPTER EIGHTEEN

ALEC

"ALEC," TARA SAYS, AND I LOOK UP FROM THE LAST OF the oysters I'm garnishing. "Ready?" She stands in the doorway, and she's simply beautiful with all the sunlight pouring in around her.

"Yes," I say, because we've had a great day in the kitchen today, after our disastrous one yesterday. Tara is a lot like me in some ways, in that she gets stressed, and then things come out of her mouth that she doesn't mean to say. At least that's what I'm telling myself, because it makes me nicer and her human.

Otherwise, she's too perfect for me, and I hate thinking I might not be good enough for her.

"I'm just finishing these," I say, lifting the tray of oysters.

"I have the ice ready," she says.

I couldn't believe we were going to serve dinner

outside, but Dawson Houser must be related to the Good
Lord Above, because somehow, the weather is cooler today
than it's been in months. Maybe it's Callie Michaels who
called in the favor. No matter what, they got a perfect
evening for their wedding.

Tara and I have been flirt-cooking all day long, and I
actually can't wait to get out of my chef (straight)jacket
and into my suit. I never thought I'd think or say those
words aloud, but I'm ready to relax.

I take the oysters out onto the deck, which Tara has
shaded to further keep it cool. She also brought over her
heated buffet units and her cold ones, and I take the time
to nestle each individual oyster down into the ice. She
covers them with plastic wrap and turns to smile at me.

I let my eyes slide past her face to the rest of the buffet,
which she's been perfecting for the past twenty minutes.
The hot dishes—chicken kabobs, creamy corn, and roasted
potatoes and veggies—are all covered with metal lids. The
cold gazpacho she whipped up after our come-to-Jesus
moment last night waits on the end of the service area,
plenty of gold-rimmed bowls next to it.

Then the cold bar starts with macaroni salad, greens,
oysters, and the dessert bar, where her strawberry shortcake cupcakes, brownie bites, and the apple and pear tarts
with oatmeal streusel—which I had to make twice—are
also covered with plastic wrap. Tara's put skewers up from
the ice under those trays and serving platters to keep the
wrap from touching the delicate tops of the desserts. We

definitely wouldn't want our immaculate decorations to be ruined.

Four tables have been set up in at the bottom of the steps, two on each side, creating a pseudo-aisle I know Callie will walk down with her father. Only two dozen chairs make up the audience beyond the tables, in only two rows. No hiding in the back row for me.

No one is hiding at this wedding, as Dawson and Callie only invited a very few people. They'd chosen to be married on a Tuesday instead of a weekend. And they'd told no one but those invited the actual date or time of the wedding.

Thankfully, the reporters surrounding me and Tara have backed off now that a few weeks have gone by. The last article that came out had hit the shelves ten days ago, and it had been a simple couple of inches about how Tara's relationship with me had lasted more than a week.

It seems love can be found anywhere, for anyone, the last line of the article had read. I smile just thinking that, because for a while there, I hadn't believed that. A year ago, if someone had told me that, I'd have scoffed, growled, and gotten behind the wheel of my SUV.

"We need to go change," Tara says, putting her hand on my chest. Her touch sends a thrill through me and forces me to focus on her.

"Yeah, okay," I say, turning to go back into her house. I nearly collide with Dawson, who grabs onto my shoulders so I don't fall backward.

"Whoa," he says, and that makes me grin.

"See?" I say over my shoulder to Tara, who's bumped into me because I stopped. "He says it too. It doesn't mean I'm a horse."

"I still hate it," she says.

I move to the side, Dawson backs up, and Tara slips through the doorway. "We just need five minutes to change," she says.

"That's fine," he drawls, already inside his professional Society skin. "That'll give me time to talk to Mother and this date she's brought." He casts a look made of thunder and lightning out the door. "Guess I better get to it."

He sighs and leaves the house, and I go with Tara through the kitchen and living room to the other side of her house, which hosts the bedrooms. She's got three, and she nods to the one where I've already stashed my clothes as she continues to the end of the hall and goes into the master suite.

I haven't been in there, and I'm male enough to admit I've thought about it. Knowing Tara as I do, I can't help but wonder what I'd find. Does she label her bathroom shelves for where to keep the body wash? Is every hook labeled with "towel" or "washcloth" the way she labels our hooks at work?

Mine has my name above it, for crying out loud. For how often she turns over chefs, I'm surprised she's labeling the hooks, but I shouldn't be. Tara likes having things where they belong, and I can't begrudge her that.

I pull off my jacket and apron and start to dress in my slacks and white shirt. Tara told me once that she likes the labels and organization, because it's something she can control. As someone who appreciates only worrying about what I can control and who's spent a lot of time obsessing over what I can't, I've decided to stop teasing her about the labels.

I finish getting dressed and rush across the hall to the bathroom to wash my face and hands, because I need to look nice. Not only as the chef of the meal some very important people will be eating, but as Tara's escort. She's Callie's maid of honor, and that means she needs someone to walk her down the aisle before the bride. That person should be her very real boyfriend, and I'm happy to do the job even though it makes me nervous to have so many eyes on me.

There's a reason I like being in the kitchen, and a reason I didn't want to be the public face of The Blackbriar Inn.

I oil down my beard and step back. That's about all I can do as a man, and I wonder how Tara's really going to be ready in five minutes. She told me her dress took five minutes to zip up as we frosted cupcakes this morning, and I'm not sure when she's exaggerating and when she's not.

I exit the bathroom to find her two dogs guarding the way between me and the master bedroom, as if I'm going to go down there and do something I shouldn't. "Not on your watch, huh?" I say to Tommy and Goose.

Goose's tail starts to wag, but Tommy just huffs and lays back down. I chuckle at the dogs and crouch down to pat them. Goose is a light brown pup who clearly isn't as old and crotchety as Tommy, and he comes over to sniff and lick my hand.

The door down the hall opens, and I straighten as Tara comes out. She's wearing a gorgeous dress the color of eggplant skin, and it looks like a second skin glued to her body. Oh, those curves would have any man groveling at her feet, but I manage to stay on mine.

"Wow," I say, forgetting about the dog barrier between us and stepping toward her. "You look amazing." I take her hand in one of mine, note her smile, and slide my other hand along that delicious hip.

The floral scent of her perfume undoes my composure. The way she's parted her hair in the middle and then pulled it into a low ponytail gives her a sophisticated, elegant look I haven't seen before.

She's wearing mascara, a light eyeshadow, and eyeliner that makes her brown eyes look twice as big. Her cheeks hold just the right amount of flush, and diamonds drip from her ears, neck, and wrist.

"You *are* amazing," I whisper as I lower my head toward her ear. I like listening to her pull in a breath, and I like the soft skin along her shoulder.

"We don't have time to kiss in the hallway," she murmurs. "You'll ruin my makeup besides."

"What about a quick question?" I ask, and though I try to swallow the words, they come surging out anyway. "Would you want to get married?"

She pulls back, her eyes wide and searching my face instantly.

"I mean, not to me," I say, realizing how stupid that sounds. "I mean...in general. Are you the marrying type?"

She visibly relaxes, but her grip on my hand actually increases. "Uh, I'm not sure actually."

My eyebrows go up. "You're not?"

"I've been married, remember? It was kind of a huge bust. Then there was the other engagement that never made it to the altar." She shrugs as Callie comes out of the room behind her. "I don't know."

"She'd marry the right guy," Callie says, resting her chin on Tara's shoulder. She grins at me while Tara tries to look at her. "Oops, I mean man. She'd marry the right *man*."

"Callie," Tara says in a warning voice.

"But she doesn't want a long engagement," Callie continues as if Tara has turned invisible. "She wants a spur-of-the-moment engagement. A wedding the next weekend. A cruise to the Bahamas."

"Stop talking right now," Tara says. She turns back to me and starts to turn me around. "Bless her heart, she's so nervous for this wedding."

"I am not," Callie says behind her, but Tara's almost pushing me down the hall now. Her dogs weave in and out of our legs, and I don't know how they do it.

In the kitchen, we meet up with the rest of the wedding party, which consists of Callie's sister and her boyfriend, Ariel and Walker, Dawson's cousin and his wife, Augustus and Emilia, and their landlord and her husband, Jillian and Tom.

"Where's Lance?" Tara asks as if she's the wedding planner, and the man steps out of the dining room.

"Right here." He does not look happy, but he does look great in his dark suit and tie, though I'm not one-hundred percent sure it matches his shirt. His flower is pinned right above his heart, and his hands hang loosely in his pockets. I'm not sure if Jessie has texted or called him yet, and I need to find out.

"You're leading us," Tara says, releasing my arm and going to brush something invisible from his shoulders. "Get up there in the front. We're ready."

He walks on wooden legs to the back exit, and Tara returns to my side. "That man." She takes my arm, shaking her head.

"Cut him some slack," I say under my breath. "His fiancée left the state, with his ring, what? Three months ago?" Four at the most, and I'm surprised Lance is here at all. I lean closer to Tara, who's frozen at my side. "If that was me—and I wasn't even engaged—I'd be somewhere in Colorado about now. Maybe Montana."

She blinks, those eyes so beautiful when she lets some vulnerability into them. "When Otis left, I slept at Callie's for three weeks."

She's told me that before. "And after Brett?"

"We went to Brussels," she whispers. "For two weeks."

"So we'll forgive Lance if he's not super-happy to lead the wedding party only a few months after what happened to him."

"Yes," Tara nods. "We will. *I* will."

He moves then, and the rest of the wedding party falls into place behind him. Tara and I bring up the rear, and since there's very few people actually in the audience, the only eyes I have to endure are Dawson's mother.

Lila Houser's sharp-edged gaze cuts me to the core, and I grin at the private knife joke I've just shared with myself. The moment Tara and I are in position, the wedding march pipes through the back yard. I lean closer to her anyway, enjoying the chance to do so.

"Wow, Lila's gaze cut me to the core, as if I were an apple."

"Oh, my word," she whispers, but her shoulders start to shake. Her laughter only increases and causes me to laugh, which is so inappropriate for the occasion. Callie reaches the top of the steps and her father, a somewhat short, older gentleman, goes up them to greet her. He gives her a kiss just as Tara's laughter hisses out of her mouth.

"Stop it," I whisper, though I'm still laughing too. "This is your best friend's wedding." Not to mention we're the professional caterers, and we shouldn't be having a horse-laugh session as the bride walks down the aisle.

Ariel, Callie's sister looks over to Tara, and she manages to control herself. I can't stop smiling though, but thankfully, that fits into a proper wedding.

"She looks amazing," Tara whispers. "Don't you think?"

"Yes," I say, because I've had girlfriends before and know when to agree with them. Callie is a pretty woman, but she doesn't press the right buttons for me. Tara seems to have all ten fingers on them at all times, though.

The bride reaches the groom, and I see the way Dawson looks at Callie. The love shining there is enough to fill a previously jaded and jilted man with hope. My smile straightens somewhat though, because Tara didn't have time to tell me if she'd get married again. At least not herself.

I want to ask her about kids too, but maybe it's still too soon in our relationship to be talking about such personal things. I'm not sure, because I've had few girlfriends where I have had those kinds of talks. And if I did, we'd been dating for much longer than a couple of weeks, with a fake-dating week before that.

Three weeks, I tell myself. *You will not ask her about having kids at three weeks.*

I want to, but I won't. I'll have to come up with a few more knife jokes to fill the silence between us.

"Do you, Callie Whitney Michaels, pledge yourself to

Dawson Connor Houser, for time and all eternity? To have and to hold, to love and to cherish, in good times and bad?" The pastor pauses, and I clue in to the fact that I've missed the advice part of the wedding.

"Yes," Callie says. "I do."

The pastor repeats the question to Dawson, who also says, "Yes, I do."

"By the power vested in me from the state of South Carolina, I now pronounce you man and wife." He grins at them, and my smile returns too. "You may kiss your bride."

Dawson grins wickedly at Callie, who's already giggling. He takes her into his arms and dips her back while a squeal comes out of her mouth.

Tara makes the same noise and starts to clap as Dawson bends over and kisses Callie. I applaud politely too, enjoying the good feeling in the back yard. And, as the cherry on top, it's time to eat.

"That was so amazing," Tara says, wiping one finger under her right eye. "You're going to watch the buffet with me, right?"

"Of course," I say as Callie lifts her and Dawson's hands. Since there are so few people there, the hugging and congratulations only takes a few minutes, and then a woman with really short, almost neon orange hair holds both hands high above her head. Callie's mom.

"There's food on the deck," she says. "Let's tuck in."

I step over to Callie and Dawson and envelop them

both in a hug. "Congrats, you two," I say, pulling back quickly. "That was really great."

"Thank you," Dawson says, and he radiates happiness from every pore of his body.

Callie grabs onto me as if I'm a life preserver. "You don't let her get away from you," she whispers. She pulls back but doesn't move her face more than six inches from mine. "She'll try, and she'll try hard. It's just what Tara does. And everyone lets her. You can't let her."

I don't even know what she's talking about, but I nod, because I'm experienced enough with women to know when they just want you to agree and when they want you to ask questions. A little tip: They hardly ever want you to ask questions.

"Okay," she says, settling back onto her feet the right way. "I can't wait to eat that cold soup you promised me."

"Alec," Tara says, and she's wearing something sharp in her voice. Both Callie and I look toward her, and I can see there's something wrong instantly. She nods toward the fence, and I'm surprised the man I catch ducking down the moment I look his way hasn't been liquified by the heat in her gaze.

"I'll take care of it," I say, already striding toward the gate in her fence. Time to go Marine on a reporter, and the only thing that's excited me more in the past several months...is Tara. I can't wait to dance with her later, hold her close, and breathe in that sexy, petally scent that goes everywhere with her.

The squawking of chickens meets my ears, and I turn back, thinking she might have a fowl emergency she needs me to take care of more than the press. I find her with a black and white hen in her arms, showing it to someone as if it's a fluffy bunny rabbit. The joy on her face fills the whole yard, and I shake my head.

I push through the gate, realizing I might have to share my dance with the woman I'm falling for...with a chicken named Hennifer.

CHAPTER NINETEEN

TARA

I WORK HARD NOT TO TAP MY PEN ON THE
conference room table, because I want this pool party on
my calendar. Martin's been talking for twenty minutes,
though, and I get it. He wants to throw an end-of-summer
bash for his high school students, because they've all left to
go back to school.

The community pool out in Sugar Creek is still open,
but they have limited hours, and blah blah *blah*. My
patience is gone, and I've been doodling in the corner of
his approved menu about which recipe I'm going to type
up next for my cookbook.

Saucebilities has a small quinceañera that night, but
I'm not going to be cooking. I just want this meeting to be
over. I've never been great in meetings, but I nod as
Martin asks a question.

"Yes," I say. "We'll use chicken breast on that. That's not a problem."

"Miss Finch?" My part-time scheduler pokes her head into the room, and I leap to my feet. I've never been so happy to see her.

"Yes?"

"I'm sorry," Lydia says. "You have tonight's client on the phone." She glances at Martin and throws him a small smile. "So sorry, Mister Powell. I can finish up for Tara."

"I think we're done," I say, looking to Martin for confirmation.

"Yes," he says, and his papers are already gathered into his folder. "I was just blathering."

He can say that again, but I'm not going to. I step over to him and give him a peck on both cheeks. "Do say hello to Jane for me," I say. His wife used Saucebilities a year or so ago for their last son's graduation party, and I probably don't need to worry about losing his business.

"I will," he says, and I gesture him out of the room in front of me. I let him go ahead and walk down the hall bordered on one side with all the conference room windows, and then I turn to Lydia.

"Thank you," I breathe. "That was torture."

"I gathered as much from your text."

"It's just that we finalized the menu twenty minutes ago, and this is all I really need." I hand her the sheet. "Will you put it in the calendar for me? It's a rush job, so I'm not sure what that does as far as scheduling."

Lydia takes the paper and glances at it. "When is it?"

"A week from Saturday. I didn't see anything on my calendar." Which is a little odd, because weekends are my busiest time at Saucebilities.

Lydia starts toward her desk, and she's at least ten years younger than me, with that early twenties body I haven't had in longer than a decade. She has regular-shaped legs that don't look like they'll snap when she walks, and her pencil skirt would make even Callie jealous.

I watch the way she swings her hips, and I try to figure out how she does it in those heels. Maybe if I wore heels, I'd be able to achieve that side-to-side movement.

I take a step and really try to thrust my hip out the way Lydia seems to do so effortlessly. My ankle buckles, and I plant both palms against the wall to keep myself from falling down. It sounds like a truck has run straight into the building, and Lydia spins around.

The paper flutters to the floor as her hand goes to her pulse. "Are you okay?" She hurries back toward me, and I really wish she wouldn't. My internal temperature has shot through the roof, and I'm sure my face is the color of the marinara sauce Alec's working on in the kitchen right now.

I wave her back as my body parts cooperate with me. Lydia keeps coming, and there's no holding her back now. She is Southern, after all, and we don't just let friends trip over their own feet and then suffer the embarrassment of that alone.

She puts her hand on my arm about the same time I straighten, and her wide, blue eyes broadcast concern. "Are you okay for real?"

"Yes," I say.

"What happened?"

"My chicken legs gave out on me," I say with a forced laugh. Jason's nickname for me runs through my mind— Legs—but there's no way I can tell her I was trying to swing my hips the way she was.

"You do not have chicken legs," Lydia says. "That meeting just went on and on. Come have some lemonade."

I go with her, this time ignoring her perfect pendulum hips. Maybe the orthopedics will never allow for such a perfect left-right swing.

No matter what, now I know why Rick is in here every day with flowers, jewelry, cookies, Lydia's favorite soda, and anything and everything else the woman likes. I can't remember the last time a man bought me a gift, and that includes Alec.

The last week since Callie's wedding has included good days in the kitchen, perfect parties, and that same, hot kissing I've been enjoying for weeks now. If our relationship was fake, I would've ended it by now, but since it's not, we're going to Mimi's for their Tuesday-night mousse tasting.

I can admit—only to myself—that our date tonight is

the reason I didn't put myself in the kitchen today. I didn't want to be oily and sweaty, rushed to shower, and then get back downtown. Alec lives on the edge of the peninsula, and I'll just go with him to his apartment while he showers.

Lydia hands me a can of sugar-free lemonade and sits down at her desk. She taps and clicks while I cool down my humiliation, with the throbbing in my ankle telling me I'm not going to try that again.

I have a pair of Callie's ankle boots in the car. She's still on her honeymoon, but she told me I could go in her house and get the shoes. She hasn't moved in with Dawson yet, but I'll be helping with that once they get back from Greece.

"Oh, honey, I don't know about next Saturday," Lydia says, and I set down the can of lemonade to peer at her computer.

"Why? What did I do?" I can cater the end-of-summer smash at the pool by myself if I have to.

"It's the Sugar Creek Fall Festival." Lydia looks at me. "You're doing a booth Saturday and Sunday."

"Noooo," I say. "That can't be right." How could I forget that? I do the Sugar Creek Fall Festival every year, at least since I opened Saucebilities, because Callie and I lived there for some very key years of our lives. She still lives there, but I moved to Cottonhill when I bought the house I'm in now.

Lydia's calendar on her screen shows the Fall Festival

in two bright pink boxes. The pool party would sit on Saturday night.

"You've already scheduled everyone to work Friday and Saturday...and Sunday."

My mind races. "Okay," I say. "I'm not sure why this didn't sync on my phone. I'll...think of something." I've called in emergency chefs before, and I can do that again.

In ten days? I ask myself, but I have to make it work. I straighten and start to text a couple of chefs who used to work for me. Jasper responds quickly and says he can't and he's so sorry.

Phillip says he's opened his own restaurant now, and hey I should come check out the small plates that he serves, since I inspired the menu with one we did of family Easter party a few years ago.

I press my teeth together and text Justin. Then Olivia. Then Sam.

None of them can come help next week.

"I'm headed out," Lydia says, and I look up. I've completely forgotten that I'm still standing out in the lobby.

"Yeah, sure," I say. "Thanks, Lydia." She goes one way, and I go the other. I wanted to work on my cookbook this afternoon before the mousse tasting, and I head toward my office. I can flip through my computer and see if I can find someone, anyone, who can come work next week.

"Maybe I can make the food for the pool party in between the Fall Festival prep." We usually do a bunch of grab-and-go items for the festival, and I can probably fit in the buffalo wild wings, the macaroni salad, and the hummingbird cakes for the pool party.

I push through the door and into the kitchen, the temperature automatically going up ten degrees. Jared laughs as he sautés something on the flat top, and Barley reaches for a stack of transportable, plastic containers. He begins to scoop mashed potatoes into them, catches my eye, and lifts his head in greeting.

I don't see Alec, though I know he's here. At least he was before the meeting-that-wouldn't-end. I frown, wondering if something's gone wrong. It definitely has for me, and my ankle shouts at me not to try the hip-swing again.

Maybe he's in the refrigeration unit, and my lips tingle just thinking about it. He's kissed me in there several times. The first time, he asked me to come help him find the mayo, though he had to know where it was.

Yeah, he did. It was just to kiss me. When I asked him what his fascination with making out in the walk-in fridge was, he'd laughed and said it was a little kissing, not making out. And that he really liked to feel like he was steaming things up, and all you have to do to produce steam in the walk-in fridge is breathe out.

I turn toward the walk-in fridge just as the door to it opens. Alec comes out of it, laughing in a boisterous, sexy way, and I smile.

That gesture slides right off my face when I see the

blonde woman following him. Also laughing. Those blue eyes twinkling.

Jessie Dunaway, his best friend.

Make that *supposed* best friend.

Or "best friend with benefits."

CHAPTER TWENTY

ALEC

I SEE THE LOOK ON TARA'S FACE AND CUT MY laughter off mid-ha. The jealousy streaming from her isn't hard to feel or see, but Jessie doesn't seem to get it. She keeps laughing and even says, "That's because you never know when to stop."

I know when to stop right now, and I wish she'd get the freaking hint. I want to wave my arms and point out the very angry brunette standing ten feet in front of us. Angry's not the right word, and Tara's really good at hiding things.

She also hates conflict, so she lifts her chin and says, "Hey, Jessie," in a voice that gets drowned out by some very loud sizzling from the stovetop where Barley has just put down a whole mess of steaks.

Tara goes by, and I want to tell her I like her hair, and hey, she's so pretty, but her cold shoulder freezes my vocal cords. I watch her walk into her office and close the door, and I wonder if she would've done that if I hadn't just walked out of the walk-in fridge with Jessie.

I have a really good reason for why my best friend is here, and once I explain it all to Tara, everything will be fine.

"Okay, I'm gonna go," Jessie yells above the steak sounds. She tips up onto her toes and kisses my cheek. I do the same to her, because we grew up in Beaufort, and that's what people do. I've probably kissed the whole town a dozen times by now.

I walk Jessie through the kitchen and the dish room to the back door and open it for her. "Good luck with the interview, Jess," I say. "Not that you need it."

She grins at me, and her smile is the happiest I've seen it in weeks. Maybe months. I close the door against the heat of the day and sigh. I need to get back to work, and I look down at the plastic tub of chicken thighs in my hand.

Chicken thighs.

Alfredo. Benedict. Pot Pie. Hennifer. Piccata. No, wait, Tara doesn't have a chicken named Piccata. Yet.

I go back into the kitchen and put the thighs on the counter. "Here you go, Jared. I need to go talk to Tara."

He twists from the massive pile of onions and peppers he's got on the flat top. "Don't take too long. We need to get those grilling."

"Two minutes," I promise him, and I'm proud of myself for being so nice. It feels good to talk to him like he's a friend, but still a little strange to think Jared might actually *be* a friend. A month ago, though, and I would've rolled my eyes and stalked away to do whatever I wanted, no matter what that did to him.

He nods, as he technically has more sway here than I do. I'm still the new man on the totem pole as the last chef Tara hired.

I hurry past the countertops and round the corner to face the closed office door. I steel myself with a deep breath and keep walking. I knock on the door at the same time I open it. "Hey, do you have a minute?" I ask. Actually two, but I've dealt with an upset Tara before, and it usually takes some butter pecan and less than sixty seconds to get her back into her happy place.

"Not really," she says. "That meeting went on forever, during which I double-booked myself in the worst way possible." She's squinting at the screen in front of her and doesn't bother to look my way.

I enter the office and leave the door ajar. "What way?" I ask.

Tara heaves a sigh and looks at me like I've just murdered all thirteen of her hens. "What do you want, Alec? Don't you have chicken Caprese sandwiches to make?"

"Yes," I say. "I do. Yes, I do." I press my hands together and commit myself to getting closer to her. "I saw your face when Jessie and I came out of the deep-freeze, and I just want you to know you have nothing to worry about."

Ice flows from her expression. "I'm not worried about you and your lifelong best friend. Your super-cute, blonde, grins-like-a-fool, and so-nice-it-hurts best friend." She glares as she stands. "I don't have enough butter pecan to deal with this right now." She strides over to her filing cabinet and pulls open the top drawer. Once she shoulders her purse, she heads in my direction. "I'm going to work at home for the rest of the day."

I start to say, "Whoa," and change it to "Wh-hhat?"

She seems to know I'm about to go equine trainer on her, and she pauses a few feet from me.

"She stopped by to tell me she finally got up the nerve to call Lance, and she has an interview with him next week." I don't say that it sure would be nice if Tara hired more people, because it's not what she wants to hear right now. I didn't used to care about that, but right now, I do.

She folds her arms and cocks that sexy hip. "And you went into the walk-in, because...?"

"Because I'm really busy with the Caprese sandwiches, and I needed the chicken thighs."

"Right," she says with a scoff. "If you want to be with Jessie and not me, just say so."

"I *don't* want that," I say, taking another step toward her and cutting off her escape route. "Baby, you have nothing to be jealous about."

"I'm not blonde."

"I don't like blondes," I say. I take another step toward her. "Listen, okay?" I put my hand on that cocked hip, fire rushing through my veins. "I've had plenty of opportunities to be with Jessie if that's what I want. It's not. She's not." I lower my head and touch my lips to Tara's temple, then her cheek. "I'm going to hold you close so you can't run away."

I tighten my grip on her, because I can feel the word-vomit starting to surge up my throat. I promised myself I wouldn't fall for her. I am a big, fat liar, because I'm definitely falling for this woman.

"I'm falling in love with you, Boss." I kiss the corner of her mouth and then her earlobe, feeling her stiffen and then soften almost instantly.

"I know what it feels like to be cheated on, and I will never, *ever* do that to someone, least of all you." I run my hands through her hair. "Your hair is pretty today," I whisper. "I like it down and curled like this."

"Stop it," she murmurs.

"Stop what?" I ask.

"Flirting with me. You're really bad at it."

The way she slides her hands up my arms to my chest says differently, but I just smile at her. "Oh, I know what'll win you over." I clear my throat. "I just got a few cats. I named them Spoon, Fork, and Knife. They're my *catlery*."

Tara looks up at me, delight sparking in those eyes. I knew she liked my knife jokes. She bursts out laughing a moment later, and it didn't even take any butter pecan.

"If you want to go, you should," I say as her laughter turns to quieter giggles. "Jared's got us on track out there.

I'll come pick you up tonight. You could have a *knife*, quiet afternoon."

Her grin stays as wide as the Great Barrier Reef. "I think I will," she says. "See you *spoon*."

I tip my head back and laugh, knowing my two minutes are up. I still take a moment to appreciate how... happy I am. I silently acknowledge that I'm definitely falling for Tara. I lean down and kiss her, hopefully in a way that would totally have the walk-in fridge full of steam so there's no doubt in her mind that she's the one I want.

"My two minutes are up," I say as I pull away. "I really need to get the thighs on the grill." I step back and meet her eyes. "For real, Tara, we're okay?"

She reaches up and wipes my lip with her finger. "You don't want to wear pink lip gloss in the kitchen."

"You didn't answer my question."

"Yes," she says, ducking her head for a moment and then lifting it to meet my gaze. "We're okay."

"Good." I grin at her. "See you *spoon*...Boss."

———

"THIS ONE IS A WHITE CHOCOLATE RASPBERRY," the waitress says, setting two small glasses on the table. The mousse goes all the way to the top of the glass, with a fine, pink powder on top.

"Oh, it's so pretty," Tara says, her eyes lit up like a

child's on Christmas morning. She looks at me and reaches for her tiny dessert spoon.

I grin and pick up my spoon too. The mousse is two bites, and I've had the white chocolate raspberry before. Mimi's always offers at least five new mousses each week, but they serve some of their bestsellers too.

"Let's take a bite together," Tara says, digging into hers.

"All right," I say with a chuckle. I scoop up my bite, and she counts down.

"Three...two...one." She slides her spoon into her mouth, which totally distracts me. I've eaten with her plenty of times, but once the kiss-barrier had been broken, I'd liked it a lot more. Those lips can drive a man to his knees.

I hardly taste the mousse, and not only because this one has a very mild flavor.

"I can barely get the raspberry," she says. "You?"

"It comes in the back of your throat," I say. "At the end."

"Ah, yes." She nods and eats her second bite. I do too, and then I reach for my glass of ice water.

"Not my favorite," she says. "Though I think I should make a white chocolate cupcake with raspberry butter-cream. I could melt down a sorbet or sherbet for that..."

I grin at her and set my glass down. "How's the cook-book coming? Did you get your recipes typed up at home?"

She scoffs and shakes her head. "No," she says. "I can't get anything done at home."

"I bet I know what you did," I say with a grin.

"Oh yeah?" she challenges. "Do tell."

I take a moment to inhale, because I feel like I'm about to get myself in trouble. "I bet Tommy and Goose talked you into taking a nap."

Tara starts to giggle, and I know I'm right.

"Then, I'm sure Hennifer required some of your attention, what with her being so high-maintenance and all."

She licks her spoon clean and points it at me. "It's Benedict that's giving me trouble."

"Really? Not Hennifer Lopez?" I fold my arms and lean back in my chair. "Seems like she'd be a Chicken Little Diva in that coop."

Tara smiles, sets her spoon down, and leans her arms into the table. "Alec, what Callie said at the wedding is right. I'd take a chance on marriage for the right man."

As I note how rapidly she changed the topic—something she's always accusing me of doing—I realize how much it cost Tara to say something like that, and I lean across the table and take her hands in mine. "That's great," I say. "Dare I ask about another serious topic?"

"Let me guess," she says, looking at our joined hands as she runs her thumb over the back of mine. "It's about having a little human like you running around."

"Or a little human like you," I say quietly, suddenly feeling the need to study the tabletop too. "Someone who loves chickens, label-makers, her friends, inventing recipes, and eating dinner really late at night."

She smiles, but it's not the usual sun-rivalry grin.

"Someone who's smart, runs her own business, is a genius with flavors, and takes time to read bedtime stories to her dogs."

"Just Tommy," she whispers. "He can't fall asleep without it."

"Hm."

She lifts her eyes to mine. "You go first."

I swallow, because I'm not great at this kind of stuff. "I'd take a kid or two," I say with a shrug. "After I find the just-right woman for me."

"Yeah? And what is she like?" She's flirting with me, and I could throw something funny back in her face. I rack my brain for a good knife joke or something self-deprecating.

In the end, my brain has gone on vacation, and I shrug again. "You didn't answer the question."

"If I ever get married again, I think kids would be part of the deal, yes."

"So...what happened with Otis? Why did you two get divorced?"

Tara blinks at me, her eyelashes fluttering like hummingbird wings. "We got married really young," she says. "Neither of us was ready." She reaches for her drink, and I recognize it as a diversion tactic.

"And?" I prompt, because I don't want her to give me a

glossed-over answer. Well, she can give it to me, but I don't want to take it. Callie told me not to let her get away from me, and that's what she's doing right now. Trying to get away.

"And he said—" She cuts off as if someone's pressed mute on the remote control for her voice. Apprehension flashes across her face, and I hate that I've done that to her. Tonight should be about desserts and fun, in this super-cool environment with low candlelight and live music on the front stage.

"It's okay," I say, totally letting her off the hook. She can swim away from the topic now. "You don't have to tell me."

"No, I can," she says. "He said I left him out to dry. I never told him how I was feeling. He wasn't even sure I *had* feelings." She takes another gulp of her water, and I can see everything she's feeling whether she vocalizes it or not.

She clears her throat and puts her glass down, shakes something invisible from her shoulders, and meets my eye again. "I have feelings. I'm not that great at saying them out loud, but I've gotten better in the past decade."

"I seem to remember you telling me that you wanted a man to talk to you," I say.

"Yes," she says. "And I tell them important things too."

I nod and glance up as the waitress arrives again. "Brand new flavor." She smiles at me, and I recognize her since I've been here before. "Toffee caramel crunch mousse."

"Ooh." Tara reaches for her spoon, our earlier conversation glossed over just how she likes it. "I like anything with the words 'caramel crunch' in it."

I like anything with Tara Finch in it, but I keep my mouth shut. I think I'm further along in the relationship than she is, and I need to make sure she's on the same page as me before I go spilling my guts.

CHAPTER TWENTY-ONE

TARA

SUGAR-FREE AND GLUTEN-FREE.

I stare at the chapter heading, wondering when I decided to include this type of recipe in my Southern Roots Desserts Cookbook. Yes, my book has a title now. It's a real book, I've decided. I've moved all the non-dessert recipes to another document, for another cookbook. Possibly delusional, but I've adopted Callie's attitude, and I don't want to throw away the work I've done.

I know lots of people who have family recipes they've typed up over the years and passed down through the generations. Driving through the small towns in Carolina, I once went into an old general store and found a spiral-bound cookbook from people who'd lived there for generations. That's what I want my cookbook to be.

I delete off the horrible words, my frustration growing. My mind sparks, and I quickly go back to the beginning of the book. Once I decided this was going to be a real book, and I was going to somehow find the guts to talk to Lila Houser about a book editor or publisher in New York, I started flipping through my cookbooks at home.

Almost all of them came with a foreword or a little something from the cookbook author at the beginning, before just diving into the recipes. I've never been trained in writing, but I can ramble on about why I decided to do the cookbook as well as anyone else.

The kitchen is quiet today, my book starts, and the same environment surrounds me now. I love coming to Saucebilities before everyone else. I love seeing it in its dormant state, because I don't get to appreciate it once things get boiling and frying.

The kitchen is quiet today, and I'm standing in it thinking about what I should make for dinner. Then I remember that I order dinner from one of my favorite Charleston take-out places every night.

There's no need for dinner recipes. Not when you can have dessert first.

I think it's a pretty decent start to my dessert cookbook, and I navigate to the end of the two pages that I've labeled the foreword, as if I really know what that word means. I don't, but I know what sugar-free and gluten-free mean.

This is not a cookbook for you if you're looking for something without sugar or gluten. These are full-fat, full-sugar, full of flavor Southern desserts from my roots—my grandmother, great-granddaddy, and more. Perfected over the years in quiet kitchens, with Southern love, by one plump chef specifically for you.

"Wow," I say, impressed with myself. I don't know if that makes me arrogant or just confident, but I do like that little paragraph. It's enough to chase away the frustration I felt a few minutes ago. I sit back in my chair and read the paragraph again, wondering why I thought I needed to include sugar-free recipes.

"For women like Jessie," I say, frowning. I'm right, and I hate that Alec's best friend has gotten into my head and pushed buttons she has no right to touch. I hate that I've let her. I hate that I've uncaged the green-eyed monster, and I wish I could chase him down and stuff him back into his cage where he belongs.

I quickly lean forward again, my fingers finding a home on the keyboard, and delete the word *plump*. I am not going to give Brett the satisfaction of knowing that he gave me fuel to use for anything. Knowing him, he'd come after me for some copyright infringement or something equally as lame.

I feel like I need an adjective in front of chef, but I'm not sure what to put. I don't mind thinking of myself as big or fat. I'm a good chef, and a good friend, and a good chicken-mother, no matter my size.

I try those adjectives in the sentence, and they don't seem quite right.

I navigate from my document to the Internet and actually go to an online thesaurus. Is this what my life has come to? Trying to think of words other than *plump* and only being able to come up with two?

"What did people do before the Internet?" I grumble to myself. I suppose I should be glad I don't have to know the answer to that question. Or, I could use the Internet to find out.

I smile as I type *plump* into the search bar at the top. Results come up instantly, and I read the top three. "Chunky...ew. No. Fleshy? This is a joke. Pudgy."

Pudgy. Stars in heaven, pudgy?

If Brett had called me that, I might be sitting in a jail cell about now, for I might have done something illegal to get back at him.

Plump is still body-shaming, and I'm still not happy about it. But at least it wasn't pudgy. Of course, Brett probably didn't have to use a thesaurus to come up with it.

I scan some other words in the list. *Beefy, buxom,* and *obese.* Dear Lord, what woman wants to be called *beefy?*

"Tubby," I read, and the word strikes me as hilarious. Giggles come, and I can't stop them. I even type tubby into my document and re-read the sentence.

Perfected over the years in quiet kitchens, with Southern love, by one tubby chef specifically for you.

My laughter rings in the quiet kitchen, and as my mind releases with the sound of it and the feeling of being wonderfully free, I think of the perfect word for my amazing body.

Perfected over the years in quiet kitchens, with Southern love, by one curvy chef specifically for you.

I don't mind being called curvy. Women want to be curvy, right? Never mind that I almost dislocated my ankle and my hip trying to achieve that curve last week. No one needs to know that.

A red light flashes on my computer, and I reach to turn off the monitor. Jared's just arrived, and that means the kitchen is about to get noisy. I probably shouldn't have come in early today, but I couldn't sleep anyway.

Mr. Reynolds will go get my dogs later today, and I even got him to agree to feed the chickens and let them out for their hour of pasturesize. I've got a full day of prep for the Fall Festival in front of me, and then hours more tonight to get ready for the pool party.

I haven't asked anyone to stay and help me with that, because I don't think it's fair. Jared has a new baby; Barley's mother isn't well; Henry's seeing someone new he's really excited about; Alec has Peaches, and he likes to lift weights and soak in the hot tub at night.

I can do the prep myself, even if I'm here until two o'clock in the morning, which let's face it, I will be. But Saucebilities is my company, and I've done worse things than cook for sixteen straight hours.

I managed to rope Callie and Jason into helping me set-up and serve the food at the pool. The party is only a couple of hours long, and though Callie's getting back from her honeymoon tomorrow, that's just a technicality.

Her and Dawson's flight touches down at twelve-fifty-seven a.m., so they'll really be home tonight.

Jason has no reason not to help me, and he can set up a buffet and carry in bins of food just as easily as I can.

I get up and leave the cookbook behind. My fingers drift over the label Alec made for me. VERY REAL GIRLFRIEND. A small smile touches my face, and I look up as I hear voices in my kitchen. One of them belongs to Alec, the other to Jared, and while I'm happy to see them both, I only want to kiss one of them. I'm only falling in love with one of them, and it has nothing to do with his knife skills—or the jokes—or how he can make a piece of chicken taste like heaven in my mouth.

"Hey, baby," he says when I come around the corner. He wears a big smile and puts his free hand around me. He leans down and kisses me, and I don't even mind that he's done it in front of Jared. "You're here early." He steps back and starts unpacking his knives.

"Yeah," I say. "Couldn't sleep, and I was finishing up that Cookie Monster salad recipe for the book."

He nods, and I turn to the hooks by the inside door. I take the apron from my labeled hook and tie it around my waist. "All right," I say with a big sigh. "We're doing fried chicken bites with dipping gravy, catfish tacos with Southern slaw relish, and banana pudding. Who wants what?"

The slaw for tomorrow can all be done today. Then we just have to put it on the hot fish to serve it. Someone will need to make and bake the tortillas, and I add, "I only want four-inch tortillas. Corn, to mimic the cornmeal batter you'd get on a fried catfish."

"We're not frying it, right?" Jared asked.

"No, one fried thing per fair is all that's allowed," I say. We have to haul in our fryers and equipment, and that makes serving two fried main dishes really hard. We'll barely be able to keep up with the chicken as it is.

"I'll prep all the chicken," Alec says. "Breast meat, bite-sized."

"Yes, sir," I say, looking at Jared. "Do you want to cook and flake the fish? Then we can just heat it up on the flat top tomorrow. Add the slaw. Done."

"I'll do the whole catfish dish," he says. "So we've got the fish, the slaw, and the tortillas." He holds up a finger for each. "Make the slaw extra sloppy for the sauce?"

"What about a tartar-slaw?" Alec asks. "That would be stellar, and you could add a couple of slices of avocado, and mmm. That would be amazing."

Both Jared and I look at him, but Alec doesn't even seem to realize what he's just said.

"Tartar-slaw?" I prompt him.

He looks up from his knives. Oh, him and his obsession with knives. "Yeah, instead of making the sauce vinegar-based or mayo-based, we make it tartar-based. Use all those flavors of tartar sauce as the sauce for the slaw." He glances at Jared. "Fish taco. Sauce and slaw in one."

"It's genius," he says.

"How about you dice up all the chicken," I say to Alec. "And do the slaw. Jared will do the blackening and flaking and get all the cornmeal tortillas done. When Barley and Henry get here, I'll get them on the gravy dipping sauce and the banana pudding."

"Okay," he says. "You'll do the sweet tea?"

"Yes," I say. "I'll do the sweet tea and get our equipment sorted and loaded."

"What time are we at the fair tomorrow?" Jared asks, his voice a little too high-pitched to be casual.

"Ten for set-up," I say. "We're serving from eleven to six." And the pool party is at four. I clear my throat. "I, uh, double-booked myself. So I have to leave at three to go set up for another event. I'll be back to help clean up and close for the night. Then I'll be there all day Sunday."

"What event?" Jared asks. "Can we combine them?"

I shake my head. "It's a pool party," I say. "Not a big deal. I'm doing the wild wings, a huge vat of macaroni salad, and hummingbird cakes. It's all easy stuff I can make in bulk and put in a single buffet."

"Why not do banana pudding?" Alec asks. "Then we can just make a ton more of it."

"Because that's not what the client ordered," I say, already feeling the pressure. "Sorry, guys. This is my problem, and I didn't ask any of you to stay and help. I'll handle it." I nod like that's that, because it is. "All right, let's get this weekend prepped."

I turn to go into the storage room-slash-pantry, which

is located right next to the walk-in fridge. I keep all of our big transport tubs in there, and I start to go through them to make sure we have what we need to get two days' worth of chicken, slaw, fish, gravy, and pudding to the fair. I've done the fair before, with a different menu, of course, so I should have the containers I need.

I set them aside, interrupt my work to give Barley and Henry instructions when they arrive, and then start to make a list of what needs to be taken in the vans tomorrow. Every time I see Alec, he gives me a strange look. At least I think he does. It feels like he's a scientist, trying to figure me out by studying me. I don't like it, but I ignore it. I have far too much to get done before tomorrow, and I razor my focus on equipment and then cleaning wings, chopping vegetables, and boiling pasta once the kitchen has gone back to being quiet.

———

"I BROUGHT JESSIE TO HELP," Alec says, and I look up from where I'm checking the temperature of the oil. It's taking forever to get high enough to fry, and my irritation is already rising.

I look at him and then the perky, smiley blonde next to him. "Great," I say with the biggest smile I can muster. I was up until two-thirty, and I didn't even go next door to thank Mr. Reynolds for taking care of my animals.

Well, I did, but only to leave a tray of banana

puddings. I gave him three and left a note to put them in the fridge as soon as he got up that morning. He's already texted to say he got them and that he's fine to have Tommy and Goose with him this weekend.

"Where do you want her?" he asks, and he hasn't cracked a smile yet. There's no *Hey, sugar's* or kisses this morning, that's for sure.

"She can do the tacos," I say, straightening. "Jared's getting the coolers right now."

"I'll go help him," Alec says, swinging his backpack to the ground under the table in the back of the booth. "Tell Jess what to do, okay?" He does flash me a grin then, but he turns and walks away so fast, I don't get to enjoy the symettricalness of it for long.

I'm left with Jessie, and she looks at me like an eager beaver, which just annoys me further. "So it's easy," I say, stepping over to the flat top and reminding myself to be nice. I am nice. I don't like confrontation, and I don't have time for awkwardness. I have to trust Alec that he's not cheating on me, and his words about he'll never, ever do that fill my mind.

I *do* believe him.

"There's a tortilla warmer here," I say, indicating the hot plate. "Jared will wrap the tortillas in a cloth, and you just take one out." I mime holding a tortilla. "The fish will be here. He'll put the fish on the tortilla, and that's where you take over." I make a quarter turn and come to a long, white, six-foot table. "You'll put on the slaw. If you wear a glove—you'll have to wear gloves—you can just use your hand. Then two slices of avocado, which we have to slice on-site so it doesn't go brown. Then fold, fold, and put it on the front table."

I make another quarter-turn to indicate the huge front table that spans the width of our booth. "I've labeled each section so people know what they're getting."

"Alec did say you like to label things." Jessie gives me a friendly smile, and it takes me a moment to return it.

"Do you and Alec talk about me a lot?" I regret the question the moment it leaves my mouth. Jessie looks like I've smacked her with a load of bricks, and I backpedal.

"Chef," Jared says, saving me. *Thank you, stars*, I think as I turn toward him. "Coolers under this table?"

"Yes," I say. "That's where the slaw and pudding goes." I move away from Jessie and her curled hair and make-upped face. She's even wearing an orange and pink blouse that looks so freaking fall-festive. "Let's get this gravy heating. Alec would you check that dang oil? I swear it's not even on."

———

HOURS LATER, the booth is really hopping. I haven't eaten anything yet, and I want to rip the next taco Jess makes from her hand and devour it in one bite. There's no way we're going to have enough banana pudding for tomorrow, which means I have to go back to Saucebilities tonight and make more.

The fryer is slow as molasses in midwinter, and my word, if I hear Jess giggle one more time at something Alec says, I'm going to go Hulk and turn over every single thing in this blasted booth.

All of my business cards are gone, though, and two full sheets on the clipboard have filled up with email addresses. I send out monthly newsletters with recipes and my booking schedule, and I've gotten quite a few clients that way.

I've just put four more chicken bites with gravy dipping sauce on the table when Callie appears before my eyes. She looks rested and radiant, and I dang near burst into tears.

"Callie." I rush out of the booth and hug her, trying to say so much without having to utter a word.

"Oh, dear," she whispers. "What's wrong? It looks like it's going so well."

I shake my head slightly in the crook of her neck, knowing I look like a fool. There's just so much to explain and no time to explain it.

She pulls away, and I wipe quickly at my eyes. "Oh, honey," she says, brushing something off my face. Probably a piece of cabbage I didn't even now was there. She meets my eyes with her glorious blue ones, sympathy from here to the Mississippi in hers. She glances down my body, but

I'm wearing my regular Saucebilities attire. I have to; I have another party in an hour.

"You do know you have a chicken nugget stuck to your shoe, right?" she asks.

I look down, horrified. This is so much worse than a piece of toilet paper. My whole body storms, and I can't even look at her again.

"Boss," Alec says behind me. "More fried chicken bites are up." For some reason—probably the boss comment, maybe that I really don't want to talk to Alec right now—that pushes me over the edge.

I don't even reach down to dislodge the freaking chicken nugget from my shoe. I can't believe I haven't felt it stuck there, but I am wearing the orthopedics, and the soles on those suckers are thick.

"I need a minute," I say, and I spin and walk away from Callie, from Alec, from his perfect best friend, from my booth, and from the chicken bite probably flapping in the wind like Old Glory.

CHAPTER TWENTY-TWO

ALEC

"Alec."

I look up at Callie, who's come around to the back of the booth where I'm frying chicken. I haven't stepped two feet from the fryer in hours, actually. I'm not complaining, because it's a beautiful day. Bright blue sky. Something different in the air—autumn. I've been laughing and talking to the others chefs in the booth, Jess, and Tara.

Everything is running just the way I like it—well-oiled. Tara's meticulous and detailed in her planning, and that makes events easy.

"Yeah?"

"Tara just left."

I blink and turn back to where the two of them had been standing. Sure enough, she's not there anymore. I try to find her, but the crowd is impossible to see through. "What do you mean, she left?"

"She said she needed a minute, and she left."

"That's not good," I say, focusing on the snapping oil in front of me again. "When she says she needs a minute, I mean. That's not good."

"No, it's not," Callie says meaningfully.

"Maybe she's going to get something from the van." I know that's not true even as I say it. We brought everything from the vans to the booth hours ago. I squirm inside my own skin, but I'm not sure why.

Callie folds her arms and sighs. She has a way of saying so much without even opening her mouth.

"Why is she upset?" I ask, jiggling the basket with my almost-done bites in it.

"Why don't you go find out?"

I look up again. "Do you know how to fry chicken?" I don't mean to sound like a jerk, but honestly. What does she expect me to do? Jared and I have been here for hours. He's leaving when Henry arrives, and Barley will work all day tomorrow. So will Henry, and I'll be the one coming in the afternoon to help finish up the fair and clean up the booth.

"She needs you," Callie says. "She doesn't really want a minute. She wants you to go after her."

I sigh and turn back to Jess. "Hey, baby," I say, realizing in that single moment that I'm a colossal moron. She turns toward me, as if she expects me to address her like that. I tell myself that a lot of people in the South call each other *baby* and *sugar* and *honey*.

It's normal...right?

No, my mind screams. *It's not normal, and you shouldn't have brought Jess here today.*

A smaller, whinier voice says, *But Tara needed the help, and it's been fun.*

"What?" Jess asks, and I realize I've fallen into a trance where two voices in my head argue with one another.

I snap to attention and say, "I'm going to do this last round of chicken. Can you serve up the gravy and get them on the table? I have to go find Tara."

Jared looks over to us from the flat top, curiosity in his expression. "I can put down more chicken. Seven minutes?"

I nod, hating that I'm going to leave the two of them to run the booth alone while I go find my boss who might be having a meltdown.

She's not your boss, the booming voice tells me. *She's your girlfriend.*

I don't wait for Jess to respond. I pull the chicken from the fryer and set it to drain, then I simply march out of the booth without a backward glance. I feel my old self returning, and I press against him. He's bossy and loud-mouthed. He's grumpy and rough around the edges. He runs when things don't go his way.

I don't want to be that Alec Ward anymore.

I have no idea where to look for Tara, and I praise the heavens that I'm tall enough to see past most people.

I haven't said a single word to Jess about Tara's jealousy. If anything, I've been extra-careful with my best friend whenever I see her, minus that *baby* slip from a moment ago. I see her occasionally, but really, she comes to my apartment and uses my WiFi to look for jobs and community classes while she keeps Peaches company. She's gone before I get home.

Sure, we text, but again, I've gone over my texts to make sure they're not flirty in any way. I may be new back in the dating pool, but I still know what flirty looks like. I haven't flirted with her. Not even a little bit. Not even anything someone could construe as flirting.

Frustration drives me forward, and I can't promise I won't shake Tara when I finally find her. I honestly don't have the energy to reassure her over and over that there's nothing going on between Jess and me. I hate that I need relationship coaching from Callie. I just want a normal, healthy, happy relationship—and I thought I had that with Tara.

You do, the smaller, quieter voice in my head says. *Just find her and it'll be okay.*

Fine, I think. *Where is she?* As if Moses has appeared and parted the Red Sea, the crowd thins and there she is. She's holding an ice cream bar and sitting on a bench, her black running shoes on the ground beside it.

I stall at the sight of her, almost seeing her for the first time all over again. The no-shoes thing is definitely odd, and that alone signals to me that something major is happening.

The booming voice in my head tells me to get to her quickly, while the softer one says I should approach with caution. I do something kind of in the middle, with me moving toward her with normal strides, but not too quickly.

"Hey," I say, taking the rest of the bench. "What's the flavor of the day?"

She looks at me, those eyes so probing and so open. "It's vanilla," she says dryly. "They had no butter pecan." She lets her gaze flutter around the crowd again.

"I'm sorry I called you *Boss*. It was a slip," I say.

"That's not why I left."

"Why did you leave?"

"I just needed a minute."

"You're not wearing shoes."

"I hate those shoes."

I don't know what to say to that, and she's not giving me anything to go on. Irritation spikes, but I press against it. "Are you going to talk to me?" I ask quietly, employing that smaller voice inside me.

"About what?'

"About what drove you to take a minute." I look fully at her, refusing to let her get away from me. "I thought things were going really well in the booth. The food has been going out quickly, and with a great response. It's busy, sure, but I can make more banana pudding tonight. There's enough chicken and gravy, so that's not a problem. Jessie's been doing great with the tacos, and Jared says the fish will hold through tomorrow." I take a deep breath. "So what's the problem?"

"No problem," she says.

"Okay." I stand up, my heartbeat thundering behind my ribcage. "If you're not going to talk to me, I'm done."

"You're leaving?" She gets to her bare feet, shock in her eyes.

"Yes," I say. "I'm done, Tara. You're the one who says you want a man to talk to you, but you don't want to talk back."

Maybe Otis was right about her, though I've never met the man.

"I don't like confrontation," she says and stuffs the last bite of ice cream in her mouth.

"This isn't a confrontation," I say, and I sit back down to make the conversation less hostile. "It's just a boyfriend coming to ask his girlfriend why she left her restaurant's booth when everything on the surface seems to be going extremely well."

Tara's fingers start to clench and unclench, and there's those feelings she's having.

"So there's something going on under the surface," I say. "But I don't know what unless you tell me. Unless you talk to me." I reach out and take one of her hands in mine. "Sit down, sugar," I say quietly. "Talk to me."

She sits, all of the fight leaving her body. "I'm over-whelmed," she whispers. I lift my arm and let her snuggle into my side. "I let Jessie get into my head. She's literally the nicest person ever, and all I can see is how she could steal you away from me."

I knew Jess had something to do with Tara's mood. I'm just not sure what to do about it. I squeeze her shoulder and rub my hand up and down her arm, but I don't say anything. She needs the space to say something.

"I feel stupid for double-booking myself. I hate that I'm gone from my dogs and chickens all the time. I've been missing Callie." Tara sniffles, and I stiffen. I'm so not good with crying women. "I only slept for five hours last night, and I'm just tired. I just needed a minute."

"Okay," I say, bending my head toward hers so I don't have to talk very loud. "I can tell Jess we're good, and she can go."

"It's fine," Tara says. "As much as I don't want to admit it, she's really good with the tacos, and I'm leaving soon. She'll have to do the chicken too."

"There is nothing between us," I say. "Honestly, cross my heart and hope to die."

Tara smiles, and I do too.

I clear my throat and look up. I need air to say this next part. "But Tara, if she's a problem, you better tell me right now. I can...I can tell her we can't be friends anymore. She'll understand."

I don't know who'll watch Peaches for me, but that's a

problem I have anyway, especially if Jess gets this job at Lance's office. Her phone interview went great, and she's going into his office next week.

"I can't ask you to do that."

"Well, I can't have you needing minutes all the time because of her."

"Have you two ever...you know? Ever?"

"No," I say. "Not once. No experimental kiss. No going to a dance together because we didn't have someone else to go with. Nothing." I can't emphasize it enough. "Never, ever, *ever* Tara. She's like my little sister, and I'm her older brother. I do..." I clear my throat. "I *am* protective of her, because I think of her like my sister. I want her to be happy, and I do things to make her happy. I can stop doing that."

"No," Tara says with a sigh. She stands and extends her hand toward me. "Come on, we need to get back to the booth."

I stand too and take her into my arms right there among the crowds at the fair. "Not until we're okay." And not until she puts her shoes back on. I shudder just thinking about all the things she could be stepping on right now. Feet are so dirty, and there's been a million people at this fair today.

"We're always okay, Alec," she says. "It's just me who's messed up."

"Maybe we should try going out with her again," I say. "A real double-date—not with Jason." I'm not sure who, because the only single guys I know are Barley and Lance. I would never set anyone up with Barley, and Lance is recovering from his broken engagement.

"Then you'll see—really see—there's nothing between us."

Tara gazes up at me. "I think I just need to figure out how to trust myself."

"Do you trust me?" I ask.

"Yes," she whispers.

"Good." I'm not sure I believe her, but I have to go with what she says. "Now, put those orthopedics back on, and let's get back to work. Jared might quit if we keep leaving him alone in the kitchen."

"Bite your tongue," she says, flying to the end of the bench to get her shoes. "I can't lose Jared."

"I think I'm getting jealous now," I say, grinning at her as she stuffs her feet back into her shoes. She brushes something off the bottom of one and stands. I take her hand and kiss the back of it, feeling a little yo-yo'ed for how up, down, and around our conversations are.

As we start back to the booth, she asks, "Will you really come do banana pudding tonight?"

"Yes," I say, because she refused to let me stay last night, and I'd done my weights and my hot tubbing with a metric ton of guilt attached to my stomach. I pull her closer as if anyone in the crowd knows me and will report what I'm about to say to Miss Opal.

"And maybe, after that, we can sneak into the clubhouse and hot tub together."

I feel her light up, though she doesn't look at me. "Did you just use the words 'hot tub' as a verb?"

CHAPTER TWENTY-THREE

JESSIE

I sit in my car, looking at the nondescript office building. It's gray. Shiny windows in the sunlight. Has a door. Some shrubs out front.

I run through these idiotic details to keep myself from throwing up. This is the closest I've come to getting a real job, ever, and I need this. Not only that, but my car shuddered a time or two getting here, and I can't afford to replace the beast should she decide to die on me.

I need this so badly, I knead the steering wheel and pray, "Please, Dear God in Heaven. It's Jessie Dunaway. Remember me?" I press my eyes closed and tilt my head back. My sister once said if you do that, the Good Lord can hear you better. I didn't think she was right twenty-five years ago, but I'll do anything at this point.

Uncle Jack is like a prowling panther, and I swear Mama calls him every single day to get the dirt on me.

I've resorted to leaving close to dawn and sleeping for a couple of hours in my car outside Alec's building, but I have to stop doing that. Last week, a couple saw me, knocked on the window to check on me, and then jumped back in fright when I sat up, drool pooled on my face.

Maybe they weren't expecting a dead body to move. Maybe they thought my beat-up sedan had been abandoned with the deceased inside. I don't know.

What I do know is that I'm exhausted, as I refuse to go back to the sprawling mansion where Uncle Jack lives with his adult son before they're having their nightcaps in the library. And let me just say that not all libraries are like the one on *Beauty and the Beast*, with ball gowns and those sliding ladders.

Uncle Jack's library is dark, dank, and very nearly a prison cell. I don't go in there if I can avoid it.

I can't avoid this interview any longer. I talked to Lance Byers on the phone last week, and it went what I would label as semi-well. He never laughed. He shot questions at me that I had to Google to answer. It's a good thing I have fast fingers, because he said things like, "fifty-eight DOM" and "pre-qual interview," and I was like, "Mm hm, yeah, of course," as if I know what those things mean.

There are entire websites on the Internet dedicated to confusing real estate terms, so I'm not a dummy. I'm just not a real estate agent.

"Yet," I tell myself. If I can get this job, I can learn the industry, and maybe I can make a career for myself out of selling houses in the Charleston area. I have no idea how much money Lance Byers makes, as he doesn't own the agency where he works.

The sign above the door reads Finley & Frank, but Lance had said "Double F" on the phone a couple of times last week. That was actually one of the things I'd had to look up to figure out what the heck he was talking about.

My phone *boo-boo-bleeps* at me, and I look down. The only people who text me are Mama, Uncle Jack, and Alec. This message is from Callie though, and she's said, *Good luck, Jessie! Remember, Lance has no idea what you're wearing under your clothes. You hold the power in that interview.*

I shake my head, because Callie is the sweetest, nicest, funniest woman I've ever met. She loves her clothes and shoes, like a lot of the ladies I knew back in Beaufort. But she's not stuffy or pretentious. She doesn't judge anyone. She works hard, and she loves deep, and she's the kind of person I want to be friends with.

Her husband is Dawson, who is Lance's best friend. Their connection to Alec and Tara are how I got this interview, and while I want to get the job on my own merits, I'll take all the help I can get.

I've already asked Callie to help me if I do get the job, because she's been working in a very busy marketing firm for years. She knows the ins and outs of a filing cabinet, and she has systems I can't even fathom.

I'm teachable, though, just like Alec said, and I really

want to do something with my life that isn't dictated by Southern Dunaway standards.

An alarm on my phone goes off, and I silence it and get out of the car. I'd set it, because I know myself really well. I knew I'd drive here and sit in the parking lot, freaking out. The alarm tells me that time is over, and it's time to get this job.

The moment I walk into the office, I'm overwhelmed. Someone has popped a bag of popcorn, and the salty, buttery scent of it hangs in the air. There's a reception desk, where a phone rings, but no one's sitting there.

A pair of giant F's hang on the wall behind the podium-desk, with the tiniest ampersand I've ever seen sitting between them. I approach the podium, which holds a bottle of hand sanitizer, along with a clipboard and a pen. It's obvious that others have signed it when they've arrived, but I'm not sure I need to do that.

I look left and right, as hallways leave this main lobby in both directions. I have no idea which way Lance's office is. Soft music plays overhead, but still no one makes an appearance.

I don't have power panties like Callie, but all I have to do is picture James Birmingham and I gain the determination that's leaked away from me in the past sixty seconds.

"Right," I say, going that way first. An office door with frosted glass stands ahead of me, but the plaque outside it reads Winifred Crockett.

Lance hasn't told me how many people work here, but

JUST HIS BOSS   265

it feels like they all got a memo to disappear at eleven a.m. on Tuesday morning, because the whole building is like a ghost town. The office is laid out in a box, and I walk two and a half sides of it until I see a conference room with a dozen men and women sitting around the table. They're all wearing shades of dark blue, black, or gray, and that's just another memo I've missed.

I look down at my black and white striped skirt and bright blue blouse. I'd chosen it, because I once won Miss South Carolina Teen in a dress this exact color of blue, and I know it looks good with my hair and skin tone.

Really accents her eyes.

The line from my critique runs through my mind, and I flinch when a woman asks, "Can I help you?"

I pull myself out of memories I don't have time for and nod. "Yes," I say, my voice sounding rusty. I do spend most of my time talking to a parrot, so this isn't all that surprising. "I have a meeting with Lance Byers at eleven?" I'm not sure why I've phrased it as a question, but I can't time travel and fix my tone.

The woman in front of me frowns, her off-white blouse made of silk and covered with a navy blazer. "I highly doubt that, but let me check with him." She turns on her heels, and I want to yell at her that I can walk in heels twice as high as the ones she has on.

Panic starts to gather in my gut. Did I get the date wrong? The time? I watch through the glass as all twelve of them look at me. I lift one hand in a half-hearted wave, like I've seen a frenemy while waiting at the bus stop. In fact, I'm pretty sure I've made this exact gesture before.

One man, a sandy-haired god of a male specimen rises from the table and buttons his jacket. It's a Tom Ford or a Brooks Brothers for sure, and that alone screams the amount of money Lance has. He probably has to look good for his super-rich clients—people like my parents.

I steel myself as the panic touches the back of my throat. I've looked up Lance's bio online, because I haven't met him in person and I wanted to be sure I was meeting with the right guy. His headshot was professional, his hair sculpted just-so, like it is right now.

I want to run my hand through it and tussle it all up. See how that ruffles the Perfect Suit that is Lance Byers.

He's frowning when he exits the conference room, and he sweeps one hand down the hall without saying anything. I guess that means I should go that way, so I do, taking care to make sure I don't trip over my feet. My skirt only falls to mid-calf, which would horrify my mother, and I catch Lance scanning me as I approach.

"You're an hour late," he grumbles under his breath as I pass.

I freeze. That can't be true. I set no less than four alarms for today's meeting. "I'm sure you said eleven," I say, automatically reaching for my phone.

"Let's just get this over with." His voice is a growl now. "I have a presentation in ten minutes." He practically shoves me down the rest of the hall and into the other corner office. So he's Big Shot Perfect Suit. Fantastic.

"If you can't be on time, I'm not sure this is going to work," he says as he closes the door behind me. "We open at ten, but I require my assistant to have her phone on all the time."

Her? I think, but I don't ask. There have to be male real estate assistants in the world, but Lance obviously doesn't employ that type. I really want him to employ me, so I don't check the text that listed the time, date, and address of Finley & Frank.

"Did you hear me?" he barks, and I jump.

"Yes," I say. "Phone on all the time."

He looks down to my sandaled feet and back to my eyes. "You can use Word?"

"Yes."

"Excel?"

"Yes." I mean, I've used them in the past. I don't have to be an expert in database construction to say yes to that question. At least that's what Callie told me.

Lance circles me and sits down at his desk. Everything seems to have a precise spot to belong, and he must have a maid walk through here every fifteen minutes to keep everything so polished and dust-free. I should know, because I grew up with maids rotating through rooms every hour to keep my mother happy.

They shouldn't have bothered. Nothing makes Mama happy. Trust me, I've tried.

"You realize the only references you put down are people I'm friends with." Lance looks up from his paperwork, one sexy eyebrow cocked.

I blink, sure I haven't thought *sexy* eyebrow. It's just a regular eyebrow.

"I'm still new in town," I manage to say, and I only sound slightly like I've inhaled helium.

He leans back in his chair. "Well, I talked to Callie over the weekend, and she said she'd come train you and just to hire you."

"Callie is very kind," I say.

"Alec said it would be great if I could only give you an evening shift so you could continue to bird-sit for him." Lance doesn't smile, but he has to find that funny.

I put a grin on my face that carries enough wattage for both of us. "Alec's just teasing. He wants me to get this job."

I'm going to kill him if he ruined this for me. Alec's my very best friend in the whole world, and I would be lost without his help and steady support. He's been there for me through absolutely everything, and I owe him so much.

Lance does not smile. "Yes, he did say that too. Said you're highly trainable and just need a chance."

"I do," I say, probably too eagerly.

"There won't be time for personal texting," he says.

"I'm new in town and have no friends," I fire back, suddenly remembering that I've dealt with men and women far richer and far more sophisticated than him. I've suffered through garden parties in July without a parasol, and I've entertained dignitaries and politicians with suits that cost four times what his jacket does.

"No social media during work hours."

"I don't do social media," I say.

That gets both sexy eyebrows to go up, and I decide I can admit that Lance Byers is good-looking. No reason to fight against it. He likely knows it too.

"There's a ton of evening work," he says. "It's your job to manage that, so we know when to come into the office and when we can get a late-start, because we'll be working later."

I swallow. "Okay."

"Lots of weekends."

"Every day is the same to me," I quip.

Lance looks like he doesn't know what to do with me. I know, because I've seen this look on my daddy's face about a hundred times. I simply smile sweetly at him and wait for him to speak. It works on Daddy, and apparently on real estate moguls too.

Lance sighs as he stands. "All right, Jessie Dunaway. I'm going to give you a two-week trial period. If it doesn't work out, that's that. No hard feelings." He hands me a packet. "Normally, I'd go over this with you, but seeing as how you were late and I'm in a meeting, you'll have to go over it alone. Bring me back the two peach-colored papers, with all the items it says, and Brenda at the front desk will get you set up on payroll, get your badge and keys, and all of that."

"Okay." I take the packet, the weight of it like Mama's jewelry case—heavy.

"It all has to be done by Friday, so you can start next Monday."

"Yes, sir," I say as he walks by me, buttoning that coat again. I see the subtle logo for Brooks Brothers, and a flash of pride fills me that I was right. I do adore fashion, and I have sketchbooks filled with ideas roughly hewn out in pencil. I have to have something to do while I talk to that parrot all day long.

I haven't told anyone about the sketches, not even Alec. I have no experience in fashion, and I don't know how to sew. I had signed up for a class at the community center, but when I went for the first time, it was full of ten-year-old girls, and the director told me it was a class for kids.

I'd left humiliated, and I haven't had time to check out the sewing center she told me to check for lessons for adults.

"You can show yourself out?" he asks, standing at the door.

"Yes, sir," I say again. "Thank you, sir." I tell myself to stop talking and start moving, and I grin at him as I go past. He doesn't return the smile, and I make that my number one goal before I get fired (probably) from Finley & Frank: Get Lance Byers to smile.

My more immediate goal is to make it to my car without passing out. I manage that, and I get behind the wheel, roll down my window to let out the stuffy heat, and turn up the air conditioner. My hands shake, and I look at the packet I've placed on the passenger seat.

Then I grip the steering wheel, and I scream. Like, really scream the happiest scream anyone ever did hear. I bang my feet against the floor and slap the steering wheel. "You did it! You have no idea how to do anything, but you got the job!"

"Uh, Jessie?"

I whip my gaze out my window, where Perfect Suit stands. Lance extends my purse toward me. "You left this inside."

Horror fills me, but I take the purse. I can't speak, and Lance frowns deeply at me. Then he simply walks away, and I stare in disbelief as he goes back into the office without firing me.

———

"I'M NOT KIDDING," I say as I walk toward the deli. "I got the job!"

Alec laughs on the other end of the line. "I knew you would, Jess. That's so great. For you, I mean. Peaches is going to be devastated."

"Do you have anyone for her?" I ask, because I do feel bad about abandoning him.

"Yeah," he says. "Turner said she can come hang out at the vet's office. That's probably what I'll do." He sighs. "It's that or allow the mom down the hall into my house, and I don't think I can stomach that."

"Which one?" I ask, too gleeful to be having this conversation. I'll just tease him about the single moms in his building who want a piece of him.

"Patty," he says with plenty of disdain. "Her youngest started kindergarten, and she's—and I quote—available."

"Oh, wow," I say with a giggle. "Better warn Tara about her." I pull open the door and go inside the deli.

"We should all celebrate together, Jess. This is a *huge* deal."

"Thank you, Alec," I say. "Really."

"Of course, baby. I know how hard you've worked for this. You just need a chance."

My chest squeezes, but I will not cry. I vowed not to shed tears after I left Beaufort. A very familiar figure stands a couple of people in front of me, and I hear Tara say something into her phone.

"Oh, Tara's at the deli," I say. "I'm going to tell her about the job. I have to go, Alec."

"Wait, Jess, that's not a—" he starts, but I hang up and tap the gentleman in front of me on the shoulder.

"I'm so sorry," I say. "My friend is right there. Can I get by?"

He scans me from head to toe too, smiles—finally!—

and turns sideways so I can get to Tara. I step to her side, all smiles.

"...honestly, I don't know," Tara says, glancing at me. She doesn't look happy I'm standing so close to her. She does a double-take and says. "She's right here, Cal."

"Is that Callie?" I ask hopefully.

Tara nods, her eyes widening with every second. "I guess so," she says, and whatever Callie's said to her, Tara doesn't like it. I can tell, because I've spent my whole life studying people and analyzing their reactions. There's so much to see in a Southern manor, even when no one is speaking.

In fact, it's during the silence that the real truth comes out.

"She wants me to put it on speaker," Tara says, her eyes narrowing. "She says you have news about your job."

"Yes," I say, and the familiar desperation to fit in with Tara and Callie punches me in the gut. I know it's hard to penetrate a friend group, and I've never had much luck making friends with women. They usually judge me before they know me, and they base everything on surface details like the color of my hair and eyes, and the clothes I wear.

I used to do the same thing, so I understand why people do it. I just hate it.

"I got the job!" I bounce on the balls of my feet. "Thank you *so* much, Callie. I know I got the job because of you."

When I look at Tara again, she looks like she's smelled something bad, and she looks away from me quickly. I'd know this response anywhere, and I wouldn't even have to be a former socialite to recognize it.

She doesn't like me, and I wonder what I did to turn her off.

CHAPTER TWENTY-FOUR

TARA

CALLIE SAYS, "DETAILS, JESS. HOW LONG WERE YOU there? What was Lance like? Dawson says he can be a real killer in the office."

Irritation flows through me like electricity through a power line. Callie is *my* best friend, not "Jess's."

"I was going to call you next," Jess says. "I just got off the phone with Alec, and he said we'll have to get together to celebrate." She looks at me with those baby blues, and I want to spin on my heel and march out of the deli. I'm not in the mood to deal with Little Miss Perfect.

Callie just seems to love her, though. She gushes over the job, and she says she's sure I can put together the *perfect* celebratory food to go with the party she'll throw at her house.

"Claude Monet hates it when you invite people over," I say.

"You should see Claude now," Callie says. "He's like a completely different cat with Dawson. He even curls into his hip to sleep. It's *so* cute." My best friend sounds so happy, and I'm happy for her. I am. I'm just not sure what my life has become, and I feel...well, I feel lost.

We'd once joked that Callie would never find someone Claude approved of, and therefore she'd be single until his death. Dawson had proved us both wrong.

I think of Alec and his conversation with Jessie, and it annoys me. Of course they talk without my knowledge or permission. Alec has reassured me and reassured me that there's nothing going on between him and Jessie, and I need to decide if I'm going to believe him or not.

When I'm with him, it's easy to believe him. When he touches me, I believe him. When I inhale that musky cologne, I trust him. When he snuck me into the hot tub and we talked and laughed and kissed a little, everything between us was perfect.

Still, there's something needling at me, and I hate it. I know it's something inside *me* that's put up a wall. I've seized onto Jessie as the reason Alec and I can't be together, and I don't know how to let her go.

In my momma's words, I'm self-sabotaging. I know I am; I can feel it. But I don't know how to stop.

"Cal, we have to go," I say. "It's our turn to order."

"Oh, okay," she says, always so nice though I've interrupted her. "Call me when you get home. I'm expecting that cookbook in no less than an hour."

I press my eyes closed, wishing she hadn't mentioned the cookbook. I catch the look of interest in Jessie's face as I say, "Okay," and hang up as quickly as I can. I don't look at Jessie as I face the front of the line.

We really are next, and while I have this menu memorized, I pretend I don't.

"What's good here?" Jessie asks me, and I sense her nerves.

Regret sings through me, and I take a deep breath and find my core. I'm not a mean-spirited person. I can't handle firing people, and I avoid confrontation. Normally, I would make an excuse and leave the deli so I wouldn't have to stand with Jessie, but today, I don't.

"The Rueben is fantastic," I say. "If you like fried chicken, their fried tender sub is life-changing." I look at her. "Have you been here before?"

"No," she says, smiling at me but glancing away quickly. "Alec told me about it; he said it was really good."

"Hm," I say before I can stop myself. I'm pretty sure I told Alec about this deli, and the only time he's eaten here was with me, only a few nights ago, after the pool party and the Fall Festival banana pudding prep.

I'd ordered nine of my favorite sandwiches and taken them back to his place, where we'd sampled them all. Since we've taken off the whole week after the craziest weekend this year, I was planning to work on the last section of the cookbook and eat sandwiches for the next few days.

"What about the Goblin?" she asks, and I nod.

"Yes," I say. "It's excellent." It's our turn, and I gesture for her to go first. "I'll get your lunch."

"Oh, you don't have to do that, Tara," Jessie says, and she is so dang nice. If she wasn't my boyfriend's best friend, I'd really like her. I daresay we'd be friends, and I wouldn't be making her work so hard for it.

This realization makes me feel like a real witchedy-witch, and maybe if I buy her lunch, I can alleviate some of my guilt.

"I want to do it," I say, because I know Jessie doesn't have much money. "Go ahead."

She steps up to the counter and the girl standing there and says, "I'll have the Goblin please."

"Wheat, white, sourdough, rye, or oat bread?"

I should've warned Jessie about the laborious ordering process here. She glances at me. "Uh, sourdough."

Oof, I wouldn't have chosen that for the Goblin, but I say nothing.

"Do you want onions?"

"Does it come with onions?" Jessie looks back up to the menu board.

"No onions," I say, smiling at the woman. I look at Jessie. "You'll thank me later." Back to the woman, I say, "Yes to the honey mustard dipping sauce. Cold, not hot."

She nods and then looks at me. Beside me, Jessie visibly relaxes, and I feel like I've done a good deed for the day. "I'll take a number three, two number sixes, a seven, two nines, and a twelve."

Her eyes widen, but I plow forward, wishing Montgomery stood there to take my order. He can do it almost as fast as I can say it. "All on white bread," I say. "No onions on any of them. All dipping sauces, and can I get double the avocado dip with the sixes?"

"Three, two sixes, seven, two nines, and a twelve."

"Yep." I dig into my purse to get out my wallet, ignoring the wideness of and the questions in Jessie's eyes.

"Seventy-four dollars and twelve cents," the woman says, putting a plastic number in front of me. After paying and stepping away, Jessie and I find a table and sit down.

"You're working on a cookbook?" she asks, and I almost flinch with the question.

"Yes," I say.

"That's pretty cool," she says. "My, ahem, brother's wife works in publishing. She's edited a few regional travel books."

"That's great," I say. "Is she in New York?"

"Uh, no," Jessie says, clearly uncomfortable. She's the one who brought it up though. "There's a publisher in Atlanta, and Beatrice works for them. Remotely. She sometimes goes into the office, but not often."

"Is she interested in a Southern desserts cookbook?" I ask, grinning and sure she'll say no.

"Maybe," Jessie says, and my hope starts beating against the back of my throat. "I, uh, don't really talk to my family very much. But Alec could call and find out for you." She puts a bright, cheery smile on her face, not realizing she's taken a knife and jabbed it into my balloon of hope.

"Why would Alec be able to call and find out?" I ask, because I apparently like to punish myself. I glance toward the pick-up area of the counter, but I don't see two bags there waiting for me. With the seven subs I'd ordered, there will be at least that many.

"Oh, well, he talks to Beatrice and Carlton more than I do."

I fix my gaze back on Jessie. "That's kind of weird."

"He's just protective of me," she says. "He knows talking to them upsets me, so he does it to let them know I'm doing fine and they don't need to worry." She must be able to read something on my face, because she hurries to add, "It's nothing. He hardly ever talks to them."

"Still," I say, and I'm not sure what will come out of my mouth next. Thankfully, they've called my number and distracted me from telling this woman that her relationship with Alec is very strange to me.

I get up and retrieve my sandwiches, ready to get away from everyone. I hand Jessie her single sandwich, and say, "I'm sorry I can't stay. Congratulations on the job."

"Thank you," she says, and I keep going toward the exit. Once out on the street, I take a deep breath, feeling a sense of relief and regret at the same time. As I drive back to Cottonhill, my self-righteousness grows. By the time I get there, I'm exhausted with thinking about Jessie and Alec, Alec and Jessie.

Tommy and Goose bark as I come through the front door, and I say, "Oh, hush," to them. "It's just me." I hold up a bag of sandwiches. "Come on, and I'll give you some turkey." As if the dogs need to be told twice.

We sit down together in the kitchen, and cut the subs into several pieces each. This way, I can have a little bite of one, and then a taste of another.

My phone distracts me for a little while, and I realize I've been home for an hour and haven't even thought about my blasted cookbook when Alec's text comes in.

I want to throw a little party for Jess this weekend. What do you think?

"What do I think?" I ask myself as I tap on the text to open the app. I think that's a terrible idea, but I can't tell him that. He wants me to talk to him, and I want to do that too.

"If you bring up Jessie one more time, he'll break-up with you," I tell myself. Maybe that's what I want. No, what I want is to end things on my terms. Otis was the one to say he wanted a divorce, and he'd filed the papers and left. Brett had sat me down and told me I wasn't making time for him.

As I eat my way through a whole sandwich without tasting it, I realize that the only man I've ever broken up with was the shy nude male model. Everyone else has ended things with me. I feel flawed, like I have some inherent thing inside me that is broken.

It'll be small, Alec says. *Me and you. Peaches, of course. Your dogs are welcome at my place. Callie and Dawson. Maybe even Lance.*

Won't that be weird to have her boss there? I send.

True, he says. *I'll cook. You won't have to do anything but show up.*

"Ah, but showing up is most of the battle," I whisper to myself. I don't know how to respond to him. I also can't break-up with him. I can't even let go of a chef who's doing a bad job; there's no way I can end a relationship with a man I want to stay with.

Tears press behind my eyes, because I don't know what to do. Alec texts a few more times, but I stay silent. He eventually calls, and I decide I can't ignore him forever. "Hey," I say, and I hear defeat in my own voice.

"Hey," he says. "You went silent."

"Yeah."

He says nothing, and the tension between us is astronomical. "Let me guess," he says, and his voice is not filled with compassion or kindness. "You need a minute."

"Yes," I say. "I need a minute...from you. From work. From everyone."

"From me?"

I nod, tears pressing behind my eyes.

"I'm going to take this silence as a yes," he says, and he actually sounds tired. Probably tired of me and my jealousy. I wish it was a string I could just snip, and it would go away. Drift by on the breeze and leave me alone.

He sighs, and says, "Okay, well, I'm having a party at my place on Saturday night for Jess. She likes you, Tara. Lord help me, she does, and she wants to be friends with you."

"Don't tell her that," a woman says, and it's definitely Jessie. They're together.

"I don't know how to do that," I say.

"Maybe you should grow up," he says, and I suck in a breath. "Forget I said that. I'm sorry. I have to go." He hangs up before I can catalog the tone of his voice, but as I stare at my phone as it goes dark, I whisper, "He didn't sound sorry."

That's because he isn't sorry.

I get to my feet, suddenly unable to stay inside walls. I hurry outside to let the hens out, but I have zero patience for Benedict and her stubbornness about staying inside the coop. "Get out of there," I practically yell at her, and I have to get almost all the way in the coop to scoop her up and force her into the pasture for her pasturecize.

I stand there, my chest heaving, and it has nothing to do with my chickens. *Maybe you should grow up.*

He sounded like the Grumpy-Cat Alec I'd met the very first time he'd come to Saucebilities, and I picture the disgust and danger in his dark eyes. He's better than me in the kitchen, and I knew it the first time I watched him cook.

He's better than me as a person, because he forgave his brother. He's talked me off the ledge a few times now. He always has butter pecan when I need it, and I spin back to the house to go get the gallon I have in the freezer. I can sit on the back deck and eat it while my hens get their hour of free time, and I do just that.

I can't decide if I'm going to go to the party on Saturday or not. If I don't, that'll be the end of me and Alec, and while that makes my stomach hollow and tighten, I almost feel like it'll be the safest thing for me to do.

You'll go, I think with my next bite of ice cream. *You won't go*, I tell myself with the next, continuing the game until the very last bite. I don't like what I land on last, but as I go back inside to throw away my empty ice cream container, I know I'll honor it.

CHAPTER TWENTY-FIVE

ALEC

I STARE AT MY PHONE, MY HEART BEATING SO HARD IT fills my whole chest.

"Who was it?" Jess asks, coming toward me.

I look up quickly and shove my phone in my pocket. "No one," I say.

She stops still, the blondie I made for her party halfway to her mouth. She blinks, and all I want to do is run away. Just when I was starting to settle too. Just when I thought I had friends.

My phone rings, and it's likely Dawson or Callie, who've both just canceled coming to Jessie's celebration party.

I'm so sorry, honey, Callie had just said. I know she means it too, because she's so nice. She doesn't want to hurt anyone. *I just can't do that to Tara.*

Tara's *not* coming, but she hasn't told me that directly. Her silence the past several days has spoken far more than she ever could with her mouth.

"You better get that," Jess says, dropping her hand to her side. "Might be your mom."

"Shoot, you're right." I pull the phone back out of my pocket, and sure enough my mother's name sits there. I swipe on the call and turn away from my best friend. "Hey, Momma."

"Alec, darling," she says as if she's just perched on a throne, tiara set in place and a cup of tea nearby. "I just heard the news about Jess. How *wonderful* for her." The sentence takes about a year to deliver in her slow, Southern accent.

"Yeah," I say, turning back to Jess. She's put the last bite of the blondie in her mouth, but her focus is on her phone now. My adrenaline spikes, because I'll bet everything I own that she's texting Callie. She's going to know any moment now that it's just me, her, and Peaches for the party.

"She's pretty excited," I say. "We're having a little party today." I've been in the kitchen since noon, whipping up appetizers and one-bites, desserts and homemade butter pecan ice cream. What can I say? I'm a fool. A freaking, hopeful fool who might be in love with Tara Finch.

I turn away from Jess as her face falls. She's going to

cry, and I'm terrible with crying women, even her. "Listen," I say. "I might have to cancel next weekend."

"What? Why?" my mother drawls.

I pace toward Peaches, hoping she'll start chattering and causing a huge scene. She chirps at me in normal bird fashion and nothing else. Traitor. My parrot actually likes my mother, and she seems to know to stay quiet during this call.

"I jumped the gun," I say as bravely as I can. "I hadn't talked to Tara about going to Beaufort, and she's got a big dinner party next weekend."

"So you'll come the following weekend."

I start shaking my head mid-sentence, my patience already thin. "I don't know, Mom. We'll have to wait and see. Will you be out of town in the next month or so?" I know she won't be. My mother doesn't travel anymore, not since the divorce. And especially not since my younger brother got married and had his first baby. Carl and Katia live around the corner from my mom, and I know she spends a ton of time with them.

Carl's the brother who fell into line. He'll inherit the mansion and land in Beaufort, and he's let our momma groom him to be the Southern gentleman she dreamed of having. I need to get down there and see everyone, and I should've gone this week while I had time off.

In truth, I sat around the apartment and visited the clubs and restaurants alone, not wanting to go too far in case Tara came knocking on my door.

Pathetic, really.

"I'll be here," Momma drawls.

"Okay," I say. "It might be a last-minute thing." Jessie touches my shoulder, and I turn toward her. "I have to go, Mom. Love you." I hang up before my mom can respond, because she's seriously like a sloth when it comes to conversations. Everything is slower in Beaufort.

"I'm sorry," I say to Jessie, taking her right into my arms.

"We don't need to have a party," she says. "We've already celebrated together."

"What am I going to do with all this food?" With horror, I realize I sound like my mother, complaining about not having the guests she wants for her prissy parties.

I pull away, unrest seating itself deeply in my soul. "She's just being stubborn."

"Alec," Jess says quietly, but I don't look at her.

"C'mon, Peaches," I say, lifting my arm for her. "Come check out these birdseed cupcakes I made for you." They're made with all bird-safe ingredients, and Peaches flaps her wings and flies over to me as I walk into the kitchen.

"Bacon, bacon, bacon," she says.

"Where was the bacon when I was on the phone with Nell?" I grumble at her.

"Alec," she chirps. "I love you. Alec. Bacon."

Fine, so I spent quite a bit of time this week teaching Peaches some new words. She can't quite say the T-sound, so Tara's name is still unrecognizable.

"Alec," Jess says again. She hasn't moved from her spot in the living room, near the birdcage and the door. "I'm just going to go."

"No," I say. "You can't." Peaches nibbles along my fingers, anxious for her treat, and I reach for the tiny, thumb-sized seed-cakes I put together for her. I give one to her, and she hops down onto the counter to wrestle with it.

I face Jess. "I don't know what to do."

"I do," she says, taking a step forward. She holds up her phone and faces it toward me. "Read Callie's texts. Then you'll know what to do."

"I don't want to read her texts to you. She texted me too."

"I bet she didn't text this." She shakes the phone, insisting I take it.

I glare at her. "You're being impossible."

"I am not," she says. "You're in love with Tara."

"So what if I am?" I bark. "Who freaking cares? *She* doesn't care. Callie doesn't care. I don't know how to choose her or you. I don't. I can't." I've never had to do this before, because I've never been in such a serious relationship that my friendship with Jess became an issue.

"Just read it," Jess says quietly, putting the phone on the counter. "I'm going to go get something out of my car."

"Jess," I say, but she turns and leaves the apartment without looking back. She's strong, and I know she'll be fine without Callie and Tara as friends. I just wanted them to get along so badly. I like Dawson and Lance, and I have so few friends as it is.

If Tara and I break-up, I'm back to having no one.

"That's not an *if*, buddy," I tell myself. "You've broken up. Neither of you will admit it, but it's true."

I sigh, my chest feeling so flimsy, and pick up Jess's phone. She doesn't have it locked, so all I have to do is swipe to open. I tap on her texts, and Callie's is at the top.

"What in the world am I doing?"

"What in the world?" Peaches repeats. "I love you. Love you."

No matter what, I'll have Peaches, but the thought doesn't comfort me the way it once did.

I tap on the text and scroll up to today's messages.

I'm so sorry, Jess. You know I love you and I'd love to be there. Dawson and I are thrilled for you. We'd love to go to dinner with you soon.

See? Callie's so nice.

We just can't abandon Tara. She's never had anyone choose her, and well, I have to choose her in this case. I hope you understand.

I understand, Jessie had said. *I would like to choose Tara too. She has to know there's nothing between me and Alec. Honestly, Callie, there's not. There never has been.*

She might just need some time, Callie had responded.

Alec says he's given her all week. She won't talk to him. She likes to push people away when things get hard, Callie had said. *I told him not to let her get away from him, and honestly, I'd like to shake that man and tell him to choose Tara. That's all she's looking for.* Jess had responded with, *I know. Alec gets too far inside his head sometimes. I'll talk to him.* Callie hasn't said anything else yet.

I look up from the phone, my mind racing. "I have chosen Tara," I say to the spread of desserts on the countertop. "Over and over, I've chosen her." I don't know how to choose her in a different way, not without cutting Jess out of my life. And if I do that, she'll really have no one.

She'll have Callie and Dawson, the small voice in my head says.

The apartment door opens, and Jess walks in. Her eyes fly to mine. "Did you read them?"

"Yes," I say, striding toward her. I engulf her in a hug despite the brightly wrapped box she carries. "I have to choose her, Jess. I'm sorry."

"I know you do," she says, stepping back. "I got you a present for being so amazing. You're always there for me, and you've been nothing but supportive since I left Beaufort." Tears fill her eyes, but she blinks them back. "It can be a good-bye present. For now. I think Tara will come around. She's too nice and too rational not to."

"She just needs a minute," I say, taking the gift. My mind seems to be moving as slow as my momma's mouth, because I just stare at the present. "I don't want you to be alone."

"I'm not alone," Jess says. "You're here, and Callie and Dawson are here, and I'm starting a new job in an office with at least a dozen people." Tears splash her cheeks, but she wipes them away quickly. "How are you going to choose Tara?"

I cock my head to the side. "What do you mean?"

"I mean...Alec." She puts one hand on her hip. "You can't just show up at her house."

"Why not?" I ask. I've done that before, after I drove to Atlanta, just to kiss her.

Jessie shakes her head. "No, honey. Sorry, but no. I know you and Tara have talked about me before. What will one more talk do? Nothing. This has to be huge. It has to be something that erases all of her doubts. It has to be...I don't know. Like writing her name in the sky." She sweeps her hand above her head, and I smile.

"You're being dramatic again." Jess loves to be dramatic.

"Here's a little tip, Alec," she says with a smile. "You know how you're always bragging that you know what women what?" She leans closer, like she's going to tell me a big, juicy secret. I find myself leaning closer. "Women like dramatic. We *like* being in the center of the stage, the spotlight on us as our man is down on one knee, begging to be with us for the rest of his life."

She pats my chest and falls back another step. "Now,

if you'll excuse me, I'm going to load up a plate with as much food as I can carry and leave you and Peaches to brainstorm about how you can shine that spotlight all on Tara."

She steps past me and heads for the kitchen.

I'm still trying to figure out if Tara likes the dramatic or not. I turn on numb feet to watch Jessie pile one-bites and appetizers onto a plate. As she starts cramming on desserts, I say, "I don't actually have a diamond ring. Do you think I need to get one?"

"Not yet, honey," Jess says. "You need to get the woman back first."

"She's the one who pushed me away. Don't you think she should be trying to get me back?"

"She will," Jess says. "As soon as you turn on that spotlight." She finishes with her plate and comes toward me again. "I'm sorry it's come to this, Alec. I'll tell Callie all about my first day on Monday, and she'll tell you."

"I hate that," I murmur.

"It'll be okay," she says. "Because you don't want to lose Tara over this." She stretches up and kisses my cheek, just like we always have. Then she's gone, and I'm alone in the apartment, wondering how to shine the spotlight on Tara.

She hates the spotlight, as evidenced by the reporters that followed her for weeks, and the articles—I suck in a breath. "That's it," I say to Peaches, who's still working on that birdseed cake.

"That's it!" I race into the kitchen and grab my keys out of the drawer. "I have to run out Peaches. Come on." I pick her up and take her and her birdseed to her cage. "I'll be back soon, I swear."

As I rush out of the apartment, I pray that newspaper reporters work on Saturdays.

CHAPTER TWENTY-SIX

TARA

"No, Momma," I say as I lift my glass of diet cola to my lips. Nothing is the same in Miami as it is in Carolina, and I'd rather have sweet tea. I don't tell my mother that. I haven't told her much of anything. "I can't stay. I have a baptism party on Tuesday."

"Seems like an odd day for a baptism party," my mother says. She sets another plate of cookies on the table between us. She and Daddy bought a condo here in Miami a few years ago, and I can admit the view is fantastic from the twentieth floor. The breeze pushes through my hair, and the people on the sand down below seem like ants scurrying about.

I've been here for a few days now, and I purposely booked my return flight over Jessie's party so I could put my phone on airplane mode. Childish, I know, but the butter pecan told me I wouldn't be going to her party.

Callie's been texting me non-stop all day, to the point that I finally put my phone on silent and left it in the guest bedroom.

"They had family out of town or something," I say. "For the actual baptism, but they're back, so we're doing it Tuesday."

"That's two whole days after you go back."

"Momma," I say. "I have to work. I have orders to put in and groceries to pick up. I have to have a staff meeting with my chefs." Alec hasn't formally quit yet, but I suspect he will. He's such a talented chef, he'll have no problem getting hired on somewhere else, and I'll need to put up a new listing for a new job too.

"It's just been so nice having you here." Momma reaches over and pats my arm. "How's the dating front going?"

"I already said I wasn't going to talk about that." I send her a glance-glare and look back out at the ocean. "I'm married to Saucebilities, remember?"

Momma says nothing, and that alone is a feat. We sit in silence for a while longer, and I finally get to my feet. "I should get going. My flight isn't going to wait for me because I don't want to leave this view." I smile at her as she stands too. "Or you." I hug her tight, my emotions balling up all the words I want to say. "Thanks for letting me come crash with you last-minute."

"You're welcome any time," she says. She smiles at me

with glassy eyes and turns to go back into the condo. "I'll call a cab."

"Thanks, Momma." I go get my suitcase and purse, which I'd packed that morning. I hug my daddy and then momma again, and then I'm walking down the hall to the elevator alone.

Always alone.

At least when I trip over my own feet, there's no one to see me when I'm alone.

From the condo in Miami back to my house in Charleston, I remind myself of all the people I have that love me. I have to extend it to living things to include all the hens, Tommy, and Goose, who I go to get from Mr. Reynolds next door.

I'd baked a whole slew of hummingbird cakes before I'd left, and I offer them to him as he opens the door. "Time for a tea party?" I ask, not wanting to be alone tonight.

"There's always time for a tea party," he says, smiling at me. "Come in, my dear."

I step into his house, which is such a comfort to me. "I can brew the coffee."

"I'll do it," he says as my two little dogs start to jump up on my legs. "You take care of those hounds."

"Hounds," I say with a laugh. I set the hummingbird cakes on the coffee table and get right down on the floor with Tommy and Goose. They're wild tonight, jumping at my face to lick me and running all around as I try to give them hello scrubs. "I missed you guys. Yes, I did. Did you miss me?"

They act like they did, and my thoughts move to Alec. Has he missed me this week? My missing for him yawns as wide as the ocean and as high as the sky. I should probably text him and ask him point-blank if he's going to quit, but the very thought makes bees buzz in my stomach. Besides, tonight is his party, and I don't want to interrupt that.

Mr. Reynolds returns to the living room with a stack of napkins, plates, and forks. He groans as he sits on the couch. "Coffee's on. What did you bring?"

"Your favorite," I say. "Hummingbird cakes."

His face lights up and then falls. "Daisy used to make hummingbird cake for our kids' birthdays." He reaches for the cake anyway. "Thank you for bringing it."

"I didn't mean to make you sad."

He gives me a quick smile. "It's a happy-sad, Tara. Reminds me of her, which isn't bad. I don't want to feel bad thinking about her."

"Of course not," I say, and I wonder if I'll ever get to the point where I don't feel bad when I think about Alec. I wasn't even brave enough to talk to him and end things properly. I sigh, and that draws Mr. Reynolds's attention.

"What's on your mind?" he asks.

"Oh, I...tell me about Daisy." I smile again, but the corners shake.

He studies me for a moment. "You know all about Daisy."

"You miss her so much." I'm not asking.

"Yes," he says. "I do. There are good days and bad days, and then there are in-between days where I get to eat hummingbird cake and remember the good times." He hands me a plate holding half of one of the mini cakes I'd made.

"Did you have bad times?" I ask.

"Every couple has bad times," he says, returning to the cakes and taking the other half for himself. "We worked through them the best way we knew how."

"What if you didn't know how?"

He takes a bite of cake, his older eyes so much wiser than mine. I can't get myself to eat right now, so I just watch him. "I think as you grow older," he says softly, slowly. "You realize more about what's important, and what's not."

I nod, though I have no idea what he means.

"So Daisy loved to garden. She'd spend hours out in the yard, and sometimes I felt neglected. Like she cared more about her plants than she did me or even the children. Which is ridiculous. They're just flowers and shrubs." He smiles and shakes his head. "The older we got, and the more I loved Daisy, I realized how the gardening for her made her into the kind, patient woman she was with me and the kids. If she didn't get her therapeutic time outdoors, she wasn't very nice indoors."

"Interesting," I say.

"It's like you with your hens," he says. "They bring

you joy." He grins at me and gets to his feet. "Or Saucebilities. It's your baby. You love it. But that doesn't mean you
don't have room in your heart to love something or
someone else too." He turns toward the kitchen. "The
coffee has to be done."

Wait, I want to tell him. I want him to come back and
explain more about what he means by what he's said. I
puzzle through it while he bumps around in the kitchen,
and when he returns, I look up at him.

"Thank you," I say, accepting the cup of coffee I know
he'll have put caramel cream and a touch of sugar into. I
breathe in the scented steam and feel myself start to relax.
"So you're saying if I don't get to work at Saucebilities, I
won't be happy."

"No," Mr. Reynolds says. "I think there are things
every person has that makes them happy. Content.
Pleased with life. Whatever you want to call it. If we don't
get to do those things, we don't feel whole."

"So then, when we have to interact with others, we're
kind of beastly."

"Yes," he says with a nod and a smile.

"So what was your thing if Daisy's was gardening?" I
ask, wondering if mine is the catering, the hens, or the
cookbook. Or my obsession with my yard, even if I don't
do the work. Or my relationship with Callie.

Mr. Reynolds starts to answer, but my ears have gone
deaf.

My relationship with Callie. If I couldn't have that, I'd be...beastly.

Alec started out beastly when he came to Saucebilities, but things got better. Those things got better the more I got to know him and the important people and items in his life. I can list them on one hand—his bird, Peaches, his best friend, Jessie, and his job. He loves his late-night weight-lifting and hot tubbing too. Those are all things he needs in his life to feel content, and that doesn't mean there's not room for me too.

I jump to my feet. "I'm so sorry, Mr. Reynolds," I say. "But I have to go."

"Yes, of course," he says. "Go."

"Come on, guys," I say to the doggos. "Let's leave Mr. Reynolds alone for a while."

He still walks me to the door, hugs me, and says goodnight. I'm leagues away from bedtime, though, and I don't even go in the house. I hurry Tommy and Goose through taking care of their business on the front grass, and then I herd them into the car.

I have to go talk to Alec right now, even if I don't want to. Even if confrontation scares me. Even if I've already ruined everything with him.

I simply can't be the reason he loses two ultra-important things to him and cause him to run again.

He's said the dogs are welcome at his apartment, and I pray that's true with every minute that passes between my house and his place.

Once there, I leash the pups and hurry up to the sixth floor. His apartment sits down at the end of the hall, and I'm panting and sweating by the time I arrive. It's barely nine o'clock, so surely the party is still in full swing.

I ring the doorbell and stand back, trying to get my heartbeat to quiet. It's not so used to running and rushing, and I really hate confrontation. I feel like I'm going to pass out, and I brace myself against the wall across from his door. Wouldn't that just be the peachiest ending to this week? Alec opening the door and finding me prostrate in the hall, unconscious, sweating, and with two dogs at my side?

It turns out that I don't pass out, and Alec doesn't even open the door. I try knocking and calling through the door, but he still doesn't answer. I work Peaches up into a real lather, though, and that only adds another dose of guilt to my already writhing gut.

"Come on, guys," I say after another minute of that blasted door staying solidly closed. "He's not home." I retrace my steps to the car, and the miles back to my house, my heart heavy.

I think about calling him as I unleash the dogs and we go into the house. But I want to see his face when I apologize. I want to look into those eyes when I tell him I understand his relationship with Jess. I want to hold him and kiss him and make sure he knows I'm not just a jealous non-communicator with a butter pecan problem.

I scoff at myself, and it sounds suspiciously like a sob.

"Butter pecan is only one of your problems," I whisper to myself.

My phone goes *boom-chicka-pop*, and I reach for it to read Callie's message.

Did you make it back from Miami? Dawson and I have something for you.

Of course she does. Callie is my savior, the one person who gets me completely. I don't know why I couldn't see that that's who Jess was for Alec too. She might still be, and that should be okay with me. They have a history I can never replicate, and I don't need to.

I know that now.

Yes, I type out. *I'm home with the dogs and thinking about ordering Chinese.*

The phone rings, and I answer Callie's call. "Don't do that," she says. "We have the Chinese and we're five minutes from your place."

"Do I have to talk?" I ask, feeling drained from the flight and then the rush over to Alec's for no reason. My adrenaline is coming down, and I just want to collapse on the couch.

"You do not have to talk," she says.

"How was the party tonight?" I ask, sinking into my plushy couch. It could seriously be called plump, and I smile thinking about that adjective for a piece of furniture.

"We didn't go to the party, Tara," she says. "I could never do that to you."

I press my eyes closed, my misery now complete.

"Cal," I whisper. "You should've gone. You like Jess, and she'll be so disappointed."

"She understood," Callie says simply. "You will always be my first choice, Tara."

"I'm such a bad person," I whisper, knowing she isn't right. Dawson is her first choice now, as he should be. "I don't want you to choose. I don't want Alec to choose. I even went over there just now, and he didn't answer the door. I ruined his party, I ruined Jess's celebration, and I ruined my whole relationship with him."

I'm such a walking disaster, and not just because my feet are too big and I wear those ugly shoes.

"We'll be there in three minutes," she says. "You're not a bad person."

Oh, I am, but I don't argue with her. I let her end the call and I keep my eyes closed. Then I just pray that Alec and Jess will find a way to forgive me once I can finally talk to them.

CHAPTER TWENTY-SEVEN

ALEC

"Pancake, Alec. I love you," Peaches chirps in the shower.

I grin at her. "I love you too, Peaches."

"Peaches," she says. "Peekaboo."

I hold my thumb out, and she presses her beak into it. "Peekaboo," I say back to her.

She makes happy birdy noises from her perch while I wash up, shave, and pull on a pair of pants. My T-shirts are once again draped over the back of the couch, and I'll have to get one when I finally brave going into the living room.

I turn off the shower, Peaches shakes herself off, and we go into the living room. I pause while she flies to the top of her cage, my mind suddenly working overtime.

I face the door. The paper should be here by now. I've

deliberately slept late, taken my time in the shower, and that newspaper absolutely *has* to be here by now.

I take a deep, deep breath and hold it. Then I open the door. I'm not sure what I expect to find there, but I jump back as if someone will have filled the hallway with snakes.

They haven't, of course. The paper isn't there either, and I frown as I look down the hallway. No one's there, and the chiming of my phone draws me back into the apartment. In all honesty, I'm surprised I haven't left Charleston yet.

After what I've done this morning, though, there's no way I can leave.

I head into the kitchen and pick up my phone. My heart falls to my feet when I see it's Tara who's texted me. I fumble the phone in my haste to get the text open, and it drops to the floor. A *crack!* fills the air, and I drop to my knees, saying, "No, no, no."

"No, no, no," Peaches chirps.

The doorbell rings. Peaches imitates it.

I scoop up my phone, noting the huge crack across the front of it, and get to my feet. "Just a second," I say, and I swipe to get to the texts.

Tara's says, *Are you home? I want to ask you about your job.*

That only gets my pulse positively hammering, and I look to the door. *I'm home,* I tap out quickly and then stride to the door. If it's not Tara on the other side of it, I'm seriously slamming it in whoever's face is standing there. Seriously.

I've been Alec-the-Grumpy-Cat, and I'm not afraid to go feline again.

I pull open the door, and Callie stands there, one hip cocked. Dawson is only a couple of feet away from her, and he's wearing a smile as wide as the sky.

"Alec Ward," Callie clips out. She brings her hand out from behind her back and lifts the newspaper she's holding. "You tell me right now: Did you do this?"

"Yes," I say, and the word is mostly air, no bark in sight. I also haven't slammed the door in her face, thank you very much.

"Do you mean it?"

"Why wouldn't I mean it?"

"You could've used a better knife joke in the fifth paragraph, bro," Dawson says. "I mean, life is *dull* without her? It's not that original."

I blink as Callie bustles past me and into the apartment. Dawson does too, clapping me on the shoulder with one hand. "You might want to put on a shirt," he says. "Callie sent about five hundred texts on the way over, and I have a feeling she called in the calvary."

"Five hundred?" Callie demands. "You exaggerate so much."

"You like it," Dawson tosses back at her, and I turn to watch them, still in shock.

"Where did you get that paper?" I ask. "Mine wasn't in the hall this morning."

"Hmm," Callie says. "That's weird." Her voice pitches up slightly, and she won't look at me.

"Callie Houser," I say, using her tone of voice. "You tell me right now: Did you steal my paper?" I march toward her, ready to rip it out of her fingers. I've only seen the article on a computer screen, and I want to see it in person.

She hides her paper behind her back, her eyes widening. "No," she says quickly. "I didn't steal your paper." She nods behind me. "She did."

I stall and spin, nearly falling flat on my face. Thankfully, there's those lovely double ovens to hold me up as I throw my hand out to catch myself.

When I see who "she" is, I sag into them.

Tara enters the apartment, and she's wearing a tight pencil skirt that makes my male side roar with want. Her red sweater only makes her dark hair look darker, and it all goes perfectly with her green-apple bag.

She calmly puts the bag on the top of the birdcage, but I catch a tremor in her hand. She plucks the newspaper from her bag and holds it in front of herself like a shield. Even from twenty feet away, across the apartment, I can read the headline.

Number one, it's humongo. Like, huge. Three-inch letters. The story takes up the whole front page, not just the Local section like Stephen said it would.

CHEFS OF ALL SIZES FIND LOVE IN CHARLESTON

I know what the first line is, because I wrote it.

At least, one chef hopes they do. See, Alec Ward has fallen in love with "plump chef" Tara Finch, and it happened right there in the kitchen at Saucebilities, the best catering company in the city.

"Does this mean you're not quitting?" she asks.

I lift my chin, though I feel naked from head to toe, and not just head to torso. "I'm not quitting," I say. "I'm not quitting at Saucebilities, and I'm not quitting on us." I take a few steps toward her, though she still grips that paper with white knuckles. I don't care that Callie and Dawson are there. I printed over a thousand words about the awesome that makes Tara Finch in the local paper. Everyone will know how I feel. Positively everyone.

If that's not a bright enough spotlight on Tara, I seriously don't know what else to do.

"I told Jessie we can't be friends for a while," I say. "You've had your minute, Tara. I need to know if *you're* quitting or not." My fingers clench, as does my jaw, and I tell myself to relax.

"I love you," I say when she still says nothing. "I want you. I don't care about anything else." I probably could've just said those ten or eleven words instead of writing the dissertation that I did. But Stephen Fyfe had given me the space, and I'd just let my soul fly.

Behind me, Callie sniffles, but I don't turn around. I

can't look away from Tara, and I can't stand the idea of her walking out on me after what I've done.

She turns the paper and looks at it, the pages rippling as her hand shakes now. "This is...well, it's just perfect." She looks up at me, tears in those eyes. "I came by last night to apologize, but you weren't here."

"I was at the newspaper office pretty late," I say, everything softening inside me.

She came by.

"Do you really love me?"

"All the way, one-hundred percent yes."

She flies toward me then, and I catch her in my arms. "I love you too, Alec," she says as she sobs into my neck. "I'm so, so sorry. I'm just this flighty bird, and I don't know. I let the wind push me this way and then that way, and there was this prettier bird, and I just got jealous." She steps back. "Then I realized that you *need* Jess to be whole, and what kind of seagull-trash-bird am I to separate the two of you? And you'll never be whole without her, and I don't want a non-whole Alec."

I have no idea what she's talking about, so I just look at her and breathe in the scent of her perfume, her hair, her skin.

"Life is dull without you," she says, looking back at the paper and rattling it on purpose this time. I want to pump my fist in triumph that she caught the knife jokes—and tell Dawson that one isn't lame. "You do make the cut."

"Do I?" I ask quietly.

JUST HIS BOSS   311

"Alec." She looks at me. "You absolutely do. Every time, at least for me. I'm sorry. Please tell me you can forgive me."

"Oh, the door is open," someone says, and Tara turns that way just as a group of no less than a dozen men and women crowd into the tiny space. The only reason they enter the apartment is because the ones in the front are getting jostled by the people in the back.

"Alec, is this true?" someone yells, waving the paper.

"Tara, are you going to take him back?"

"Does he make the cut?"

"Why do you use knife jokes? Is there an inside joke between the two of you involving a knife?"

I start to laugh, because I can't believe that's the question they have.

"Get in closer," someone says, and they're not talking to me or Tara.

"There's Peaches. Be sure to get a shot of her."

"Where's Jessie, Alec?"

"Is she going to pull you apart?"

I slide my hand along Tara's waist, the touch so intimate and so delicious, I can almost taste it. She shivers and sags into me. "You better answer their questions, baby. They're asking a few I have too."

She tilts her head down, her mouth toward me. "What do you think? Answer with a kiss and not a single comment?"

"Oh, I like the way you think," I whisper, gripping her

a little tighter and turning her into my body. I meet her eyes, and yes, I forgive her for the "minute" of silence she needed, and then I lower my mouth to hers.

I wasn't going to really *kiss* her—after all, there are other people present. People with cameras. But the moment her lips touch mine, all bets are off and all explosions are happening, just like the first time we kissed.

I can't even imagine what next weekend's headlines will read like, or what kind of accompanying photos they'll have. I don't care. I got Tara Finch back in my life, and I'll do whatever it takes to keep her there.

Somewhere among the cheering, that small voice tells me to keep it clean and wrap it up. So I do, pulling away while I'm only breathing hard, not panting, and my hands are still in an appropriate place.

"Alec," someone says, and I know that voice. "Excuse me," Jessie says, pushing her way through the crowd of reporters. "The show's over. Get out. Back up, please." She muscles them all out of the way despite her smaller frame and closes the door behind her. She turns to face us, and I can't help grinning at her.

She's not looking at me though. "Tara," she says, but she doesn't turn her head when Peaches blurts out, "K-kara, I love you. Love you."

CHAPTER TWENTY-EIGHT

TARA

I'm not sure where to look first. Jessie, who's standing there with a wide, pie-eating smile on her face? Or Alec, who rushes toward his bird's cage and says, "Shh, Peaches. Not yet," as he throws the blanket over the wire? Callie and Dawson, both of whom are chuckling in the kitchen?

I honestly feel torn in thirds.

"She's here," Jessie says.

"I'm aware," Alec growls at her. "What are *you* doing here?"

"I came to see if you'd really done this." She holds up the paper.

Alec glares at her and turns to face the rest of us. I'm stuck in between everyone, but I can't help smiling. "Why does no one believe I did this?"

"It's just so romantic," Jessie says. "I didn't know you could write like this."

"I worked with a reporter," he says, sounding semi-disgusted those words come out of his mouth.

"I think it's beautiful," Callie says. "In fact, Dawson and I are going to find all the copies we can. That way, I can make a scrapbook page of it for my bestie." She steps over to me and hugs me tight. "Love you, my friend."

"Scrapbook page?" I ask when I should say *I love you too, Cal.* "Who has scrapbooks anymore?"

"*You're* going to have one," Callie says, stepping back. She gives me a stern look before reaching for her husband's hand. "You can put it on the shelf next to your cookbook." Callie speaks as if what she says is law. When she'd showed up on my doorstep about ninety minutes ago, with a newspaper in her hand, my whole world had changed.

She'd helped me get dressed, and we'd driven over here. I'd kyfed Alec's newspaper so I'd have a copy of my own, and we'd waited like stalkers on the sidewalk below until we'd heard Peaches start to babble. Lucky for us that Alec likes to keep his windows open. Also that there were no cops lurking about. Been there, done that.

Callie opens the door, and shouts fill the air again. She and Dawson slip out into the hallway, pulling the door closed behind them and shutting out the shouting.

I press my palms together and face Alec and Jessie. I've already apologized to him, but I still have some awkward conversations to endure. "Jessie," I say. "I'm so sorry. If you weren't so awesome, and so you know, pretty. And perfect." I blow out my breath. "I'm not very good at this kind of stuff, but I want to get better."

"What stuff?" Alec presses.

"Talking," I say. "And realizing that not everything is about me. That you have things and people you need to feel complete, and Jessie is one of those people."

He looks at her, his eyebrow cocked. "She's not wrong," Jessie says. "Get over there and kiss her."

"I already kissed her," Alec says, grinning from her to me.

"I wouldn't object to another kiss," I say, returning his smile.

"I'll get out Peaches," Jessie says, and Alec comes toward me again.

"What's this about me being complete? Whole?"

"So I was talking to Mr. Reynolds last night, and he said he used to get mad at his wife for working in the yard all the time. Jessie's the yard. She's important to you, just like the gardening was important to his wife. She needed it to find her center and be her real self. Her whole self."

I run my hands up his chest, enjoying the way his eyes darken with desire. That's all for me, and I can scarcely believe it. "When you're your whole self, you're not Mister Grumpy-Cat. You're brilliant in the kitchen. You're sexy, strong, and smart. You're the guy who drives five hours to make amends with his father and his brother.

You're everything I want in my life, so I can be happy too."

He watches me for a few moments. "And what's your thing, Tara?"

"Saucebilities," I say. "Or tea parties with my neighbor. Letting the hens out for their pasturecize. Making sure my yard is perfect. I don't know. The stuff I spend my time and energy on, because I like it."

"I think it's the hens," he murmurs, lowering his head toward mine again. He pauses before kissing me. "You forgot Peaches for me."

"Mm, yes," I whisper, the strength of his arms around me igniting a fire inside me. The warmth of his hands on my back sends pinpricks of excitement through my blood. "Seems like you taught Peaches some new words."

"You picked up on that, huh?"

"You have to get up really early to pull a blanket over that bird's cage...so I don't know," I say, but my quip makes no sense.

Alec starts to laugh, saying, "I have no idea what you just said," among all the ha-ha-ha's.

"Do you want her?" Jessie asks, and Alec takes the green and white parrot from her.

"All right, Peaches," he says.

"Peaches, peaches," she responds.

"No," he says. "Let's practice what we do when we see Tara." He nods toward me, but the bird has never liked me much. That's because I don't like her much. Being attacked the first time we met has definitely cast a shadow over our relationship.

"Tara," he says again.

"Kara, I love you," Peaches says. "I love you."

"That's right." Alec grins at the bird and holds up his hand. She leans out and boops her beak against it, making a kissing sound as she does.

My heart melts watching this tall, muscled, ex-Marine-turned-chef interact with a four-ounce bird. He loves her with his whole soul, and his expression doesn't change one iota when he switches his gaze to me.

"Tell her. Tell Tara." He faces Peaches toward me. "Tell Tara."

"Kara, I love you," Peaches chirps. "Bacon, love you. Motor-bike!"

Alec laughs again, and so do I. He slips the bird to his shoulder and takes me into his arms again. "I do love you, Tara. Something clicked inside me when we went to Florida, and it might be fast, but I've never been very slow at anything."

"I'm a little scared," I admit, leaning into the steadiness of his body.

"No rush," he says. "You can take all the minutes you want, but I do have one favor..."

"Oh, yeah? What's that?"

"My mom found out about us, and she wants me to bring you to Beaufort to meet her." He nuzzles my neck, lowering Peaches closer to my ears.

"What in the world?" she screeches, and that about sums up how I feel about meeting Alec's mother.

But I say, "Sure, baby. That sounds fun."

———

LITTLE DID I know that when he said, "She wants me to bring you to Beaufort to meet her," that we'd literally be going that day. But we do. I have an overnight bag in the back of Alec's car, and he's brought Peaches in her travel cage, along with a duffle of his own.

It's only an hour and a half drive, and we go over a couple of bridges to an area he calls Ashdale.

"This is super nice," I say, gazing up at the huge, sprawling white house with six columns along the front porch.

"Some places have private docks," he says. "They're right on the water."

"Let me guess," I say. "Yours is one of those."

"I mean, my momma," he says.

"You did grow up here," I point out.

"Yes," he says. "That one right there is Jessie's family's place. The Dunaways."

Since they grew up next-door to each other, I automatically look down the street. But there's far too many trees between the properties, and these are more like estates than just plots. I realize that she's not right next door the way Mr. Reynolds is to me, or the way Callie was before I moved to Cottonhill.

If Jessie had been crying in her backyard, Alec wouldn't have heard her. "I'm nervous for some reason," I say, looking away from the cream-colored mansion that is Jessie's childhood home.

"My momma is just a person," Alec says. "Since I gave her warning, I'm sure my brother and his wife will be there."

"Carl and Katia," I say. "Right?"

I can't believe how nervous I am. I've only met Otis's parents, because even though Brett and I were engaged, he had never taken me to meet his family. My parents had just moved to Miami, and we'd gone there twice.

"Right," Alec says, kneading the steering wheel. At least I'm not the only one who's nervous, and at least I've left my orthopedics at home today. "They have a baby boy named Houston. That's my momma's maiden name."

"How very Texan," I say.

"She's from right here in South Carolina," he says, smiling. "She used to travel a lot, but not anymore."

"Like you," I say, and Alec looks at me, surprise in his eyes. "You're not going to run away again, are you, Alec?"

"No," he says quickly. "I've returned to my southern roots, and I'm sticking around." He grins at me. "You won't be able to get rid of me."

"Good," I say. "I don't want to get rid of you." I reach

for his hand and lace my fingers through his. "What are you thinking for a wedding?"

"Oh, we're talking about that already?"

"I'd like to," I say.

"I'm thinking you should tell me what you want, and I'll do that."

"You have no thoughts?" I'm sure his momma will.

"I think you should dress up the hens in little flowery dresses and let them cluck down the aisle for their back-yard-cize."

"It's pasturecize," I say, but I want him to go on.

"Okay," he says. "But they won't be in the pasture. They'll be in your backyard, leading the two of us to the altar. And we'll be married in a small ceremony like Callie, and then I'll whisk you away to the huge Rocky Mountains for a couple of weeks. We'll sleep in the back of a truck or a tent or a cabin, and I'll brew coffee while the sun rises, and we'll stay up late and watch the sunset too."

"Oh, wow," I say, laughing at this picture-perfect life he's describing. "From sun-up to sun-down, huh?"

"And we'll sample all the restaurants in Boulder or wherever, and then we'll come back to Carolina. You'll find someone to publish your cookbook, and I'll work for you until I figure out what kind of restaurant I want to open."

He makes a turn to go down a lane, and I lose track of what he's said as I peer up at the white house with two large windows on the blocky right side of the house, which matches perfectly with the left side of the house. A bright red door sits smack dab in the middle of that, with two more smaller windows on either side of it.

Five peekaboo windows line the roof above the middle section of the house, and he takes us past plenty of trees that are probably two centuries old to the driveway. There aren't any other cars there, and I think maybe his brother hasn't arrived yet. We sure didn't give them very much notice that we were coming.

Which is probably a good thing, I think as Alec brings the vehicle to a stop. If I'd have had more time to think about meeting Alec's mother in a plantation-style home like this, with a private dock right onto the water, I'd be a puddle of blubbering goo right now.

"There she is," Alec says. "She's not the subtlest of people. She's going to love you." He nods toward the front porch, but I've already found his mother. She's a tall woman, or maybe she's wearing nine-inch heels under that prom dress.

"My goodness," I say.

"It's the Sabbath," he says. "She likes to get everything and everyone all dolled up at least once a week."

"Is that tulle?"

"I don't even know what that is," Alec says, and he hasn't moved to get out either. "Oh, she's folding her arms. Come on, let's go." He gets out of the vehicle and comes around to hold my door for me. He gets Peaches out of the back seat and we face his mother together.

Then he's laughing and darting ahead of me, taking his momma into a big Alec-Happy-Bear hug. She giggles too, and he twirls her around, that massive skirt billowing out with at least ten yards of fabric.

When he sets her on her feet, her smile is as wide as this mansion where she lives. She faces me, and I'm about as opposite of her as a person can get. At least Callie put me in a pencil skirt today—one of hers—and made me bring my fancy-pants purse.

"You must be Alec's Tara." She extends both of her hands toward me and I put mine in them. I like the way she drawls, though Alec said her slow speech drives him crazy.

"I am," I say. "You must be his momma, Nell."

"My momma," he says quickly. "Nell. Momma, Tara." He beams at me, as I lean in to kiss his momma's cheek. First one, and then the other.

"Well, well," another man says. "Look who the cat dragged in."

"Carl," Alec says, and the two brothers hug. He steps back and reaches for my hand. I move past Nell and he says, "This is my younger brother, Carl. Carl, this is Tara Finch." He looks at me, those eyes that used to glitter so much distaste and disgust now like bright stars in a gorgeous navy sky.

"The woman I'm in love with."

"Well, butter my butt and call me a biscuit." Carl grins

at me, grabs onto me, and pulls me into a hug while Alec protests against his brother's Southern slang.

I just laugh and hug him, glad I've been so accepted into Alec's family. I step back to his side and take one of his hands into both of mine and gaze up at him.

"Okay?" he asks, leaning down to touch his lips to my forehead.

"Okay," I confirm, because I'm feeling more okay than I ever have before.

CHAPTER TWENTY-NINE

ALEC

"THERE'S JASON," I SAY, AND I REACH FOR THE DOOR handle. In the passenger seat, Jessie sighs. "You don't have to date him." I give her a look, and she does seem exhausted. She started at Lance's real estate office this week, and she's being the most Positive Polly on the planet about it. But even makeup can't hide the watery weariness in her eyes.

"Good," she says. "He's drop-dead gorgeous, but my goodness, he's such a player."

"Tara says he's a good guy."

"Sure, he is," Jessie agrees. "He just doesn't want to settle down."

My eyebrows go up. "Do you?"

She shakes her blonde curls over her shoulder. "I mean, yes. I do, with the right man." She tears her gaze from the windshield to pierce me with it. "And look at

you. I never thought in a million years you'd get married."
She grins, and I shake my head.

"A million years? Come on." I get out of the SUV and
step onto the sidewalk. "Hey, man. Thanks for coming." I
shake Jason's hand and indicate Jess. "You remember
Jessie."

"Of course." Jason grins at me and then her, steps into
her and kisses both of her cheeks. "How's the new job
going?"

"It is wonderful," she says, wiping away her tiredness.
"I've got the afternoon off today, because we've got a big
open house in the morning." She indicates the jewelry
store we stand in front of. "I asked around, and this is the
best place for custom pieces."

I look at the glass door, which bears the name Henson
Handcrafted Jewelry, and I tug on the bottom of my polo.
"Okay," I say and take another deep breath. "Let's just go
look."

"You're not going to buy today?" Jason asks, stepping
over to the door and opening it for me.

"Maybe," I say. "It just depends on what we find."

"Callie says she's two minutes out," Jess says, and
neither of them will enter the store first. I'm in love with
Tara, and I want to marry her. I have the perfect proposal
all written out—and yes, it's got a knife reference in it.
Maybe two or three.

Our relationship is still new, though, and we both still
need time to get to know each other well. I'm starting the

search for the perfect ring to go with the perfect proposal —*I can't wait to make you my knife. Oops, I mean my wife* —and that gives me the courage to enter the store.

Jess follows right behind me, always such a support for me, and Jason comes in right after that.

"Good afternoon," a sharply dressed man says. "How can I help you today?"

I freeze, the cases and cases of rings and watches in front of me seemingly going on for miles and miles.

"He's looking for something for his girlfriend," Jason says, glancing at me as he passes. "She's a chef—an amazing chef, so he wants something that has diamonds but that can be removed or worn separately."

"So she has a ring she can wear in the kitchen without gems," Jess says, stepping to my side. She puts her hand through my arm. "And one with diamonds he can show to his momma when they go visit." She grins up at me, and somehow that thaws me.

"Right," I say, moving forward to shake the man's hand.

"I think I can help you find that," he says. "My name is Tom, and most of our two-piece rings are over in this case." He indicates the right side of the store and glances to the door as the bell sounds.

Callie walks in, a smart red purse on her arm. "Jessie." She gives her a hug and then grabs onto me. "How's it going? Sorry I'm late. You would not *believe* what Claude Monet got into." She shakes her head. "He's still adjusting to the new house and the fact that Dawson comes home with me at night, every night."

She smiles at Jason and then the salesman and leans toward him. "Honestly, so am I." She laughs lightly, and she has this way of making everything full of unicorns and sunshine. I honestly have no idea how she does it. "Anyway, if you see feathers anywhere on my clothes, just brush them off. We're down a couple of pillows as of right now."

Jessie giggles, and Callie's smile grows. She has no feathers anywhere, and I step to the front of the group to go with Tom to look at the two-piece rings on the right side of the store. I'm expecting silver and gold, and I definitely see those. But there are some darker metal rings in the case too, and I say, "Tell me everything. I've never bought an engagement ring before."

Tom smiles at me as if he's a lion and I'm fresh meat. I suppose I am, and I just smile back.

"We have the traditional gold, silver, and white gold," he says. "But since this is a specialty shop, and all of our rings are handcrafted by a master metal-worker and gemologist, we have some unique metals too."

"Like those darker ones?" They almost look reflective, and some of them have designs carved right into the band.

"These are men's rings," he says, taking out the ones I've indicated. "They're made of high-carbon steel."

I look up at him. "You're kidding."

"I'm not," he says. "Some of this lighter patterning you

see—that's stainless steel. Some of them are silver. They're all one-of-a-kind and made right here, in the back of the shop."

"Who makes these?" Callie asks, picking up one of the bands. "Why didn't I know about this place when I was buying a ring for Dawson?"

"Because you didn't have Jess," I say. "She's the best at finding the most amazing shops." I smile at her as she steps up to the case.

"I know what you're thinking," she says.

"Yeah? What am I thinking?"

"I really like these," Jason says before Jess can answer. "If I ever get married, I want one of these." He picks up one of the male wedding bands too.

"That one's called the cowboy," Tom says. "It's completely flat so it won't catch on anything while you're working. But it's got these ornate designs underneath." He indicates them with a slim pointer, almost like a pencil.

I really like the ring in Jason's hand, and I meet Callie's eye. I've brought her along, because she knows Tara better than anyone, but she can also tell Tara what I like. I'll tell her too, but I know she listens to Callie in a different way than she does me.

"Callie, do you know what the best chef's knives are made of?" Jess asks, pressing one hip into the case.

"I have no idea," Callie says, peering past the male bands on top of the case to the rings still inside it.

"High-carbon steel," Jess says, and that brings Callie's

eyes up. She wears surprise and delight there, and I know exactly how she feels.

I turn my attention back to Tom, the knife jokes flowing through my mind now. This couldn't be more perfect. "Do you have female bands made of the high-carbon steel?"

"Only one right now," he says.

"But this is a custom shop, right?"

"That's right." He pulls out another six rings on a display case. "This one is high-carbon steel." He takes the ring off the support and hands it to me. "We can lighten it up with some silver or white gold. It would go well with..." He searches the case and pulls out another strand of rings.

"See this setting? How the top of the ring can go down next to the main band?" He looks up at me, and I nod. "So she can have the bottom band for the kitchen, and again, if you don't like how dark it is, we can add in some other metals. Piper is absolutely amazing with patterns, and the high-carbon steel is such a strong metal that it can hold others."

"Piper is your master jeweler, right?" Callie asks.

"Yes, ma'am," Tom says. "Piper Newman."

"Is she here?" Callie asks. "I'd love to meet her."

"Unfortunately, she's not." He looks genuinely sorry too. "She's in Belgium, getting some new diamonds for a client."

"Fascinating," Callie says. She faces me too. "Tara would like a ring like that."

"What are we talking for a custom ring with the high-carbon steel, some of that inlaying, the diamond..."

"Our custom pieces generally start in the five-thousand-dollar range."

I pull in a breath, though the money isn't really the problem. My mother has called me every day this week, and she's said she'd love to help me get Tara the perfect ring.

"Okay," I say. "I'm not going to propose right away. I can start saving." I don't want anyone to know my momma is going to help with the ring. Well, I'll tell Tara, but no one else needs to know. "I mean, this is the rest of my *knife*, right?" I glance at Jess to see if she's caught the pun.

She rolls her eyes. "You're such a dork."

"It'll be *knife*," I say. "Really *knife*. Five-thousand-dollars *knife*."

Jason shakes his head though a chuckle comes out of his mouth. Callie looks from me to Jess, and I'm grinning like I'm the world's next amazing comedian. "What is happening here?" she asks.

"Alec thinks substituting the word *knife* for a variety of words is so funny," Jess says, plenty of eyerolling in her tone.

"It is," I say, glancing at Tom. He's grinning too. "Right?" I ask him. "She's my sig-*knife*-icant other. She should have the *knifest* ring possible, right?"

Tom starts to laugh, and even Jessie does. Callie still

looks like I've pulled a knife on her, and she blinks rapidly as she tries to decide what to do.

"Piper will be gone through Wednesday," he says, still smiling. "I can schedule a consult with her for when she gets back, if you'd like."

I look at Jess. "What do you think?"

She cocks her head to the side, and she looks happier than I've ever seen her, even if she is tired. "I think... No *cuts*, no glory."

I do the blinking now, and then all of us burst out laughing.

———

LATER THAT DAY, I stand behind Tara as she wrestles her stubborn hen out of the coop. "I'm going to make you into your name," she grumbles at Pot Pie. "First Benedict, and now you too?" She drops the brown and white hen on the ground, pushes her hand through her hair, and faces me.

I don't see her with her hair down all that often, and I sure do like it. I smile at her as the chicken warbles and struts away like she's done nothing wrong. "You'd never eat these hens."

"Come hold the basket for me."

"Yes, ma'am." I already have it in my hands, and I simply take a couple of steps to stand beside her as she starts to gather the eggs from the coop. "Can we use a few of these for dinner tonight?"

"I don't cook dinner at home, remember?"

"Right, but I do," I say. "I'm thinking...fried rice. Beef fried rice."

She glances at me. "Can I order Chinese food to go with it?"

I grin at her and lean over to kiss her. With my lips still on hers, I whisper, "You can do whatever you want, baby. It's your house and your party."

She smiles against my lips and kisses me again. I drop the basket of eggs, some of them clacking against one another as they hit the ground. Neither of us seem to care, and I push my hands through her hair and deepen the kiss. With no reporters around, I can put my hands where I want, and Tara has no objections.

"Can I have a few eggs for a cake?" I ask, sliding my lips to her neck.

"I guess," she says as she sighs into my touch.

I straighten and smile at her. "It's your birthday, baby. You have to have a cake."

"My birthday isn't for a few more days."

"Yeah, and you scheduled someone else's birthday party over your own." I bend to pick up the basket, noting only one egg is actually leaking the white through the shell. "Which I have to help you cater." I smile so she knows I don't care.

"Yes, and it's a very important birthday," she says.

"Who's is it?" I don't keep the schedule. I work when Tara tells me to, and I make what she tells me to. She used to be just my boss, but she's so much more now.

She nods next door, across the pasture. "Mr. Reynolds, and it's a surprise. His kids hired me, and we're all invited, so keep your big mouth shut tonight."

"My big mouth?" I abandon the eggs again and grab onto her. "*My* big mouth? You're the one who told my neighbor about my after-hours hot tubbing, and now Miss Opal says I might not get to keep doing it."

She giggles as I swing her away from the chicken coop. "I'm sorry," she says, though we've already talked about *her* big mouth. She glances down to my lips and back into my eyes. "It won't matter for much longer, though, right?"

"Why wouldn't it?" I ask, though I know what she's saying. I just want to hear her say it.

She swats at my chest and rolls her eyes. "You'll move in here when we get married. We can put a hot tub right there on the deck."

"Mm." I look over to the deck as if inspecting it. "And you'll order Thai while I lift weights and soak, is that it?"

"That's about it, baby," she says.

"And you don't want a long engagement."

"No, sir."

I almost drop to my knees and propose then, but I don't have the ring, and I'm still working with Peaches on her part of it all. "Well, I guess the appointment I made for next Friday at the custom jeweler won't be a waste of time."

Her eyes widen, and I chuckle. "I love you, Tara."

"How long until you propose?" she asks.

"Honey." I touch my lips to her forehead and then her cheek. "A man needs time to prepare something perfect for the woman he loves."

She sighs, her fingernails in my hair like magic. Deep, Southern magic. "Okay," she says. "I'll be patient."

"Heard anything about the cookbook?" I ask, still working my way toward her mouth. If I'd known how amazing egg-gathering could be, I'd have been here every night to help her with it. Of course, Tara has an erratic schedule, so sometimes her hens get their "pasturecize" in the morning and sometimes the afternoon or evening. Or even a late-night hour out of the pen.

"Nothing yet," she says, melting into my touch. "But Lila's only had it a few days." She cups my face in her hands and forces me to look at her. "I love you, Alec."

My smile is soft and probably the realest it's ever been. "I love you too...Boss."

Read on for a sneak peek at Jessie and Lance in **JUST HIS ASSISTANT**. **It's available now in paperback!**

SNEAK PEEK! JUST HIS ASSISTANT, CHAPTER ONE: JESSIE

WHEN MY ALARM GOES OFF, I GROAN AND ROLL OVER to silence it. It's been the longest, worst week of my life—but also the very best—and it's only Friday morning. It's almost October in Carolina now, and that means it's not exactly light at five-thirty in the morning.

I'm not one-hundred percent awake. But I will be, because my boss and I are meeting this morning to go over the open house happening tomorrow. It's my first open house—this week has been stuffed full of firsts for me—and I want to get it right.

There's very little that's gone right this week, other than the fact that I keep showing up—on time, thank you, thank you. I wasn't late for my interview last week either. I have the text from Lance Byers to prove it, though I've never told him that.

He still hired me, and I'm still one-thousand-percent

determined to figure out the real estate business. "Don't be one of those people," I sleep-mutter to myself. I once dated a guy who said stupid stuff like, "One hundred and ten percent, Jess," for everything. It grated against my nerves then, and now I'm using the nonsensical figure.

There's only one hundred in a percentage. Anything above that just makes no sense.

I roll over and sit up, taking a moment to stretch left and right. The bed my uncle has provided for me is very much appreciated, but it is not very much comfortable. I've also put on about twenty pounds since arriving in Charleston six months ago. All that sitting on Alec's couch with his parrot on my shoulder and eating the delectable food in his fridge hasn't exactly added to my physical fitness. Neither has the stress of being away from home for the first time and trying to figure out my life.

I don't care about my weight, despite the looks Uncle Jack gives me when I butter my cornbread muffins in the morning. If he doesn't want me to eat them, why does he have his chef make them every dang day?

Because he can, I tell myself as I finally stand. I go through my morning routine, which includes complete skin and hair care, carefully inserting my contacts, doing my makeup, and the careful selection of clothing. Lance told me yesterday that I wear too much red, and I could only stand there in my very crimson dress and stare at him.

He'd sighed—a sound I have memorized after only four days of working with him—and gone back into his office. His has a door and walls—windows on two of those too—while mine doesn't. I just sit at a desk that faces his office, the wall across the hall to my right, and a huge bank of copy machines on my left.

If someone uses the machines, they can't actually see me, because there's a six-foot divider there. Still, when those things heat up, that hot air just comes right around the divider. I've said nothing to anyone about it, because we're Southern, and we understand heat.

A woman named Brenda sits at the front podium-desk most of the time, and if the wall with the giant F&F wasn't behind her work area, I'd be able to see the front door and her desk too. As it is, though, I'm pretty isolated at my desk. I have a great view of a clock though—and Lance's door.

That's the most important part. I'm his assistant, and apparently that means I'm supposed to be able to read his mind. Somehow. He even said on the first day, *Jessica, I need you to anticipate my needs and have things ready for me.*

"Anticipate his needs." I scoff. I know what men need, and that's constant fuel for their egos. At least all of the men I've ever known or dated, with one rare exception in my best friend, Alec Ward.

Alec does like being the best though, and people constantly praise his food, myself included. So he probably has plenty of fuel for his ego. He also struck the jackpot when he got his job at Saucebilities, because they're now the top-rated catering service in Charleston, and he's about to get engaged to the owner and his boss, Tara.

I smile just thinking about the two of them, which is such a different reaction than what I'd been doing only a week ago. I carefully paint the pink lipstick onto my lips, pressing to really seal it in. I have permanent lip staining, but it requires some touch-ups from time to time. Lance gives me the up-down, check-out-in-a-non-sexual-way, look every single time he sees me, and I know if I didn't meet his requirements, he wouldn't hesitate to tell me.

I finish up with my makeup and shimmy into a pair of navy slacks I've borrowed from Tara. She said I could keep them, because she literally wears the same thing to work every single day and they don't fit her anymore. But it feels like charity to me. I don't need to be given clothes.

I go back into my bedroom and open the closet. I adore clothes, and I've kept all of mine that I brought from Beaufort when I left. Some of them I can't wear anymore due to that fourscore increase in poundage, but I can't get rid of them. Fabrics and patterns inspire me, and I reach out to touch an off-white dress with bright butterflies on it.

It makes me feel like I can spread my wings and fly too, and a smile moves through my soul. I could probably let out the dress and still wear it, though I'm not attending charity luncheons or non-profit fundraisers anymore.

No part of me yearns for that past life, with all the fake smiles, false eyelashes, and phony friendships. No, thank you. Not for me.

A wave of loneliness washes over me, and I close the closet. "It's Friday," I say. "You're only working half the day. You can do this." I started listening to affirmation podcasts a couple of months ago, and I do feel better about myself and life in general.

I also know I won't only work half the day, because everything that Lance knows how to do instinctively, I don't. I have to learn it, and that takes twice as long. But I only have to be in his presence until lunchtime. Thankfully.

After that, Callie, one of my only friends here in Charleston, said she'd come over and help me institute a filing system. Right now, the precarious stacks of folders on my desk aren't really getting the job done right. Lance even eyed them yesterday like they were a giant slimeball that might attack him next time he strode past my desk to use the restroom.

Honestly, the man is a like a big, black fly in a perfectly pretty glass of lemonade. He's the party-crasher. The killer of fun. He probably laughs when babies cry—that's how surly the man is.

I remind myself that he's in the top five real estate agents in terms of sales in the whole state of South Carolina, and I'm very lucky to be learning from him. "Very, very lucky," I tell myself as I leave my bedroom and head into the main part of the house. Hopefully, it'll still be too early for Uncle Jack or my cousin Rufus to be out and about.

They're about as insufferable as the hundred-degree temperatures on a Carolina Sunday, and I'm *this-close* to being able to move out. I need my own freedom, and in any spare time I have, I've been looking at apartments around the city.

The trouble is, everything is more than I can afford. I'm almost hoping Alec will get his plan together to propose to Tara, and then I can ask if I can sublet his apartment from him. He'll probably let me, and I can even say I'll take care of Peaches for him when I'm not at work.

The cornbread muffins sit on the kitchen counter, but I don't see any evidence of nearby humans. As I split and butter a muffin, footsteps approach. I know the sound of shiny, leather shoes that have literally never seen the outside of this mansion. They belong to Uncle Jack.

Busted.

"There you are," Uncle Jack says in that ultra-smooth voice of his. It's like he polishes his voice box in one of those rock tumblers before using it. He swoops his medium brown hair to the side just-so, and I've never seen him with an ounce of stubble. Not even a half-ounce.

Where else would I be? I wonder, but I say, "Here I am. Good morning, Uncle Jack." I step over to him and give him a kiss on both cheeks. I am a proper Southerner, after all, and I've been taught to respect my elders no matter what.

No matter that he tried to set me up with someone fourteen years older than me. No matter that Rufus keeps brining home these little weasels for dinner, as if it's an accident they're all dressed up in suits and silk ties.

I may be from a rich family, but I'm not stupid.

"Thanks for always getting these muffins," I say, slathering on more butter though it's a little heavy-handed, even for me. I smile and take a big bite, immediately regretting it. Way too much butter, and I didn't think that was even something that could happen. Still, I chew through the slippery butter-muffin in my mouth like it's the best thing I've ever tasted.

My uncle gives me a terse smile, which is actually step up from his tight ones. "I'm glad you like them." He reaches for the coffee pot and frowns. "Oh, brother. Wesley didn't make this in the last hour." He looks around as if his personal assistant will be hovering there, waiting for his approval on the brew.

"I have to go," I say, because the last thing I need is a display of Uncle Jack's money. We get it, he's got money. Enough to have a personal assistant make his coffee and a personal chef cater all of his meals. Enough to have a shed full of cars and motorcycles. Enough for a pool, a theater room, and that prison-like library.

Big freaking deal. BFD, as I like to say. Tons of people have money, and it doesn't make them special, just like it doesn't make Uncle Jack better than anyone else.

Outside, my sedan sticks out like a whore in church on Sunday, but I smile at her. I've nicknamed her Lucy, because Lucille Ball is a personal heroine of mine. She opened doors for women in comedy no one had before, and she was the first female to head a production studio.

Mama hates my idolization of Lucille Ball, but she's not here in Charleston, and I don't have to answer to her anymore. I get behind the wheel and pat it. "All right, Luce. Just to work and back today, I swear."

Sometimes we go all over town—or at least to Alec's—but since I'll spend the day at the agency and I have that open house tomorrow, I have no detours planned today.

She starts up on the second try, and her engine seems to chug along pretty nicely. I ease away from the front of the house and along the graveled drive until it turns into hard-packed dirt. Uncle Jack lives on the outskirts of the suburbs of Charleston, in a town called Sugar Creek. Barely in Sugar Creek, which is where Callie lives. Lived. She moved in with Dawson, who's in another small town kissing up against Charleston—Cottonhill.

Lucy and I go down the road, really gaining some momentum when we hit the road that leads into a more populated area of town. The downtown area of Sugar Creek is straight out of the historical South, and I love every old brick and all the crumbling façades.

Lucy doesn't seem to love the quaint buildings as much as I do, and she starts to sputter just as I go through the single stoplight. I ease her over right in front of the bakery, noting the steam starting to rise from the hood.

"That's not good." I get out of the car and stand on the sidewalk. I've seen people open the hoods of their cars, but

I'm wearing a silky white blouse with orange trim on the sleeves to signal my support of autumn arriving. A single smudge would ruin the entire outfit.

This might be the end of Lucille Ball the Camry, but I still have to get to work. Callie doesn't own a car, and she and Dawson go to their downtown office together.

Lance lives in Cider Cove, and while it's not exactly on the way through Sugar Creek, it *is* on the way into the city. Since I left over two hours before I need to be at work, surely he'll still be home.

I pull out my phone, who I've named Missy Rings-A-Lot, though she doesn't, and tap when I see I've gotten a text from him. *Confirm that you've received the Hudson docs.*

"Would it kill him to say please?" I mutter to myself, and I tap on his name to call him. I'm sure I got the docs, and I can just tell him I did and then check my email. I mean, do people not get emails these days?

"Jessie," he says. "You got the docs?"

"Yes," I say. "But actually, Mister Byers, I'm calling for a favor."

"A...favor?" he asks as if he doesn't know the meaning of the word.

"Yes," I say, lifting my free hand to my mouth to bite the thumbnail. "My car broke down in Sugar Creek, right in front of the bakery." I turn and look at the building, which already has a line out the door. "I was wondering if you could stop by and pick me up on the way to the office. I can get a Carry home."

Why I can't get a Carry there, I'm not sure. Maybe because my bank account has seventeen dollars in it, and I tell myself in a stern voice, *no maple bacon doughnut for you, Jess* as the scent of the treat reaches my nose.

"Fine," Lance says as if I've asked him to rip off his arm and feed it to his dog. "I'll be there in an hour."

"Thank you," I say, my voice small and tinny. The call ends, and I face my nemesis: the bakery. A maple bacon bar won't be seventeen dollars, but I figure I better go take care of my money situation before treating myself to a second pastry that morning.

SNEAK PEEK! JUST HIS ASSISTANT, CHAPTER TWO: LANCE

I SEE MY ASSISTANT, JESSICA DUNAWAY—JESSIE, SHE'S asked me to call her—sitting on a bench, her blonde hair reflecting the morning sunshine in so many haloes of gold light. I clench my fingers around the steering wheel, because I have a soft spot for blondes.

Scratch that. I have no soft spots anymore. When my fiancée left Charleston with my diamond ring on her finger, everything turned hard. My heart is hard. My chest always feels stuffed full of concrete, so my lungs can't really get enough air. I've been pouring myself into the treadmill and the gym since Hadley's departure, so my muscles are hard too.

Life, in general, has been hard for me lately.

I flip on my blinker and ease up to the curb in a spot several yards down from where Jessie sits with an older gentleman. She pinches off a piece of doughnut and tips her head back as she laughs. I can't hear her, as I've got my windows up and the AC blowing. Watching the two of them feels like a scene from a peaceful movie, and I long for the easier days of this year, when everything seemed to be going my way.

A doughnut sounds amazing, and I get out of my truck and walk down the street in my casual Friday clothes—a black pair of slacks and a light blue button-up shirt. I'm wearing a red and white checkered tie that my mom gave me for my birthday at the beginning of the year, and I feel patriotic and put-together at the same time.

Jessie's wearing a gorgeous silk blouse that looks like God Himself reached down and touched it, making it glow white. Dark orange strips of fabric rim the sleeves, a very subtle nod to the calendar, which is almost to October. She's paired that with a dark brown leather skirt, and I lick my lips and swallow the sudden extra saliva in my mouth.

It's because of the mini pecan pie on the bench beside Jessie. Yeah, that's it. It's not because she's the type of woman that ticks every single box I've ever thought of when it comes to a girlfriend.

I'm not dating for a while. I need to figure out where I went wrong with Hadley, and where we deviated. I hadn't even known it, and that unsettles me the most.

I'm cursing Dawson's name when Jessie turns toward me. I'd told him I couldn't hire her, but my two previous assistants hadn't even lasted a week. Not even long enough for his wife and secretary—who's seriously one of the best in the city—to come train them. She's coming this afternoon, though Jessie wasn't the one to tell me.

Callie told me, because she said I better have Cayenne's there for lunch, and plenty of Skittles to help her get through the Friday afternoon at the real estate agency. I'd promised her she'd have it all, and I'm actually pretty proud of Jessie that she's made it through this whole week.

She has no idea what she's doing, but she tries. I can tell that much.

"Mister Byers," she says, rising to her feet. "I got this for you." She collects the miniature pecan pie and extends it toward me, as well as a friendly, if professional, smile.

I simply stare at it as I take it from her. "Thank you."

"Is this your sweetheart?" the older gentleman asks, his voice raspy like sandpaper over rough wood.

"Oh, no," she says waving her hand. She darts a look at him, back to me, and then to him. "I'm just his assistant."

"She's just my assistant," I say, smiling at the older man. My heart pounces through my chest, and I hate that. I feel like I'm falling for a minute, and then I look at Jessie again. "Should we get going?"

"Yes," she says. "I'm sorry you had to go out of your way. I'll use a Carry from now on." She tucks her hair behind her ear, but the thick lock just flops right back out. Her hair isn't quite long enough to tuck and have it stay, and I smile at the rebellious curls.

"It's fine," I say. "You'll have to deal with Cha-Cha's

hair, though I did try to brush it off." I had, but only for a second at a stoplight on the way here, when I'd thought about it.

"Cha-Cha?" she asks, looking at me with those big, beautiful blue eyes.

"My dog," I say. "She's a corgi, and she's shedding her summer coat to grow her winter one." I open the passenger door for Jessie, because I'm not a complete ogre. I'm just on a female fast. I also don't mention that I open the door for Cha-Cha, and that I have to lift the stubby-legged pup into the front seat so she can ride up front with me.

"Interesting name," Jessie says with a smile and a glint in her eye that says she really thinks it's silly.

"I didn't name her," I say as she slides by me and gets in the truck. Her skirt pulls up as she steps up onto the runner, and I stare at the extra thigh I can see. My whole body flushes, and I feel like I'm sinking in quicksand. Everything is moving quickly around me, but I'm stuck moving at sloth-speed.

That's why I don't realize Jessie is stumbling before she's falling backward. All I have time to do is open my arms in a wide splay and catch her as she hits me. I grunt and fall to my knees, but that's as far as I have to go.

I'm touching so many inappropriate things, but I can't let go of her. Her body shakes even as she says, "I'm so sorry. My heel slipped."

I can't speak, so I just steady her as she gets to her feet, trembling all the while. She brushes her hands down the front of her body with her back to me, and after several long seconds, she turns to face me.

Bright pink patches decorate her cheeks, and she extends her hand toward me. "Did you rip your pants?"

"I'm sure it's fine," I say as I take her hand, not that I need her help to get up. I do need help with something else—my erratic heartbeat and the way my hands now have muscle memory of the feel of her body against them.

I manage to stand up, and I glance down at my slacks. Sure enough, there's a rip in the knee on my left leg. Jessie sucks in a breath and starts to apologize again.

"Stop it," I say, and I don't mean to sound so much like a scoundrel. I sigh when our eyes meet and hers are filled with anxiety. "I'm sorry," I say. "I didn't mean to bark that. I'm just...tired of listening to you apologize. It's not necessary."

The expression in her eyes changes to one of defiance, and she nods just once, barely any movement at all.

"Ready to try again?" I ask when I realize we're just standing there staring at one another on the sidewalk.

"Do you need to go home and change?" she asks.

"No," I say. "I have extra clothes in the office." I indicate the truck. "I'll help you up this time."

"My heel just slipped," she says again, turning. This time, she does grab onto the bar just inside the truck, and I put my hand on her hip to balance her. She doesn't flinch, and my skin tingles though I'm really just touching the leather on her skirt.

She makes it into the passenger seat, and I close her door for her. I go around the front of the truck, straightening my sunglasses and wishing I could straighten out my thoughts and my pulse. Well, maybe not my pulse. A straight heartbeat indicates death, and I don't want to be dead.

I just don't want to be duped again.

I get behind the wheel and cast a quick glance at Jessie. As I buckle my seatbelt, I say, "All good?"

"Yes, sir," she says. We ease away from the curb, and she clears her throat. "Who named your dog if you didn't?"

Everything tightens again, and I work to release it, the way I've been learning to do in therapy. "My ex-fiancée." It's my turn to clear my throat. "The first one."

"Oh." Jessie adjusts her purse and grabs the pecan pie as it starts to slide. "How many have you had?"

"Just two," I say, though that's a lot of fiancées, in my opinion. Especially if you can't get them to become wives.

"Ever been married?"

"No," I say. "You?" I'm not sure why I ask. Seems like the right thing to do. Someone asks you how you are, you answer and then ask them how they are. Right?

"No, sir," she says. "Never been engaged either, much to my mama's disappointment."

"Yes, well, it's not all that fun to tell your mama that your fiancée has called off the wedding either." I'm aware of how dark my voice comes out, but I don't know how to lighten it. Hadley left four months ago, and I feel like I should be further along than I am. The truth is, I have good days and bad days. Some days where I think I'm going to be okay, and I could probably, definitely, take a new woman to dinner. Some days where I think I'll never figure out who I am and what I want, and getting it is never going to happen.

Today is kind of in the middle, to be honest.

"I'm sure it's not," Jessie says. "I'm sorry, Lance."

"Jessie," I say in a warning voice.

"Oh, sugar honey iced tea," she says. "I apologized again. I'm sor—" She clamps her mouth shut and claps one hand over it. She isn't one of those women with fake nails and fake eyelashes and a fake chest. I know, as I basically just felt her up while she fell backward.

I smile and look away from her before I drive us right off the road. I need to get us back on safe ground, and there's nothing safer for me than work. "All right," I say, maybe adding on a little thickness to my Southern accent. "What did you think of the Hudson docs?"

"Oh, uh, I thought they looked good," she says, and I hide my smile. She has no idea what the Hudson docs even are, and in all honesty, I shouldn't expect her to.

So teach her, I think but that's very dangerous ground. If I start to teach her, that means I care about her, and I absolutely, cannot—will not—start to care about Jessie Dunaway as more than just my assistant.

But I do want to have a good, competent assistant. I

sigh as I turn toward her. "It was a letter of intent to purchase," I say. "Shiela Hudson wants that riverfront property I showed her a couple of weeks ago, and she doesn't want anyone to slide in an offer before she can get hers in."

Jessie turns toward me, and she looks like she's ready to soak up every single thing I say. "Okay," she said. "Is there an acronym for that?"

I grin at her. "Yes, Jessie. LOI."

"LOI," she repeats, plucking her phone from her purse and starting to type a note into it. "Got it. Was there anything else in the docs?"

I like that she's eager to learn, and I shake my head. "Not in that email."

"Yes, sir," she says, going back to her phone as I continue the drive toward the downtown agency. I tell myself that telling her about a letter of intent was not an attempt to get closer to her. It wasn't flirting, because that would be pathetic with a capital P.

It was just me being...nice. Yes, I do know how to be nice, and I'm proud of myself for achieving it so early in the morning.

———

She's just his assistant, which is exactly how this Southern belle wants it. No spotlight. Not anymore. But as she struggles to learn her new role in his office—especially because Lance is the surliest boss imaginable—Jessie might just have to open her heart to show him everyone has a past they're running from.

Read JUST HIS ASSISTANT today - available in paperback!

BOOKS IN THE SOUTHERN ROOTS SWEET ROMCOM SERIES

Just His Secretary, Book 1: She's just his secretary...until he needs someone on his arm to convince his mother that he can take over the family business. Then Callie becomes Dawson's girlfriend—but just in his text messages...but maybe she'll start to worm her way into his shriveled heart too.

Just His Boss, Book 2: She's just his boss, especially since Tara just barely hired Alec. But when things heat up in the kitchen, Tara will have to decide where Alec is needed more —on her arm or behind the stove.

Just His Assistant, Book 3: She's just his assistant, which is exactly how this Southern belle wants it. No spotlight. Not anymore. But as she struggles to learn her new role in his office—especially because Lance is the surliest boss imaginable—Jessie might just have to open her heart to show him everyone has a past they're running from.

Just His Partner, Book 4: She's just his partner, because she's seen the number of women he parades through his life. No amount of charm and good looks is worth being played...until Sabra witnesses Jason take the blame for someone else at the law office where they both work.

Just His Barista, Book 5: She's just his barista...until she buys into Legacy Brew as a co-owner. Then she's Coy's business partner *and* the source of his five-year-long crush. But after they share a kiss one night, Macie's seriously considering mixing business and pleasure.

ABOUT DONNA

Donna Jeffries loves everything about the South, from the big ships to the food. She loves dogs, the beach, and anything with bacon in it. Find her on her website at
feelgoodfictionbooks.com

Printed in the USA
CPSIA information can be obtained
at www.ICGtesting.com
LVHW070312200923
758631LV00050B/912